BEYOND THE PALE

Vivien Armstrong

Severn House Large Print
London & New York

This first large print edition published in Great Britain 2002 by
SEVERN HOUSE LARGE PRINT BOOKS LTD of
9-15, High Street, Sutton, Surrey, SM1 1DF.
First world regular print edition published 2002 by
Severn House Publishers, London and New York.
This first large print edition published in the USA 2002 by
SEVERN HOUSE PUBLISHERS INC., of
595 Madison Avenue, New York, NY 10022

British Library Cataloguing in Publication Data

Armstrong, Vivien
    Beyond the pale. - Large print ed.
    1.   Police - England - Fiction
    2.   Detective and mystery stories
    3.   Large type books
    I.   Title
    823.9'14 [F]

ISBN 0-7278-7170-6

Printed and bound in Great Britain by
MPG Books Ltd, Bodmin, Cornwall.

BEYOND THE PALE

For Charlotte Redman

One

The Pendleburys occupied a duplex at the top of a new block in Pimlico. It had been the show-house suite and, overlooking the Thames, the view was unparalleled. Nevertheless, it was not an area Madeleine would have chosen. Had she been an animal, the delicate spoor of Madeleine Pendlebury would have left a single track between Belgravia and South Kensington. But the proximity of the Pendleburys' small business just across the river designated this un-chic district the perfect roost, the abrasive cliff of redevelopment immured from the continuous roar of traffic along the Embankment, a luxurious bastion of solid comfort. Victor could drive to Lambeth in fifteen minutes even in the rush hour and, as the estate agent had assured him, even go home for lunch.

Not that he did this. Madeleine prepared his breakfast eggs each morning, he left promptly at eight fifteen and their ways diverged for ten hours. Mr Pendlebury's girls made lampshades. Very expensive, hand-sewn lampshades, much sought after by the smarter decorators. Hours were long, jobs often rushed, clients' resettlement patterns bunching urgently in spring and autumn, as seasonal as the migration of Canada geese from the royal parks to the ultimate wilderness.

Madeleine Pendlebury had her life in control. At forty-three years of age her programme was, of necessity, rigidly structured, proof against the chaos which raged beyond the fortress of routine.

On Mondays she swam at the Queen Elizabeth pool. Twenty lengths exactly. A stately progress up and down, up and down. Afterwards Max styled her hair in the chintzy bower which disguised the most exclusive salon in London. On Wednesday afternoons she played bridge and took tea with Mary and Ursula and generally Kate. Though Kate was unreliable. Kate had children who sometimes inconveniently intruded on the bridge afternoons and then Glenys or Ulla was permitted to stand in. The Pendleburys had no children. No unsightly stretch marks marred Madeleine's flat belly. Her schedule was undisturbed by half-terms or chickenpox.

The rest of her week was gratifyingly filled with aromatherapy on Fridays, a session with Sean, her personal fitness trainer, on Tuesdays and, of course, shopping. There was tennis at Queen's, summer and winter, with Pixie, the only friend to have known Madeleine before her marriage and whose rumbustiousness sometimes struck a harsh note in the smooth progression of Monday to Friday. But Pixie's tennis was as fast, accurate and punishing as her conversation. Madeleine reluctantly conceded an astringent dash of Pixie was as necessary as the slice of lime in her vodka.

Madeleine Pendlebury looked wonderful, one had to admit that. Graceful posture, perfect skin and a clear, untroubled blue gaze like water in an empty swimming pool. Her manner was gentle if a little vague, her arrangements for the sexual and material comforts of Mr Pendlebury flawless, her virtue being she was utterly without guile. Until her introduction to murder, she was, in fact, a dull creature, her immaculate appearance and empty mind both, by a perverse trick of fate, enhanced by the violence of the storm which shattered the still surface of her life.

The Pendleburys dined late, often off trays in the little TV room because Victor required regular doses of the news and weather forecasts. Madeleine failed to comprehend his predilection for world affairs, famine, violence, pestilence and the greenhouse effect. Madeleine never concerned herself with any of these apart from a guilty unspoken gratitude for the rift in the ozone layer, which seemed to have made the English summer so much more delightful in recent years. Meteorology was a matter of indifference to her. Good heavens, the weather hardly affected the Pendleburys, did it? If it rained, there were taxis, if it snowed, there was central heating, if it blazed down through a relentless city summer there was air conditioning. Anyone might think they were farmers, she mused, what with Victor's avid concern with showers in the west of Ireland or a hosepipe ban in the Home Counties. Lampshades, after all, required no spell of dry weather for harvesting.

They ate sparingly. Grilled fish and white meat and a delicate variety of salads, all prettily arranged and deliciously dressed by Madeleine herself. She kindly bullied Mr Pendlebury about his waistline and devised cunning little exercise routines to fend off the back pain which mysteriously struck the moment he was seated at the opera. Victor bowed to the inevitable in respect of the opera. Madeleine did not care for the theatre, not even for music if the truth be told, but they did occasionally entertain business contacts at Covent Garden. Madeleine adored the crowded gaiety of the Crush Bar, the interval being, in her estimation, the real performance of the evening. He shrugged off these excursions. It was little enough to ask. His wife was a good woman not given to boredom, discontent or avarice. Once a year to the West Indies and Easter in Paris and not a murmur in between. And the poor girl did suffer the occasional weekend at his old family home without complaint, an uncomfortable country house where he and his sister kept horses, a fascination engrained by formative years he and Genista had spent in Argentina. Victor considered himself a very lucky man: Maddy kept herself fully occupied. What more could a man ask?

After all, she never required his company at the cinema, another taste he did not share. Between the confines of her week's busy schedule she fitted in a matinée at the Curzon. Always alone. Madeleine was addicted to the movies, losing herself in the darkness, munching chocolate brazils – her only vice – in the secret gloom of half-empty auditoria.

But, ticking away, its fuse lit, her life was set to explode. Out of the blue, Madeleine Pendlebury fell in love. Fell in love for the very first time and to a man quite unsuitable, whichever way one regarded it. A man unkind acquaintances might brand Love Rat, a man with an eye for a vulnerable lady with money to burn.

At first it had been a delicious flirtation. Fun. Flattering. Lighting an unexplored landscape both thrilling and terrifying to a woman whose heartbeat had, until now, ticked away like a metronome. But why not, she asked herself. Why not? Had she been burnishing her fading good looks all these years with only Victor's tepid devotion as reward? A husband of whom Maddy had been known to remark, only half jokingly, 'I don't think I've ever said anything he found interesting.'

Not that this placid existence had chafed, Madeleine being an unimaginative soul not usually given to introspection. Until she was struck with this unforeseen passion, Madeleine had considered her marriage a perfectly acceptable state of affairs. Un-eventful, but by no means unhappy. She had married young, had been cared for with affection and had never been tempted to believe her lot was in any way lacking. And yet...

Secrets were always dangerous. And it had to be a secret, of course. Her friends seated around the bridge table would have found her blissful capitulation to a man so 'common' and so 'young' quite beyond the pale.

Madeleine was giving a party for her tennis partner two days before Christmas. Pixie Bowles was about to depart to Zambia to join her husband, a civil engineer, on a pro-ject likely to keep him away from England for several months. In a curious way, Madeleine was relieved to lose her closest friend just now. She doubted her ability to keep her secret for much longer. Dissimulation was a skill Madeleine had never perfected and Pixie knew her far too well.

Pixie Bowles was different from Madeleine in every way. A big-boned woman, cheerful and with a wry humour, totally unconcerned with appearances. Their unlikely friendship, struck up at school, spanned periodic gaps when Pixie was overseas, often living in uncomfortable campsites with Tom's road-building crew. The women did not correspond. Pixie, never much of a letter-writer, knew, in any event, Madeleine would not thank her for accounts of setting up a succession of makeshift homes, marking the progress of Tom's new road schemes in one unhygienic foreign location after another.

Pixie had one sister, in truth a half-sister, Judith. Their mother – an art potter of some distinction – having embraced the easy life-style of the sixties, never elaborated on her daughters' paternity apart from a reluctant acknowledgement that they did not share the same father. But even to the casual observer, this was patently obvious.

Judith Pullen was a detective sergeant and, in both looks and manner, clearly out of a different stable. Several years younger than Pixie, Judy was deceptively fragile-looking with straight blonde hair and sherry-coloured eyes. Despite the age gap, the sisters were like two parts of some strange exotic fruit, one side sun-kissed and the other, Judith's half, with a delicate bloom, pale and unripe: shaded from the sunny side of life.

Pixie's sister had been invited to Madeleine's luncheon party along with the current man in her life, Laurence Erskine, an inspector with Special Branch, a linguist and a good-looking, if somewhat abrasive, young man who could have been typecast in a film about war-time codebreakers. The single-minded type. True blue. Judith could never quite make up her mind if she was serious about Erskine, their yo-yo relationship having swiftly taken on a closeness which disconcerted her. Sometimes, she was not even sure if she *liked* the man. Judy didn't believe in Fate and was more than wary of these Special Branch bods in their smart double-breasted suits. But, despite all her resolve, Erskine's undeniable appeal was hard to resist and perhaps the trouble was they were both too defensive, reluctant to lay themselves open to deeper emotions which could prove double-edged.

They had met, eighteen months before, on a murder hunt in which Special Branch had been called in, after which Judith eagerly accepted a transfer to the Serious Fraud Office. It had been a squalid case, brutal and involving peripheral victims apart from the dead man, a lawyer called Francis Swayne.

One of the injured parties was Judith's ex-boss, an irascible Yorkshireman who took early retirement as a direct consequence of inter-departmental clashes over the conduct of the inquiry. It had been in all the papers and had created no end of a dust-up at the Met, what with accusations and counter-accusations, most of them fermenting between Laurence Erskine and Judith's former inspector, Ralph Arnott. Judith had been more than relieved to escape to the relative sanity of fraud investigation after that.

In time, the wounds healed and Arnott and Judith remained on friendly terms. Her reluctant fascination with Laurence had bloomed into a semi-attachment which neither of them could quite make up their minds about. Christmas was a funny season and Laurence, aware of his own burgeoning feelings for Judy, was not a man to walk into the Pendleburys' penthouse with his eyes shut. A farewell bash laid on specifically for the sister might turn out to be a family 'do' and he was nervous about being cornered. Christmas has a special magic and had it not been for the airline ticket tucked in his wallet, his exit visa to a skiing chalet party over Christmas, Erskine might well have excused himself from a ding-dong near Vauxhall Bridge. He had heard about Pixie Bowles. Pixie did not sound the sort to mince her words, especially where her little sister was involved.

Erskine was still turning over these possibilities in his mind when an informant's tip-off sent him racing across London and, for a while there he thought, with no little satisfaction, that he would have to give Madeleine's lunch party a miss.

The emergency call had turned out to be a bomb alert in Kilburn, a political plot hatched by a group of small-time anarchists, so far unnamed. In the course of the arrest, Laurence got himself caught up in a full-blown fist fight. Had it not been his last chance to see Judith before flying out to Tignes that evening, he would have buzzed straight home after making his report and left it at that. In the event, a brush-off by phone was no easy option even for Erskine. He always found it difficult to summon up yuletide bonhomie and it was only the gift-wrapped package zipped inside his jacket, his deposit on Judith's affections until his return from holiday, which tipped the scales. Stone-faced, Erskine strode away from the hiatus surrounding his informant's nest of vipers, his mood distinctly unfestive, tasting the blood seeping from his split lip. Erskine knew then why he hated Christmas. He had been here before. In Jerusalem, milling about with tourists, blood and hatred spilling over into the dust of what was supposed to be the festive season.

He brushed down his leather jacket and hailed a taxi, wincing as he dabbed at the bleeding cut under his eye.

It was after one o'clock when Judith Pullen opened the door of her flat to admit the dishevelled figure of Erskine. He held up a blood-caked hand in mute apology.

'Larry! What on earth...? Have you been in a crash, for God's sake?'

Quickly, she drew him inside, unable to take her eyes from the raw graze along his cheekbone. She closed the door and he hugged her briefly, tired to death with yet another doom-laden Christmas. Why did these things always crop up when he was within an ace of jetting out?

'I'll explain on the way,' he said with a grimace. 'It looks worse than it is. I hadn't time to change, I'm afraid. This party for your sister – it is unavoidable, I take it?'

She nodded, holding out a hand for his jacket as he passed her in the tiny hallway, smoothing the L-shaped tear in the leather sleeve.

'Madeleine's laid on this special lunch before Pixie goes to Zambia. We're driving down to spend Christmas with my mother straight after the party. I must go, Laurence.'

'Romney Marsh in December – what a prospect!' he muttered, moving into the sitting room. 'I could do with a drink, Ju.'

She emptied the last of the whisky into a tumbler.

'You don't *have* to come to this bloody lunch, Laurence. You look awful. What happened?'

'Give me five minutes.'

He made for the bathroom, leaving Judith holding his empty glass and totally confused. Laurence's job encumbered their so-called romance with secrets. She had learned to accept the blank patches, the sudden depart-ures, the missing explanations. In fact, when he emerged, considerably spruced up and much more cheerful, he was, for Erskine, almost loquacious. He told her about his informant's tip-off about the safe house in Kilburn, the possible bomb alert involving an unnamed VIP on the diplomatic list.

They clattered down the stairs with Judy's luggage and Christmas parcels, discussing the arrest. Presumably a terrorist plot, in which case some sort of organization would shortly make its political claims. It was a pity Judy's car radio had been stolen – they could have listened to the news on the way.

She said, 'How is it the so-called season of goodwill always incites violence? I thought we were in the middle of a peace process?'

'You're assuming it was the Irish? Other people live in Kilburn, believe it or not. Mind you, now you mention it, Lockerbie turned out to be an Arab stunt pulled off just

18

before Christmas. I'll be glad when it's New Year,' he added bitterly.

'Perhaps it was a hoax?' she ventured.

'No way. Anyway, I'm flying out tonight, sod the lot of 'em!'

'Your skiing trip means that much? You're a key witness, Larry – you won't escape as easily as that.'

Judy was surprised by his response. He seemed determined to keep out of it, which struck her as odd in a man for whom terrorism was his daily bread. Not to mention the kudos involved in being the one to instigate the alert. Laurence Erskine was an ambitious character, the last, she would have thought, to disappear and let someone else take the credit. There was probably more to it. Covering up his source of information maybe? He never gave her more than the bare bones of the story and certainly never anything she couldn't have discovered for herself from the newspaper.

They stacked her bags in Judy's ageing VW parked outside, Erskine folding himself awkwardly in the passenger seat. Despite the bitter cold, the engine started first time and they exchanged grins. The 'beetle' was a running joke between them.

'You driving your sister to Kent in this crappy vehicle? Doesn't Elfie have a decent car of her own?'

'It's Pixie. And she doesn't drive. She's

19

going abroad for months. That's why she agreed to spend Christmas with Claire before she leaves.'

'Claire?'

'Our mother. She's what used to be called a "hippy" type. Still an oddball. She doesn't care for labels. Pixie and I have always called her Claire.'

Judith had never discussed her family with Erskine. There never seemed the time or inclination. Only Christmas could have put them on this collision course.

'A middle-aged flower child, eh?'

She glanced sharply at him but his face was turned away, the tilt of his smile erasing the tension of the round-up in Kilburn. But the graze on his cheek flared painfully raw.

Two

The Pendleburys' flat was situated in a curved modern block which rose like a cliff against the Thames. Judith gave Erskine a quick rundown on their hosts as they waited for the lift.

'Victor runs some sort of decorating business. Silk lampshades principally, I think. Madeleine's known Pixie since they were at boarding school. Claire used to teach art there and Pixie got a free place as part of the deal. A very classy establishment – heaven knows how our mother's weird antics fitted in but they must have appreciated her, keeping her on even after I put in a surprise appearance. Pixie stayed as a boarder and we were shunted to a staff cottage in the grounds. Perhaps they needed an on-site illustration of the wages of,' she paused, '—unfettered pleasure.'

This last remark was uttered with surprise as if it had never occurred to her before. 'Anyway, Maddy's staging this send-off before Pixie's six months incarceration in a caravan on an African building site –

Madeleine's idea of purgatory.'

The lift arrived, cutting short Laurence's pithy retort. Two other guests bearing fancy parcels hurried to join them.

Pixie's farewell celebration had overflowed on to the top landing, the front door of the Pendlebury apartment wide open, loud chatter and music spilling out to greet them.

A voice screamed through the crowd, 'Judy! Where on earth have you been?'

A tall woman, wearing a silk tent-like dress which might have graced the Field of the Cloth of Gold, detached herself from the scrum in the hallway and flung her arms around her. Erskine tagged along, determined to snatch a private farewell with Judith before making a quick getaway from what promised to be the worst sort of pre-Christmas thrash.

The marble-tiled foyer featured a cantilevered looking-glass overhanging a gilded console table heaped with parcels and unopened cards. The maisonette had a Continental feel, Parisian chic devoid of holly but liberally sprinkled with sparkly decorations and strongly scented with an indefinable fragrance for all the world like incense. Not that this was any sort of religious bolthole. Here, Christmas had reverted to paganism. From the next room the muffled beat of an old Mick Jagger hit was almost drowned in the hum of excitable small talk. They edged past a bubble-wrapped antique desk protruding from under the stairs causing a minor obstruction, presumably recently delivered and as yet unpacked. Erskine sighed. The whole place was throbbing, the party noisily well under way.

Judith touched his arm and spoke to Pixie. 'Darling, this is Laurence Erskine. My sister—'

'Priscilla Bowles. About time we met, Laurence.' She held out a hand to the surprisingly battered-looking man confronting her, his grazed cheek and lopsided smile offering an attractive but dangerous image, not at all the type she would have guessed to appeal to Judy.

'Don't start the big sister quiz,' Judith warned, well aware of Pixie's ability to unpick boyfriends like knitting. 'Where's Madeleine? I'm sorry we're late. Laurence got held up.'

Pixie raised an eyebrow. 'At gunpoint?'

'Got it in one, Priscilla,' he replied, hurriedly tacking himself on to Judith's heels already tapping away across the parquet to the main room.

Here the crowd was thinner, the party moving in on a buffet table laid out in the adjoining room. Large windows took up an entire wall, presenting a riverscape as breathtaking as a Canaletto. The sky, broodingly overcast and promising snow, posed a threatening backdrop to the glitter of the overheated drawing room, where a silver Christmas tree hung with golden pears touched the ceiling.

Judith pulled him forward to meet their hostess, plucking at her sleeve. Turning to greet them, Madeleine's fair hair swung smoothly across her shoulders like a shampoo advertisement. Erskine felt her eyes slide across his leather jacket and stained slacks and knew now he should never have agreed to come. Not that this reed-thin, perfumed creature was unwelcoming. On the contrary. Her smile was genuinely warm, the girlish hug enfolding Judith no mere gesture. But...? Erskine was puzzled: this fashion-plate female had an indefinable quality, a vulnerability at odds with the gloss. His security work often drew him into the swirl of diplomatic receptions, leaving him distinctly unimpressed with the so-called beautiful people. But he had never before been knocked sideways like this before. He could not take his eyes off the bloody woman. It was not sexual attraction either; Madeleine Pendlebury was too perfect for that. Lovely, but as untouchable as a portrait behind glass. She nattered with Judith unaware of the impression she was making – or perhaps such reactions were commonplace? Introductions to the others in the group slid over his head like the indecipherable dialogue of a Noh play and Erskine found himself holding a glass of wine, murmuring responses, his mind floating. Maybe the punch-up had left him in a state of delayed shock? The thought was unnerving. Suppose he was losing his grip? That brought him to his senses.

'—and Judith tells me you used to work together,' someone was saying. Erskine shook his head like a swimmer shaking water from his ears before answering the plump, middle-aged American lady who had buttonholed him.

'Originally – er – yes, sort of,' he agreed, casting about for Judy and a means of escape. 'Judy's with the Serious Fraud lot now. Tell me,' he insisted in an effort to veer the conversation, 'what do *you* do? I'm afraid I didn't catch your name. The noise in here ... my name's Laurence Erskine by the way.'

'Sophie Neuman. I work in London. When my husband died I decided to stay on. Chuck and I lived in this neighbourhood for years, you see. It felt like home.'

'Ah.'

Judith had vanished into the crowd. He craned his neck, seeking her out – the only person who could drag him to a shindig like this and she runs out on him ... The American was well into her stride.

'I've gone into business, Laurence. A year ago now. Perhaps Maddy mentioned my club, Chiaroscuro?'

'Club? Night club, d'you mean?'

Her laughter belted out, a real guffaw, plump cheeks trembling with amusement at the very idea.

'An *art* club, honey. Bruce Foxton, my partner, hatched the notion. Art study courses. Lectures in fine art and practical courses in decorative techniques. Sotheby's and Christie's run similar schemes but we've gone one better at Chiaroscuro. Bruce has turned over his entire house as club premises. We encourage members to drop in any time. We have a coffee room, a studio for slide lectures, of course, and a nice cosy study area – real "homey".'

'Like a health club without the need to exercise?' he suggested, po-faced.

'You bet! Very exclusive, naturally. A strictly private membership by personal introduction only. Mostly folks with time on their hands – not everyone's dying to spend their leisure organizing charity lunches, you know. And we're getting a name for ourselves for excellent guest speakers, not to mention our own staff lecturers, of course. We have just started a few evening sessions for busy young men like yourself, not to mention our weekend breaks staying at private homes by special invitation. The "country house set", Brucie's friends, are just dying to accommodate us. Judith told

26

you she's joining our Bath cultural tour, of course.'

Erskine flinched. He could imagine nothing worse.

'In January,' someone else chimed in, a low-pitched Canadian accent claiming his attention. Erskine dropped back, looking haunted. Sophie Neuman's companion made herself known, holding out a cool hand.

'Fenella. I never bother with surnames at parties. Life's too short.' She smiled, guessing Erskine's discomfiture. Being hedged about by art lovers was clearly not his bag at all. 'Let me take your coat,' she said, drawing him aside. 'It's hot as hell in here and if we can find Victor I'll get you a proper drink.'

She led him across the room ignoring his protests about leaving early. People closed in behind them like the Red Sea, stranding Sophie Neuman still rhapsodizing about her art club.

He allowed himself to be divested of his jacket and lit a cigarette, appraising his rescuer. He had spent a couple of years in Quebec and felt at ease with Canadians. His new friend was small and pert with eyes so black that the irises were indistinguishable. Thirtyish and smart as paint. He relaxed, watching her waylay a tired-looking fellow in a city suit bearing a tray of drinks, presumably their host, Victor Pendlebury. Fenella offered a sizeable slug of bourbon on the rocks and Erskine loosened his tie. Things were looking up.

He said, 'You a friend of Pixie's?'

'Pixie? Oh, no. Sophie Neuman's my connection here. She introduced me to Madeleine at one of her ghastly lecture evenings recently, though between you and me I've known Victor for years, he's an old chum of mine from way back. I run a little flat-finding agency in St John's Wood. Sophie's dear departed, poor old Chuck, was with the American embassy. I used to help him locate accommodation for the diplomatic crowd. They like to deal with people they can trust, who know what's required: a nice little apartment near the shops and a Californian kitchen. Wheels run smoother if the wives are happy. Bored, you see, poor darlings. Living in a foreign city, feeling lonely, no career to keep them amused. Sophie and I help out. I find the flats and the interior decorators and schools and Chiaroscuro fills the gaps. "Something cultural, honey",' she mimicked with a wicked Texan drawl as if 'culture' was some new beauty aid to be indulged secretly like plastic surgery or adultery.

Erskine chuckled and let her run on, Fenella's acerbic summary of Sophie's clientele unsparing.

Across the room a rowdy group was urging

someone to play the piano which stood on a shallow dais. A lively girl bounced on to the stool, discarded her bangles and started to play, quietly at first, chattering all the while and laughing like a jolly schoolgirl, entirely unaffected by her formidable talent.

'Who is that?'

'The redhead at the joanna? Now there you see a genuine Goldilocks – she's got the freckles to prove it. That's Victor's Girl Friday, Tricia Carroll. Turns her hand to anything that girl. Helps out with the accounts, organizes Madeleine's dental appointments and tinkles the ivories at parties.'

Victor's versatile secretary swung into a sparkling jazz routine which had her small circle bopping. Laurence idly took in the scene, half-attending to Fenella's continuing commentary.

With a start he recognized a familiar figure across the room and grabbed her elbow. 'Excuse me, I've just spotted a friend over there.'

She glanced towards a knot of young men clustered round a dark girl wearing spangled turkish trousers and a bolero.

'Suki Nadhouri, our beautiful Lebanese? Oh, Suki's *everyone's* friend, Laurence.'

Erskine ignored the innuendo. 'No. Morton Playle. The guy she's with used to be attached to Army Intelligence. Do you know him?'

She shrugged and fell in behind Laurence as he made a beeline through the crush. Sophie's hand snaked out, waylaying Fenella as Erskine placed a hand on Morton's shoulder.

Morton Playle was a dab hand at this sort of party and his swift assessment of Madeleine's guests missed nothing. He had noticed Erskine's arrival, surprised to see him at such a do. They had not met since Egypt three or four years before and he was unenthusiastic to renew the acquaintance. Laurence Erskine carried a whiff of danger about him like cordite. Morton Playle, at fifty-three, desired only a quiet life and a rich wife. Or vice versa. He sighed as Erskine shook his hand, resigned as a stoat in a trap.

'Your girlfriend mentioned you were involved in this arrest in Kilburn today, Laurence. Newsflash on my way here claimed some crackpot pro-Palestinian outfit calling itself "the Sioux" is involved. A new one on me. You heard of it?'

'You know anything, Morton?'

He shook his head, genuinely nonplussed. 'Only that the bloke you put the handcuffs on owns a restaurant called Tiki's off the Bayswater Road.'

'You been there?'

'Tiki's?' He shrugged. 'Once or twice. Great nosh: delicious bits of lamb in lemon juice, rice like snowflakes.'

'Come off it, mate! Spare me the foodie spiel. Don't try to tell me you haven't got your ear to the ground.'

Erskine pulled him aside out of earshot, smiling apologetically at the Lebanese girl.

Morton wriggled on the end of Erskine's line. 'I've been to Tiki's a few times,' he admitted. 'Contacts. My bread and butter since I left the Army. I freelance now. Articles for specialist journals. Some broadcasting for the World Service. A bit of translation work for the Foreign Office. Hammad introduced me to Tiki's place.' He nodded towards the girl in the gold lurex now laughing with the younger, livelier element clustered round the piano. 'Suki's brother, Hammad Nadhouri, runs a news-sheet in London. Knows everyone.' His voice dropped to a whisper. 'All the exiles, the dissidents, the fixers. Plus the usual hangers-on, of course. The Nadhouris are powerful in a discreet way. I just go along for the ride. Pick up a few tips from time to time.'

Laurence scribbled on the back of a business card and passed it over. 'My home number. I thought we might have a natter, compare notes on an informal basis. A mutual exchange and mart. Could do us both a bit of good, Morton.'

He reluctantly accepted Erskine's note and slipped it into his pocket. 'OK. Let's get together in the New Year. For "auld lang syne".' Morton's smile was wintry.

'I'll be back in London then. There's a special favour I'd like to ask of you, Morton.'

Their careful exchange was interrupted by the arrival of someone clearly unembarrassed at being a square peg at Madeleine's party. She breezed into the room like a gust of fresh air and stood in the doorway wearing a hacking jacket and jodhpurs, the brazen lack of conformity singling her out in the sparkly crowd. She caught sight of Erskine in his fight-stained gear and grinned, their eyes meeting like tricksters pulling the same scam.

'Hello, everyone. Happy Christmas!' she said, joining Morton and Laurence, ignoring Suki Nadhouri, who petulantly turned aside. Victor called to her over the heads of his guests, waving a half-empty bottle of champagne, and she abruptly moved off to greet him, striding across the room in her spattered riding boots, leaving a trail of woody scent, sexy as a romp in the heather.

Erskine nudged Morton. 'Who's that?'

'Genista Pendlebury. Victor's sister. Strictly speaking she's off limits here. Madeleine and Genny prowl their own part of the forest as a rule. It *is* Christmas, of course,' he added.

He was perfectly serious. Morton had no sense of humour.

From his vantage point, Erskine studied

Madeleine's sister-in-law. No one could be more of a contrast to Victor's wife or to her sophisticated friends. Her glowing looks were enhanced by very pale blue eyes and, even more dramatic, springy hair, prematurely white, cut close to her head and curling into the soft nape of her neck. Far from being a drawback, the hair emphasized the woman's sheer vitality, her neat head poised on a long neck, alert as an egret's. From the glimpse he had already caught of their host, Victor Pendlebury, the sister was younger – no more than early forties certainly – fitter and a good deal more intelligent than her brother. Erskine had an eye for it. He'd put a tenner on Madeleine's husband being under stress, under par and underperforming between the sheets. On the other hand, the sister...

'Do you remember that joke we had about excessively pale blue eyes?' Erskine muttered in Morton's ear.

'That nurse in Cairo, d'you mean? The oversexed one?'

'That woman wasn't oversexed – she was a bloody nymphomaniac.'

'Well, don't get any funny ideas about Genny Pendlebury, old man. She's never shown the slightest interest in men. She's exclusively in love with horses.'

Three

Judith regarded Laurence's smooth assimilation into Madeleine's crowd with a tinge of envy. He was the picture of relaxed affability, a glass in one hand, a cigarette in the other, exchanging jokes with strangers: entirely at his ease.

Sophie Neuman, Erskine's middle-aged American art club proprietor, by now more than a little tipsy, joined her, deepening Judy's dark mood with a boring monologue on the personalities who comprised the Pendlebury coterie. Then she proceeded to give the lowdown on Victor and his sister.

'Madeleine is insisting they all stay in London over Christmas. Genista's livid.'

'Oh?' Judith glanced at her watch, wondering how she could winkle Pixie from the party in decent time for the long winter drive to Kent.

Sophie nodded vigorously, setting her earrings a-wobble. 'Genny just told me it's the very first time they will miss the Boxing Day meet at Finings since she and Victor moved back from Argentina. Wonderful

English country home. A former medieval priory. Do you know Finings?'

Judy shook her head, getting crosser, wondering if her absence would even register with Erskine when she slipped away. The man was a chameleon, fitting in absolutely anywhere.

'—and all because Maddy invited her pa for the holidays. Alain Lambert, you must have heard of him, Judith, the French movie actor.'

'Lambert? Er, no. I'm not much into foreign films.'

'Your friend Laurence is a fan, I feel sure. He's a linguist, Pixie says.'

'Yes, but I wouldn't say he was any sort of film buff, Sophie.' Judy snorted at the notion of Erskine on the bijou cinema circuit. James Bond was more his mark.

'But Genista's insisting they all go down to Finings to see in the New Year. She's put her foot down over that.'

'Bully for Genista.' The tired irony was lost on Sophie, now getting into her stride and firmly blocking Judy's escape.

The American's bleary eyes focussed and she dropped the gossipy tone to move in even closer, suddenly perfectly sober.

'Judith, I need your professional advice.'

'Fraud at Chiaroscuro?'

'Hell, no!' Sophie shook her head. 'Theft,' she whispered. 'From the lockers, for

Christ's sake! My partner, Brucie's at his wits' end.'

'Have you reported it?'

'Are you mad? The people involved have been wonderful. Chiaroscuro can't take any bad publicity, we're only just keeping our heads above water as it is.' She produced a full-colour brochure and handed it to Judy, saying, 'Discretion is absolutely vital.'

'What's gone so far?'

'Madeleine was the first to call my attention to it. Her wallet, credit cards, you name it – all gone from her locker while she was doing a workshop in the basement. Suki claims to have lost the keys from her handbag, though she's such an airhead she probably just mislaid them. We keep several private lockers on the landing outside the coffee shop where folks can leave a change of gear; the guys come straight from work and like to get into jeans and sweatshirts before the evening sessions. We've been running a series of practical design courses recently – marbling, special paint effects, stencilling, you know... The girls keep their pinnies and valuables locked away in case they get mussed up.'

'Were the lockers broken into?'

'No, keys were used, Christ knows how. Brucie has been terribly careful. Another girl, Lucienne, had a ring stolen. She's being much more tiresome about it – Belgian, of course, they're always difficult – a nation of moaners, if you ask me. Being the butt of French jokes makes them touchy, I guess. Judith, as you're booked in on the West Country tour next month you could give us some pointers. In a quiet way, of course – we don't want to frighten the horses!' The edge to her laugh was unamused.

Judy was momentarily taken off balance by the false assertion of her own membership of the snobby club and concluded Sophie's apparent insobriety was only skin deep. Poor woman was certainly frantic. It was a pity 'Brucie' was off in Thailand for the holidays, leaving the poor old trout to sort it out on her own. Judith protested her own lack of experience in the petty theft and security line and was glad when Victor appeared and broke up the discussion.

The man looked strained. A pre-Christmas rush on lampshade orders perhaps? She choked back this unfriendly thought, realizing that his pallor was more basic, signalling something more fundamental than stress. Was the poor fellow ill? Victor must have weathered the recession better than most small-time manufacturers if Madeleine's unaltered spending power was any guide, but the effort of keeping commercially afloat must have taken its toll and Maddy was hardly the wife with whom to share the tribulations of Value Added Tax or the new business rate.

Luckily the Pendlebury family gene which had produced the premature greying of his sister's hair had bypassed Victor. His own fairish, faded thatch counteracted the ageing effect of his slack profile and hinted at a former handsomeness now all but submerged by business worries. Also, Victor had retained his slim build. Judith could imagine the dash he and Genista had cut on the polo fields of Argentina before their return to England, home and much diminished glory.

Sophie gloomily accepted a fresh glass from his tray. He smiled sympathetically at Judy, a diligent host, sensitive to the entrapment of the poor girl. Judith had always liked Victor Pendlebury, doggedly setting about any task in hand, his quiet manner undervalued it seemed by both Genista and Madeleine. He went through to the kitchen and Judith snatched at her opportunity to slip past Sophie in his wake and run upstairs.

The women's coats had been laid on Madeleine's bed and it took a while to find her own. It was well after three, almost dusk and the light filtering the net curtains was fading fast. Halfway downstairs she caught sight of Madeleine and Pixie jammed by the front door. It was now their turn to be skewered by Sophie Neuman's attentions. Judy signalled over the heads of a couple sitting on the stairs and Madeleine waved to her to come down. She squeezed past and joined them.

Judith said, 'Pixie! We must make a move.'

Her sister looked flushed, obviously delighted with the tremendous send-off but, Judy guessed, incandescent with Victor's champagne and probably relieved 'au fond' to have a deadline. She was right. Pixie's feet hurt. She looked down at her swollen ankles with disgust and apprehension.

Madeleine was radiant. As always, Judy conceded with a grin. Nevertheless, there was something different about her – like a myopic with her first pair of spectacles seeing outlines clearly for the first time. Madeleine had lost that vague and languid quality which to a stranger could seem disconcertingly as if the woman was ever so slightly bored with the conversation. Even so, it proved all that attention to creams and exercise paid off in the end. Especially if one geared one's whole life to it like Maddy. Judy inwardly blushed at her frank appraisal. The truth was Madeleine was uncomplicated. Maybe her new glow was, after all, something to do with Sophie's insistence that Pixie's best friend had 'discovered Art'. Judy's more earthy suspicion was that the woman had simply discovered Botox. Poor old Victor. No wonder he looked so groggy.

The doorbell rang, breaking up this interesting line of thought and Madeleine opened up. A motorbike messenger held out a small package.

'Mrs Pendlebury?' he said. 'Sign here, please. Special delivery.' Madeleine signed and stepped back to close the door just as the couple on the stairs descended to the hall and the three of them collided, the man falling back against the antique desk which projected from under the stairs. Sophie leapt upon him in alarm, grabbing his arm.

'The escritoire! Oh, my God.' She knelt on the floor checking the bubble-wrapped corners of the elaborately carved piece. 'God dammit, Maddy, isn't there somewhere *safe* you could store this?'

Madeleine shrugged. 'Sophie, there's not a spare inch till the party's over. It's on its way to Finings later. Genista's taking it in her Range Rover.' She turned to Pixie. 'It's my Christmas present from Victor,' she said with a small moue more expressive than words.

'Don't you like it?' Sophie wailed.

'Not much. A bonheur-de-jour wasn't on my Santa list. I hate all those fiddly little bronze knobs and pigeonholes. It's not French, you know,' she said, dismissing it with a wave of the hand. 'It's a Victorian copy.'

'But the workmanship's superb, Maddy. I bid for it myself. Victor thought you would like it for writing letters...' Sophie lamely concluded, sagging with dismay.

Madeleine patted her shoulder, all concern. 'Sophie, darling, I am so sorry. I had absolutely no idea Victor had involved you in all this! Don't take it to heart, my dear. It's just – j-just that I n-never write l-letters,' she stammered.

Mollified, Sophie perked up. 'I'll show you something really wonderful about this desk, Madeleine. Sophie's little surprise,' she said, pulling Madeleine into the alcove. Judith and Pixie crowded in behind.

'Just you take a little peeky-boo at this, darlings.'

Sophie's inebriation made her dramatic flourish as she whipped open a secret drawer between the pigeonholes as comical as a conjuror on *Amateur Night Special*.

'No one at the auction knew about that – not even the vendor or the price would have rocketed,' she crowed. 'Stuff like this fetches thousands of dollars in the States. A secret drawer's real icing on the cake. I didn't tell Victor, of course – we all need our little hideyholes.'

Madeleine grinned. 'What would I put in it?'

'Hairdressing bills? To hide them from Victor?'

She laughed awkwardly. 'Well there is my silly diary.'

'It's the spelling she's ashamed of,' Pixie quipped.

41

'Seems like a secret drawer's wasted on you then.' Sophie sounded depressed. It was probably the booze.

Madeleine squeezed her arm and tossed the Special Delivery parcel in the shallow aperture and closed it with a flourish, the fascia of the pretty desk now blandly innocuous. 'There you go. First item to go under cover! A secret drawer's just what I needed, Sophie. Can't think how I've managed without one all these years. Trust you to find the perfect present for the Spoilt Bitch Who Has Everything. Our secret,' she confided, her finger pressed to her lips.

Laurence emerged from the party scrum just in time to catch Pixie's noisy departure. He pulled Judith aside and they muttered on the threshold, tossing her bruised ego back and forth in the undertones of a public squabble. At last a truce was agreed and Erskine persuaded her to accept the gift-wrapped parcel, which in all honesty had almost slipped his mind. So much seemed to have happened since Burlington Arcade that morning.

As they wrangled, Pixie fielded enthusiastic farewells and now waited by the front door, frankly curious, watching the gusts of this hot and cold relationship her sister had contracted. The telephone jangled on the console table at Sophie's elbow and she automatically dealt with it. Holding the receiver above her head she bawled into the main room, 'Suki! Suki Nadhouri!! Your brother's on the phone. Been calling all over London for you, for Christ's sake.'

The girl in the gold harem pants pushed her way through, waving a sprig of mistletoe, the essence of Christmas fun. Sophie handed her the receiver and tottered out into the lift area on the landing, where partygoers were giving Pixie a final send-off. Laurence kissed Judith and promised to ring her from Tignes on Christmas morning. They clung together like lovers on a station platform and it was only afterwards that Judith remembered he didn't have Claire's number. Pixie's eyes filled with sentimental tears and she hugged Madeleine as the gang of wellwishers waved them off. The lift doors closed.

Out in the street the wind whipped their ankles and Judith bundled her sister into the VW's passenger seat and stowed her suitcases and gifts. As Judy was about to step round the car, the swing doors of the apartment block flew open and Suki, a full-length silver fox thrown around her shoulders, ran down the steps, hotly pursued by Morton Playle. Judy hesitated, assuming for a moment Pixie had left something behind, but the girl fled past to her own vehicle, a gleaming red Ferrari Testarossa parked in the next slot.

As the girl nervously fumbled with her keys

43

Morton caught up and took them from her, opening the car door himself and pushing her inside. Judy stood open-mouthed, astonished at the sudden change of party mood – Suki white-faced and apparently mute with shock. Morton took the wheel and revved up, the tail lights disappearing into the dark.

'Pixie, did you see that?'

'Her house must be on fire.' Pixie's response to emergencies was unfailingly laconic.

'No. Not the panic exit. Didn't you see what was pasted on her windscreen?'

'A parking ticket?'

Judy started the ignition. 'No, you fool. SUKI AND KILROY stuck inside the windscreen of that beautiful sports car! You know, on a rainbow strip, capital letters you get from motor shops. Like TRACEY AND KEV. Real council estate style.'

'Oh, that's just Suki's idea of a naff joke.'

'Good grief. It's sacrilege. Defacing a Ferrari like that... Anyway, who's Kilroy? The middle-aged boyfriend?'

'No. That's Morton. Kilroy's Suki's Afghan hound.'

Four

They drove along the Embankment in an unbroken line of traffic dragging its way out of the capital for Christmas, snowflakes sticking to the windscreen in soft melting blobs.

Pixie shifted in her seat, fidgeting already, not daring to mention her need to stop off for a pee before too long. She wondered if the stomach bug contracted on that last Java tour had flared up again. For the past fortnight she had been feeling distinctly nauseous, the last thing she needed on the brink of this Zambian trip. She decided to keep any hint of this from their mother over Christmas, Claire's invariable reaction to any sort of ailment being a stiff dose of herbal tea. Pixie shuddered at the prospect and glanced at Judith's profile set stonily against the jam of cars and lorries stuck ahead. She turned to stare at the black river reflecting the fairy lights strung along the opposite bank where the dense vegetation of Battersea Park lay dark as the shores of the Amazon. Judy's voice startled her.

'I hate to ask this, Pixie, but would you mind terribly if we stop off at Mortlake? Just a quick call to drop off a present for my old boss?'

'I *knew* you were driving the wrong way,' she crowed. 'Be my guest. I'd like a break myself, get sorted out before the long haul.' She glanced at the back seat piled with Christmas parcels and wished the heating in Judy's car actually worked.

'He's a widower, retired early after the Swayne case I told you about.'

'Wasn't Laurence the nigger in that particular woodpile?'

'Mm. Old Arnott was pretty pissed off when Special Branch horned in on his investigation and started moving the goal posts. Laurence's abrasiveness can get to anyone and Arnott's a cantankerous old sod.'

'Must you swear? I thought your conversation would be more ladylike once you settled with the Fraud lot. No more murder cases, just polite city crooks.'

Judy laughed. 'Sorry. Wouldn't have guessed your ears were so sensitive after years as a camp follower.'

'If you came out to visit us sometimes you'd realize that road workers are perfect gentlemen when females are around. Quite old-fashioned, in fact. You'd be surprised. Anyway, as we were saying, if your bloke,

Laurence, fell out with your boss and he lost his job over it, I wouldn't imagine he'd ever want to set eyes on either of you again. The season of goodwill's not magic, sweetie.'

'We made it up. Arnott finished the case in his own time, to his entire satisfaction. I haven't seen him for ages. I thought I'd just like to wish him a merry Christmas. Poor old devil's on his own, has no family and, as far as I know, no friends. He wasn't popular at the station. They were glad to see the back of him as a matter of fact.'

'Oh, so you are playing Lady Bountiful now? Fancy that! Judith Pullen visiting the poor and unloved, bringing yuletide cheer.'

'Arnott's no pathetic old pensioner, believe me. Anyway, I've had an idea. I think I've got something for Arnott.'

They pulled out of the snarl-up at Old Chelsea. Judy swung the little car through a dozen narrow streets and by a devious series of back routes they were soon clear of the traffic jams. Her impatience evaporated once they were able to pick up speed and they breezily chewed over the send-off Madeleine had staged for Pixie.

Judith said, 'Madeleine looked pretty perky, I thought. Does she really know anything about furniture? I was astonished when she was so dismissive of the dear little desk thing Victor bought for her.'

'Maddy's a dozy female on the whole but

she learned a lot about furniture in Paris in the school holidays.'

'Have you met her father?'

'Alain Lambert – the heart-throb of the Left Bank? Oh yes. She took me to France one Easter when we were teenagers. Alain had just acquired a new wife though he bunked off a year later, I heard. He's been living with an American starlet until recently, Madeleine told me. Anyway, Eloise, Madame Lambert mark II at that time, was a collector. She trailed Maddy and I round the galleries and auction houses with her just to keep us two girls off the streets, I suppose. Actually, it was quite a lot of fun though I felt a bit out of it because my French was so lousy. Still is.'

'And Madeleine's bilingual, of course.'

Pixie nodded. 'Absolutely fluent. I sometimes wonder if all that bobbing about between London and Paris caused the stammer.'

'Claire's convinced it's affectation, of course. All part of the act.'

'It's not, you know. Though it is attractive, don't you think? When someone looks so stunning, a human frailty like that is awfully alluring. Madeleine's dyslexic, you know, barely literate, poor love. That's why she was so shirty about Victor assuming she wrote letters. Stupid man. You would think he would notice after being married for years that his wife is paranoid about her spelling. She was always hopeless at school, hardly opens a book even now. I was totally bowled over when she agreed to join the art club. I pushed her into it because Sophie was having such a bad time. Sophie has sunk her widow's mite into it and obviously a thing like an art club takes a while to build up a solid membership. It costs Madeleine no more than she spends on her exercise classes and even if she drops out after a bit the cash is in the till now. She certainly can afford a little charity.'

'If you ask me, Sophie's left it a bit late to start even a charity. Poor old duck is obviously totally out of her depth. She even thought I was a member. Convinced I had booked to go on some potty jaunt to Bath. I didn't argue. She was obviously pissed.'

Pixie shifted in her seat and coughed. Judith felt a sudden chill, warning bells ringing through Pixie's uncharacteristic silence. 'Come on, Pixie, spill the beans. What are you up to?'

The response came in a rush, the tone aggressive and defensive all at once. 'Actually, you *are* booked on the Bath weekend. You don't have to go, of course, but I've paid for it now. I thought you were *interested* in art, Judith.'

Judy clashed the gears in her confusion. 'Not enough to get myself banged up for three days in one of Sophie's "bee-ute-i-ful private homes" with a crowd of dowagers and culture-crazed foreigners.'

Pixie pursed her lips, clearly hurt.

'Judy, Chiaroscuro's hanging on by its fingertips. It just needs a little time to get established, that's all. I thought a nice arty weekend away would be fun for you. It's not exactly Open University stuff. Good Lord, even Madeleine enjoys it and her idea of exercising her brain cells is an afternoon at the pictures with a box of popcorn.'

'Maddy would never touch popcorn – the smell might get in her hair!'

Despite her show of temper, Pixie could see the funny side of it.

When the giggles subsided, Pixie blurted out, 'I tell you what, Judy. Why don't you go to the pre-tour lecture evening at Chiaroscuro the week before the "off" and make up your mind when you know the score? It's all listed in the itinerary I was going to give you on Christmas morning – "my wee giftie",' she added with mock demureness before continuing in her own naturally bantering tone, 'The whole thing's bloody expensive, you ungrateful cow.'

'Perhaps my big sister could confine herself to book tokens in future,' Judith briskly retorted.

Luckily, at that moment, they pulled up outside Arnott's house.

'Good. The lights are on. I thought he might be at the pub. Pixie, pass me a bottle from the floor behind you.'

Pixie scuffled about and came up with a beribboned bottle of Glenfiddich. 'Morton gave me this,' she grumbled. 'I hope this Arnott bloke's worth the gesture.'

'Don't be such a Scrooge – it *is* the season of goodwill, etcetera.'

Judith slammed the door, gripping the whisky in her gloved hand, skidding on the frosty pavement. The snow had turned to slush but the ground was treacherously patchy. She opened the gate and was rushing up Arnott's path as Pixie shouted from the car. Judy twisted round, slid on an icy puddle and, in an effort to save herself, fell awkwardly, taking the full force of the fall on her free hand. She lay spreadeagled on the path, winded by the pain.

'Shit!'

Still cradling the bottle, she sat up, holding up her wrist to the light which streamed out as Arnott opened his front door.

'Bloody 'ell, Pullen. You're a big lass for playing slides in the snow.'

He helped her up just as Pixie slithered to a halt beside them. 'You all right, chicken?'

'No, I'm bloody well not all right. Why did you have to shout at me like that, Pixie?'

Arnott put up his hand. 'Hush now. Come inside. Let's look at the damage.'

He led through the narrow hallway, the smell of stale tobacco seeming to seep from the very wallpaper. Pixie felt queasy and wished she had gone easy on Victor's champagne.

The small sitting room rocked with the heat from a gas fire. The women sat down and Arnott took the whisky from Judy and gently removed her overcoat, Pixie anxiously watching the scruffy man in the baggy cardigan examine Judith's wrist with all the expertise of a trained medico.

He laid her throbbing hand in her lap and moved to a stainless-steel drinks trolley shoved in one corner. It looked like a pharmacy with the bottles and glasses lined up for sterilization. In fact, the whole room looked pretty spartan. He poured a brandy and passed it to his patient.

'Just a sprain, lass. I'll get some aspirins.'

'I can't drink this, Arnott. I'm driving.'

'Not no more you ain't, not tonight any road. But please yourself, woman. A cup of tea'd suit me.'

Judith started to weep. It was all too bloody much.

Arnott patted her shoulder. 'I'll make the tea,' he said and went out of the room.

Pixie squeezed Judy's good hand. 'Don't sniffle, darling. It's not the end of the world. I'll ring Claire and put her off. We can stay in London for Christmas.'

'We *can't* do that! Claire's been talking about nothing else for weeks. And I can't ask Laurence to drive us. He's flying to Switzerland or France or somewhere tonight. Skiing – that's if he's allowed to escape the investigation of the business in Kilburn. Oh, God!'

'What about a train?'

'Just before Christmas? We'd never get seats.'

Judy felt fresh tears well up and fiercely blew her nose as Arnott returned with a tray of tea plus bandages and a bowl of iced water.

Pixie took off her coat, making herself at home.

'I'll be mother,' she insisted, drawing the cups towards her as Arnott dealt with Judith's sprain.

'And where were you two girls gadding off to in this weather?'

'Romney Marsh. Our mum's expecting us. And as I'm often abroad at Christmas she's set her heart on it unfortunately. We can't cancel – I'll telephone and say we'll be late. We can get a minicab to drive us down. I've never learned to drive, you see,' Pixie explained, passing a cup of very strong tea to Judith. 'I'm her sister by the way. Pixie.'

Arnott eyed Pullen's ginger-haired sister sitting opposite, all bundled up in a fancy frock, entirely filling his Parker Knoll and looking not a bit like a fucking fairy.

'May I use your loo, Mr Arnott?'

'Upstairs, lass. Turn right, off the landing.'

Pixie nodded, pausing at the door to explain. 'That's what I was trying to call out to you when you slipped on the path, Judy. I needed to come in for the bathroom.'

'Don't make a drama out of a crisis, Priscilla,' she snapped.

Arnott hurried to intervene before they started scrapping again.

'It was my fault,' he said. 'I should have put some ash on the bloody concrete. Sugar, Pullen?'

When Pixie had gone upstairs, Judith gazed round the little sitting room, which was now entirely disencumbered of Peg's furniture, the place furnished – apart from the one comfortable armchair – like Arnott's old office at the station. Even the glass-topped coffee table which had loomed so large on her last visit was less obtrusive now Peg's knick-knacks had all been cleared out and, in fact, was hardly visible under mounds of newspapers. Judith smiled, watching him light a cigarette, glad his evil-tempered anti smoking crusade had burned itself out.

'Well, Arnott—?'

She had never managed to get her tongue round any other form of address since his retirement and still had the utmost difficulty in omitting the 'sir'. 'How are things? Looks

54

as if you've settled down here after all. Not moving back to Yorkshire?'

'Housing slump's put paid to selling up for now.' He sipped his tea, regarding the girl by his fireside cradling her bruised hand. 'I bought this boat in the summer, see. A leaking bloody tub but with all this time on my hands I can do it up meself. It's at a yard near Rye. Lucky you caught me. I'm off down there tomorrow. Can't stand rattling round here all Christmas fending off the neighbours. And who wants to spend the 'oliday gawping at the telly?'

'While Pixie's upstairs, I want to give you this.' Judith fished in her bag for a biro and scribbled a note of introduction in the margin of Sophie's Chiaroscuro brochure and passed it across.

'This friend of mine, Sophie Neuman, badly needs a security survey. On the QT. I immediately thought of you,' she lied. 'Just up your street, Arnott, and she'll pay handsomely. Help refit the leaking tub.'

His nicotine-stained fingers handled the flimsy leaflet as if it were blue touch paper and might easily cause a big bang.

'Nay, lass. I 'aven't worked since that Swayne caper. She know I'm retired, this Neuman woman?'

'I didn't mention your name. I wanted to speak to you first. Think it over. Give her a call in the New Year, Arnott, if you're interested. See what's involved. No hassle.'

They both looked up as Pixie ambled in and Arnott hurriedly shoved the brochure in the pocket of the baggy cardigan as if it were a billet-doux.

Pixie asked, 'May I use your telephone, Mr Arnott? I've decided I'll have to tell Claire we can't make it. I can't believe we would get a taxi to take us all that way in this weather.'

Judith sighed. 'Here, use my mobile.' She scrabbled in her pocket, producing the smashed remains of her little cellphone.

'Oh, bugger! It must have got broken in the fall. And to think I was nursing that bloody bottle of whisky!'

Arnott smiled, the familiar foxy grin Judith had almost forgotten.

'What about if I drive you down in my motor? I've got a big Jap four-wheel drive now,' he said in triumph. 'An endowment policy came up and I thought I'd treat meself. Peg would never have stood for it, a great bus like that. It's grand for carting all the boat junk up and down the frigging motorway. Better in snow than that VW of yours, Pullen. Safer for your sister. Reckon she's had enough excitement for one day.'

Judith's eyes widened at the possibility.

'Would you, Arnott?' Toting two women down to the country in a near blizzard was not, she imagined, top of the pops with Arnott.

'I wouldn't bloody well make a silly offer like that for laughs, Pullen.'

Judy massaged her wrist, reminded of the unexpected bumps in any exchange with ex-Inspector Ralph Arnott.

'Your language hasn't improved with retirement then?' she retaliated.

'Why should it? I'm not ready for the Golden Oldies Bingo Club yet by a long road. Peg used to keep the lid on my four-letter words but I can please meself now, can't I?' he said sourly. There was no answer to that.

He grinned again, breaking the tension. Pixie restacked the tea tray and moved towards the kitchen. He followed her out. She liked Judy's cranky old devil. It would be fun to see Claire's reaction to their unlikely knight errant, a woman who herself had made a life's work of being unpredictable.

Pixie looked round the tiny kitchen, tidy as a galley, and at the man impatiently stuffing the rest of the bandages back in the first aid box. Things had certainly taken a funny turn since Madeleine's smart party. She heard Judith dialling Claire's number as she started washing up and called out, 'Tell her to lay an extra plate. Say we're bringing a new man down with us.' And then, grimly under her breath, 'Claire'll love that.'

Five

It was the second day of January before Arnott found himself crossing Romney Marsh again. He was due to pick up Judith Pullen for the return to London.

To his surprise he had enjoyed a right old knees-up over Christmas at a place up the coast from Rye run by a former 'working girl' now turned seaside landlady called Brenda. There were six others staying over the holiday, a mixed bunch but more than ready to whoop it up. They all got on a treat – quite a party in fact – and not a bit like mince pies and sherry in Mortlake. Arnott let nothing slip about his police pension, which would have gone down like a lead balloon with the other lodgers, who all, he would bet a pound to a penny, had some form. 'Sea View' suited Arnott's floating situation. He was more at home with the semi-criminal element these days than his well-meaning neighbours at Mortlake, whose sympathies since Peg's death left him feeling out of step with people, a state of affairs not improved by his uneasy retirement. The limbo of a seaside boarding house out of season provided more than enough company for oddballs like himself with no real homes to go to over the so-called festive season.

He sat hunched in the driving seat tapping the steering wheel in time with a brass band concert from Easington blasting from the car stereo. The sun glittered over the chaste landscape with its rolling meadows of eye-popping viridian. Smooth as a vicarage lawn. Not a patch on the Yorkshire moors, he decided, but a fair prospect even to Arnott, who had tunnel vision when it came to geographical prejudices. The last time he had battled this way, having dropped off the Pullen girls at their ma's, the view had been as impenetrable as a Scotsman's purse, the snow banked in mounting drifts and still falling. Arnott, bullied by Pixie, stayed to supper at the cottage that night and had, in truth, been glad of the break. But he should have pressed right on. The weather didn't let up till late and Brenda Clegg must have been the only landlady on the south coast to whom two in the morning was a reasonable hour to book in.

The snow that night had blanketed the roads, reducing the lines of cars leaving London to a bleak caravan winding across the white desert of Kent in a blizzard. The

Pullen sisters would never have made it in the VW – they would have frozen in the attempt.

Pullen's mother was plainly relieved to see them arrive safe and sound and welcomed them into the comfortable chaos of Pike End Cottage with an obvious delight which he had been warned might well be absent. The girls freely admitted that their ma was a quirky character, unpredictable and not overly concerned about the opinions of others. It must have been one of her good days.

To Arnott's eye, the thin brown-eyed woman all wrapped up in a long tartan skirt and holly-green jumper looked very attractive indeed and, at a rough guess, not a day over fifty-five, which couldn't be right, of course, not unless that big, red-haired gel of hers with the silly name had been the result of a romp in the bushes on the way home from school. Claire Pullen was an arty version of Judy and no mistake, her direct glance sweetened with a smile which instantly turned Arnott's craggy mug to that of a telly advert Saint Nicholas, his terrier's eyebrows dusted with real snowflakes.

Arnott had allowed himself to be fussed over by the three women, astonishing himself with his own goodwill. The journey had been a brute and without the flattering challenge of getting Pullen and her sister to the godforsaken spot he would never have set out from Mortlake. Serves you right, you silly old sod, Peg would have said, ever ready to puncture his propensity for showing off. He frowned, recognizing the imaginary commentary which so often flared up in his mind these days. You'll have to watch it, Ralph lad, you'll be talking to yourself out loud next.

The cottage at Pike End was a rambling affair with several outbuildings merging together to form a low byre-like habitation sheltering from the east wind in a wooded hollow. Arnott could never have found the place on his own even in good weather and was interested to see it again in daylight. His Mr Punch nose was a navigational beacon: Arnott never lost his bearings twice.

He turned off the ignition and clambered out, stamping his boots up the path to shake off the dry mud before ringing the bell. Judy came to the door, dressed for the journey, and put her finger to her lips.

'Pixie's having a lie-in. I said goodbye last night. Claire's in the yard, firing the kiln. Come and see.' She stacked her luggage in Arnott's 'Trooper' and they tramped round the back.

Claire Pullen emerged from one of the outhouses and greeted him with a vague smile.

'I can't take my eyes off it this morning. Bloody thing's on the blink,' she said. Her eyes had the same hazel warmth as Judy's and her hair, already greying and wispily drawn into a topknot, retained the gleam of former glories. Arnott had an eye for a pretty woman but it brought out a latent stiffness of manner making him seem abrupt. But though she smiled and took his hand in both her own to wish them a safe journey, he guessed her mind was elsewhere, his awkwardness unremarked.

Distracted, she hugged her daughter as if to remind herself of the formalities of leavetaking and followed them to the gate. But her heart was not in it and they were barely seated before the woman in the spattered jumper had turned back to her workshop.

'I didn't ask you in for coffee, Arnott. Claire's restive after a whole week away from her studio and Pixie needs no excuse to come downstairs.'

'She confined to barracks or summat, this sister of yours?'

Judith nodded, frowning at the empty lane ahead. 'The doctor called in and read the riot act yesterday. Her temperature's way up again ... there are complications. He insists Pixie has total rest for a month at least. Mind you, Pike End's the perfect place for it.'

'Can she take it? Used to the country like your ma?'

'No way! Pixie's a real townie. Poor Tom

will never manage to peg her down in London the way Claire can here. He's due home in February but by then the worst will be over – he can make her keep her feet up for the last bit, if she's still sane by then that is. I must admit Pixie's been a bit screwy lately...'

Arnott was out of his depth with all this women's talk and started telling her about his boat.

'A nice little centre-board gaffer,' he said with pride. 'Clinker mahogany, gaff sloop rig and roller headsail. Champion little begger. Needs a bit of work mind, but next summer, by 'eck, you won't catch me in bloody Mortlake! I've got to drop off an outboard motor with a pal of mine at St Katherine's dock on the way in. Won't take a tick.'

Judith was somewhat stunned by all this. 'Never thought I'd see you playing Popeye.'

'Watch your tongue, you saucy tart,' he said with a grin. He accelerated on to the motorway and launched into an incomprehensible monologue about engines, moorings, paint treatments and an inch-by-inch description of the wooden marvel which he had mysteriously renamed *Pamina*. This rang a bell but before Judy could follow it up the traffic snared up again and Arnott's mood lost its buoyancy. They gloomily pursued their own thoughts.

After ten minutes' silence, Judy chipped in

with, 'Arnott, can I ask you something personal?'

His bushy brows lifted in unspoken comment. During their many car rides together in their professional capacity before his retirement, Arnott's former DS could barely bring herself to ask him the time. But everything had changed and he reluctantly accepted his place in the no-man's-land he now inhabited.

Taking his silence for assent, Judy hesitantly put her question.

'Do you miss your family?'

Arnott, taken completely off balance, roared with laughter.

At last he said, 'You serious, Pullen? You doing a bleeding survey for the *Police Gazette*?'

'Forget it,' she muttered, shifting abruptly to stare out at the unmoving traffic clogging all three lanes. 'Just curiosity. Sorry.'

'Won't take a shake of a monkey's tail to set that one straight, lass. I ain't never had no family. Not on paper, any road. I was reared by Uncle Barnardo.'

'You were?' Judy assimilated this, then ventured, 'I only asked because I had this terrific row with Pixie last night. We don't seem to have any relations at all – I couldn't think who else to ask. Everyone else seems to have dozens of cousins and what-not, especially at Christmas.'

64

'You and that sister of yours squabble *all* the bloody time? Like a couple of starlings the pair of you, always on the twitter.'

'Pixie's virus makes her run hot and cold but this is really bothering her, she's making herself ill over it, worse at any rate. It involves Claire and while they're boxed up at Pike End everything's getting out of proportion. I've never talked about this to anyone; in fact, it's never bothered me, I'm not a worrier like Pixie. You've met Claire ... You can see how she is – she's always gone her own way, done her own thing. A real tower of strength in an emergency and never tied us down emotionally, if you know what I mean. But Pixie and I have different fathers, you see. That's all Claire would ever say about it. She brought us up on her own and as far as I'm concerned that's been more than enough. But all over Christmas Pixie's been nagging at Claire to tell us more. To put it in a nutshell, Pixie wants to put the record straight. She wants to know about our family, our roots...'

'Left it bloody late, ain't she?'

Judy nodded, looking solemn. 'Claire won't cooperate. Pixie reckons she owes it to us. She thinks we're entititled to more of a background than Claire's willing to offer.'

'Did me no harm. What good's it going to do, dredging up some rotten relatives thirty-odd years on?'

65

'My sentiments exactly. Forget it, Arnott. Three women cooped up in a small cottage over Christmas was just too much. No wonder the psychiatric clinics are busting at the seams every New Year.'

The traffic lurched forward and the 'Trooper' picked up speed. Arnott fiddled with the stereo and the mood lightened over *Star Choice*, a programme in which the famous were interviewed about their choice of music and books, mostly PR whitewash but mildly entertaining on a long run. Judy wondered if it was a traffic police ploy set up with the connivance of the broadcasting company to calm drivers stuck on the motorways. Nice soothing stuff.

The jams built up again once they hit Tower Bridge Road and Arnott's temper seriously frayed when they found themselves at a standstill once again. Judith's sprained wrist had stiffened and she rubbed at it, glassy-eyed, gazing out, thinking about Laurence Erskine, hoping for a postcard on the mat when she got home. Suddenly, she jerked forward, clutching Arnott's sleeve.

'Hey! Look there!' She pointed at the crowded pavement outside a pie and mash shop lit like a cinema foyer, its art deco interior gleaming with mirrors and fantastical tiling. Arnott stopped at a zebra crossing.

His face lit up. 'Pie and mash and a slosh of liquor. By 'eck, Pullen, that's a grand idea.

I could down a plate of that and it wouldn't even touch the sides. Surprised you go in for all that stuff though, a skinny bird like you.'

'I never have. No, look at that woman in the red ski jacket. The one with the long blonde hair just going in with the guy with the yellow cycle cape slung over his shoulder.'

Arnott's lizard's eye assimilated the young man in denims guiding his glamour girl to the entrance. 'Lucky soldier. The tart looks a bit flash for a pie shop though, don't she? A mate of yours, Pullen?'

The woman in the red parka stood out in the scruffy crowd like the Snow Queen in downtown Harlem.

'That's Madeleine Pendlebury. Pixie's best friend. She's absolutely loaded. Pie shops must be the "in thing" all of a sudden. Just goes to show how wrong you can be about people, Arnott. I've known Maddy for years and if you asked me who was the very last person to try a fast food junkshop like that, Madeleine Pendlebury would be way up on the world list.'

'Hang about, lass. Eels is good nourishing stuff. Nowt to beat it. You don't know what you're missing. That chum of yours looks ruddy pleased with herself any road. More sense than you, by 'eck. Why don't we pull over and have a couple of bobs' worth? My treat.'

The test cricketer on the radio programme chose his last disc, a seasonal number about a partridge in a pear tree. Arnott made a ribald remark about the plump partridge Pixie's best pal looked surrounded by the motley bunch going in the pie shop and they laughed, staring in at the brilliantly lit tiling gleaming behind the steamed-up windows. Cars started hooting behind. He hurriedly let out the clutch and the traffic moved on. Judy stared over her shoulder, mesmerized by the couple disappearing inside.

'Let's give it a rain check. It looks like Madeleine wouldn't welcome us. That wasn't Victor Pendlebury widening her gastronomic horizons.'

'The bloke in the Tour de France get-up?'

Judith laughed, grappling with the concept of Victor on a bike.

'Just drive home, Arnott. You can introduce me to the pie and mash shop tomorrow.'

'You're on, my lass,' he said with relish.

Six

On the way home from Arnott's house at Mortlake Judy called at her office to check the post and acquaint herself with the new files, which seemed to breed like wire coathangers in her absence. Serious fraud took no holidays. In fact, it appeared to flourish in the press twilight of the Christmas break when dubious transactions went unreported. Most people seemed to be taking the rest of the week off, the pace in the city curiously muted, faces on the street bearing the tribal marks of the 'morning after'. The temperature had risen: it was starting to drizzle.

Picking up some shopping from the late-night delicatessen on the corner, she approached her apartment building at seven o'clock with all the dismal ennui of an empty evening ahead. As she dropped her bags inside the hall and turned to close the door, a man in a belted trenchcoat carrying a flight bag bounded up the steps. She recognized the all-purpose grin of Craig Thomas, an Australian journalist who occupied the two-roomed flat on the first floor though he seemed to be constantly in transit. He picked up a pint of milk from the porch and greeted her.

'Hi Judy! Great to see you.'

He hugged her briefly and shut the door on the weather outside.

'Hello, Craig. Happy New Year.' She nodded towards his battered bag with its fluttering airline labels. 'Just back?'

'New York and Washington,' he answered with relish.

'Work or play?' Judith sorted the post into neat piles, extracting her phone bill and a postcard.

'Congratulate me, sweetheart,' he drawled à la Humphrey Bogart, tilting the brim of his hat. 'Just landed a staff job with *Manhattan Magazine*. Kiss me quick, I'm feeling lucky.'

Judy giggled, fending off his exuberant advances. 'Craig, that's absolutely wonderful. You moving out?'

'Next month, God be praised. Can't wait to have a regular paycheque again. I've been angling for this for months. You just back from the country? Good time?'

'Mm, so-so.' Judith scanned the postcard – the snowy alpine scene almost as glacial as her own feelings towards Laurence just now. His habit of penning postcards from glamorous locations round the world didn't seem funny any more – the joke had worn distinctly thin.

'What? Sorry, Craig. I was thinking of something else. What did you say?'

'I said why don't we two go out on the town tonight? I feel like an enormous steak after living off plastic airline trays since Boxing Day. We could celebrate my new status – offload the price of a dinner and a night out clubbing on my expenses. What do you say?'

Judith tore up Laurence's card and tossed it with the rest of the mail on the hall table.

'Why not? Sounds a great idea. I've had enough turkey to last me to the Day of Judgement.'

Craig looked slightly stunned. His luck really was in. Judy grabbed her things and called out, 'Give me half an hour,' as she ran upstairs, leaving him nursing his bottle of milk.

They started off at the Admiral Codrington, which seemed to be the wailing wall for all the Australians skinning the bloom off their suntans on their first winter in Europe. Craig Thomas was out to enjoy himself, showering his good news in a wide arc of bonhomie. Judy and her new escort found themselves the focus of the attentions of the 'Freebies' as they were collectively known, all chronically short of girls and beer money after a week-long celebration of the nativity.

'The Freebies. The Bonzo Boys from Bondi, three Bs – get it?'

Craig and Judith finally escaped, grabbed a cruising taxi, and left the Aussies behind. They decided on a lively bistro-bar in Soho and bagged a corner table with no problem. The festive crowds had either gone underground after New Year or were, like the Freebies, out of funds.

He beamed at Judith, seated opposite in the half-light of the candlelit cellar restaurant, her sequinned sweater sparkling like her eyes. Craig Thomas briefly regretted his imminent move to New York. He could hardly credit this date with Judy Pullen, all his previous propositions having been cheerfully turned down. The tall guy from Special Branch was the stumbling block and Craig was not going to press his luck. But nothing ventured...

The Australian was good-looking in the outdoorsy style of male models on knitting patterns, Judy reflected. In fact, the sporty image was, she knew, entirely false: Craig made his living exposing high-society scandals. His investigative journalism had earned 'Sneak' Thomas – as he was known in the Belgravia jet set – many enemies and he had almost run out of rope. It was time he moved on. Tap-dancing on the sensibilities of the glitterati was a dangerous game. He himself felt light-headed with the imminent move to the States, where the brashness of his appeal would enjoy a smoother passage than on the London snob circuit.

They ordered pasta followed by charcoal-grilled steaks. The waiter lit the candle on the red check tablecloth and Judith, knowing it would amuse him, described Pixie's pre-Christmas lunch party. Craig knew several of the people involved, including the Chiaro-scuro crowd, and impressed her with his instant command of biographical detail. The man's mind was a computer!

'Bruce Foxton started the art fanciers' club with an American woman called Neuman. Do you know them?'

Judith shrugged, concentrating on her spaghetti.

'Foxton's a lawyer, a very shrewd operator by all accounts. He used to be with some financial investment outfit until last year. Accepted a golden handshake when they suddenly closed the London office, and hatched Chiaroscuro on the proceeds. Actually, it's not a bad idea though personally I think the art club racket's no longer the 'in thing'. Chiaroscuro arrived on the scene a year too late – no one wants to be seen enjoying themselves too conspicuously just now. The big auction houses have been running art courses for years but Foxton's notion was to make it more palatable to the affluent layabouts with a penchant for culture – hence the clubby image. You been there, his place behind Gough Square?'

'Not yet. But my sister gave me a weekend art break as a Christmas present – a West Country tour centred on Bath. I'm due to attend the precourse lecture evening on Thursday week.' She made a small grimace in response to Craig's quizzical glance. 'Don't say it!' she warned.

He tactfully assured her it would probably be a whole load of fun but his lack of conviction propelled Judith to attack her steak with fierce misgivings about Pixie's gift.

He said, 'Surprised to hear Madeleine Pendlebury's involved. Did she put money in it?'

'Not that I know of. I doubt whether Victor would agree. Horses are his luxury interest, not art.'

'Madeleine's not dependant on the Pendleburys for her pocket money, love.'

Judith sipped some wine and regarded Craig over her glass.

'And what does that mean? Are you suggesting Madeleine has a sugar daddy on the sidelines?'

'Madeleine Prissyboots with a lover?' He stifled a laugh and poured more Valpolicella, his eyes flickering with the irrepressible spark of the professional gossip. Judith drew back, suddenly wishing she had not impulsively agreed to this date. It was all Laurence's fault. Laurence and his bloody postcards.

Craig, sensing her subtle recoil, swiftly added, 'Of course, you know Madeleine from way back, don't you? I'd forgotten. You must have met her grandmother then, the incomparable Celia Goddard, the doyenne of the interior design dictators.'

'Actually, no. Madeleine is Pixie's friend. Celia Goddard really was the tops, then?'

'Absolutely. I went to her funeral last year. Over eighty when she finally dropped off the perch but working right up to the end. It was Celia who gave Victor Pendlebury the lamp-shade business, you know. A sort of wedding present. He used to work for her in the showroom – one of Celia's pretty young men who fluttered round the Queen Bee. For a woman with a hawk's eye for quality and taste, Celia Goddard had no nous at all when it came to men. Just like her daughter, of course.'

'Madeleine's mother?'

'The glorious Roseannagh Goddard. Ran away with a French actor and died in a pile up on the Paraparique soon after Madeleine was born. I researched Celia Goddard for an obituary tribute in *House and Garden*.'

Judith leaned across the table, back on the hook, her reservations about Craig Thomas pushed aside. 'Celia Goddard *gave* the lampshade business to Victor? Are you sure?'

'Cross my heart. After her only daughter died, poor old Celia practically kidnapped the baby and brought her up in England, keeping a firm foot on Madeleine's neck and marrying her off practically from the schoolgates to this prune Pendlebury who worked in the front office. La Goddard was having no more elopements in the family and Victor seemed a nice sensible bloke with a country estate and the right sort of school tie. The lampshade set-up was a flourishing offshoot to her decorating firm; handmade silk shades and unique bronze lampbases. Positively the *only* source of the inimitable Goddard style at that time. To be fair, no one could foresee the way the Chinese would jump on the bandwaggon at a fraction of the cost. It wasn't entirely Pendlebury's fault the business went stale on him and I doubt whether his heart was in it in the first place. I interviewed him for the magazine syndicate after the Goddard funeral and he seemed a nice enough guy – just no push. Once the old girl had disappeared from the decorating scene there was no one to bully the clients and funnel business in Victor's direction. The Goddard firm was sold almost immediately and I've heard on the grapevine the lampshade workrooms are going the same way. Fetch next to nothing in the present climate, I'd say.'

'But Victor's wealthy. He and his sister have this marvellous place in Somerset which belonged to their mother. "Finings".

They run a stud farm or something there. Victor's not dependant on the decorating business, Craig. He was left a fortune by his father, Pixie told me all about it.'

'Peter Bloch alias Pendlebury? The mysterious recluse who spent his declining years breeding snowdrops? Pull the other one, baby! Don't tell me the Fraud Squad's wiping the slate clean these days.' The hint of a secret about to be revealed hovered on his lips but he thought better of it and changed the subject, saying, 'Was the delectable Tricia Carroll at Victor's party?'

Judy nodded.

'I bet she had to play the piano. Poor Tricia certainly sings for her supper. And what about Suki, the glamorous Lebanese spy?' he added in a melodramatic whisper.

The waiter brought coffee and Craig sipped his cognac, surveying the smooth fall of Judith's hair through the haze of cigarette smoke blurring the atmosphere. The conversation slipped back into inconsequential chat after that and they eventually decided to give the dancing a miss and go straight back to Kensington.

In the hallway, Judith snatched up the torn fragments of Laurence's postcard and slipped them in her pocket. The aftermath of Christmas seemed to chill the whole house and Judy's half-hearted invitation to Craig to share a nightcap was agreeably shelved on both sides. It had been a long day, the mood had shifted and as Judith found herself mouthing platitudes about 'beauty sleep' and 'work in the morning', the jagged pieces of postcard touched her fingers like a promise unfulfilled.

They parted on good terms and Judith breathed a sigh of relief, closing her door with a careful quietness. She made a pot of tea and lit the cold flames of her gas log fire. It blazed with all the cheeriness of a real fire as she sat on the floor and opened Laurence's Christmas gift once again. The dark blue velvet interior of the jeweller's box enhanced the platinum shimmer of a single pendant earring, a delicately wrought squiggle like a question mark. Judy sipped her tea and read the message again.

'I'm keeping the other one till I see you so you can thank me nicely. Love always, L.'

Seven

Judith was glad to get back to work. The office was quiet and Laurence was not due back till the weekend. It presented the chance to start the New Year with a clear desk. The Serious Fraud Office suited her. The pace was relentless but not subject to the constant emergencies which inevitably accompanied her former job with Arnott. Office routine and diligent research – anathema to many who joined the Force – came as a relief to Judy Pullen and she was increasingly fascinated by the intricacies of fraud. Laurence found this incomprehensible, delighting in the power-broking and undercover manouvering of Special Branch. Perhaps this was why they hit it off: the attraction of opposites.

She was still in bed when the phone rang just before eight on Saturday morning. She snatched up the receiver, certain it must be Laurence back from Tignes.

'S-sorry, Judy. Did I wake you? It's Madeleine.' The stutter was appealingly hesitant. 'Could we meet? I went down to see Pixie yesterday and there's a problem.'

Judith stiffened, gripping the receiver. 'Not again? Pixie's not in hospital again?'

'N-no, no. S-sorry. I didn't mean to alarm you. P-Pixie's fine. At least, she was when I left but ... something came up and I seem to have put my foot well and truly in it. I've been worried sick all night. I wondered if you could smooth things over for me? C-Claire threw me out of the house!'

Judith relaxed. 'Goodness, Madeleine, you gave me a fright. I thought something serious had happened. Don't give it another thought. Claire's always flying off the handle. I've been chucked out lots of times.'

'I must tell you about it in case Pixie rings you. P-put you in the p-picture. I'm dreadfully worried I've upset them both.'

They arranged for Madeleine to come over and Judy put down the phone with a wry smile. Poor Maddy. She wasn't used to the rough and tumble of Claire's mood swings. She leapt out of bed and flew about the flat straightening cushions and uselessly rearranging things. Madeleine had never visited before. The flat was, in truth, no more than an enormous L-shaped bedsit with a kitchen tucked into the angled space contrived by the construction of the bathroom. But the treetop view of Kensington Gardens was worth it by a mile in Judy's opinion.

She lit the fire and arranged cups on a

table near the sofa. Suddenly remembering it was the twelfth day of Christmas she swept all her cards into a drawer, smiling at the remembrance of Arnott's astute comparison of Madeleine to the festive partridge in a pear tree. He was right, of course. Maddy *was* an innocent game bird perched on a magic bough just asking to be shot at. A natural target.

'Out of milk, dammit.' She checked the time. There was no help for it: she would have to steal Craig's. He was never up at this hour anyway. She ran downstairs and snatched up a bottle, scribbling a note of contrition to leave on the hall table with his mail.

The postcard was all too evident – Damascus, palm trees and an azure sky – it could only be Laurence up to his usual tricks. She turned it over. 'Sorry. Duty calls. Put the champers on ice. Happy New Year. L.' Posted in London? Odd. Presumably stuffed in some diplomatic bag by a crony of his and mailed at Heathrow. Or perhaps Laurence was not in Damascus at all. Maybe he kept a stack of postcards at the ready and had posted it himself? She felt deflated, cramped with disappointment. What a fine bloody love affair this turned out to be! If Madeleine was the 'partridge in a pear tree' Laurence was certainly not one of the 'two turtle doves'.

She was about to go back upstairs when the doorbell shrilled. Madeleine stood on the step, breathlessly apologetic, cheeks glowing with the cold.

'Judy, I'm early. Do you mind? Parking's a doddle round here at weekends, isn't it? Everyone's still away, I suppose.' She looked distracted, jingling her car keys and glancing over her shoulder like a bad actress in line for an audition.

Judith led the way to the top floor, flinging open her door with a touch of bravado. Madeleine hesitated on the threshold, her nervousness intensified. Did she imagine Claire to be lurking behind the door, malevolent as Snow White's stepmother?

Drawing her inside, Judith realized she was seeing Madeleine without make-up for the first time. It was no secret that Pixie was nearly three years younger than Madeleine but no one ever guessed that. The two had been thrown together at school, Madeleine's dyslexia having kept her back and Pixie's cleverness shooting her forward. Maddy's total absorption in maintaining her looks had placed her in that ageless vacuity of photographic models. In the clear light of a January morning, dark shadows under her eyes emphasized a fine tracery of lines and Judith warmed to Madeleine's uncharacteristic vulnerability.

She persuaded her to sit by the fire and

poured coffee, wondering what could have caused Madeleine's panic. Surely, a spat with Claire was not that devastating? She didn't have to wonder long. Madeleine plunged straight in, words tumbling, her stutter almost obliterated in the rush to unburden herself.

'I telephoned Pike End from London yesterday and Claire invited me down for lunch. I simply had to talk to Pixie. There was no one else to turn to, you see. It was a glorious day and Victor and Genista are still at Finings. Victor's closed the workrooms till next week.'

'They've been in the country since New Year?'

'Oh, Victor can't get enough of it. It's the horses. I drove back to London with my father on Monday to see him off at Heathrow and I've been alone at the flat ever since, worrying my guts out.'

'What happened?'

Madeleine plunged on. 'I couldn't stand the empty apartment. Going round and round in circles, not knowing what to do. I suddenly took it into my head to drive down to Pike End and take some books and jigsaws and things for Pixie. She's been awfully good, you know. Stays in bed every day, takes all her medication like a lamb.'

'Claire would make a perfect prison warder. She's just what Pixie needs just now.

You didn't upset the routine, I hope.'

'Oh, no.' Madeleine leaned forward, all contrition. 'Honestly, Judy, I blew down there with the very best intentions, thought it would cheer her up and take my mind off things at the same time. I shouldn't have bothered her with my troubles, of course. But, you see, Pixie's always so sensible. She's my rock. I needed her advice.' Madeleine fiddled with her rings, her immaculately manicured red nails catching the light like wounds.

'Go on.'

She hesitated for a moment, gathering her thoughts, and then continued, her low voice almost inaudible.

'Claire had laid on one of her enormous vegetarian casseroles and to begin with everything was absolutely fine. I told them about Christmas in town, which, not to put too fine a point on it, was pretty stressful with Papa in tow. He was dreadfully bored, poor man. In fact, he cut short his stay, his car's still in London.'

'This is Alain Lambert you're talking about?'

Madeleine nodded. 'I managed to put off us all going down to Finings till New Year's Eve.' She sat bolt upright, her coffee un-touched, anxious to get her story straight. After pausing again she looked directly at Judy and said, 'I had better come clean. By the purest mischance I discovered Victor is having an affair. Do you remember at the party a bike messenger delivered a parcel for Mrs Pendlebury? I shoved it in the antique desk Sophie made such a song and dance about.'

'Victor's Christmas present?'

Madeleine sketched a wintry smile and continued, the entire episode still raw. 'Genista took the desk to the country and installed it in the morning room. Papa and I were alone at Finings on the Sunday morning, Victor and Genny were with the horses. I was scrabbling about in the ghastly desk trying to show Papa the secret drawer and when I opened it, there inside was this package which had, in fact, completely slipped my mind. When I unwrapped it, there was a covering note from the manager of some hotel in Ireland where Victor stays all the time. Apparently, "Mrs Pendlebury" had telephoned to say she had left her charm bracelet behind and would he keep it in the hotel safe until Victor's next visit. The stupid manager decided to be ultra-helpful and dispatch it straight back to London. Typical Irish cock-up. That's Victor's cross, of course – looking so respectable merely invites an excess of service. I stood there in the morning room beside Papa simply gawping, holding this horrible bracelet jangling with gold charms like a Christmas tree. There was no mistake. I recognized it.'

'You know who this woman is?'

She nodded. Madeleine looked not so much emotionally bruised as totally shell-shocked. After a conscious effort, she pulled herself together.

'Judy, I hate dragging you in on all this but as I seem to have upset Claire so dreadfully you'd better hear the whole story. Naturally, I was totally poleaxed by this monstrous thing which had been sitting in that bloody secret drawer all over Christmas like an unexploded letter bomb. I just couldn't take it in ... Victor of all people! Always so correct, so dependable, never so much as a hint...'

'Perhaps it's just his mid-life fling. A temporary flirtation, nothing serious,' Judith ventured.

'Oh, no. It's too deep for that.' Her gaze focussed with something of the old Maddy's assurance. 'Mind you, he hasn't been well for months. Victor had a slight heart attack shortly after my grandmother died. I'm useless when it comes to business and Victor had to sort out things with the lawyers. It was all rather complicated ... Everything seemed to come at once – there was a lot to arrange, of course. The doctor suggested he moved his bed downstairs at Finings. Just for a while Victor said. But he still sleeps in his study. He even cut out riding for a month or two. Things seemed to settle down and I

86

thought ... I thought, things would eventually get back to normal but...'

Her voice trailed off and she jumped up and hurried to the window, staring out at the chimney pots and rooflines sharply outlined in the crisp morning air. She turned back and stalked about the room, shoulders stiff with tension, her eyes glazed. Madeleine saw nothing of the pretty room.

'You had a bust-up with Victor?'

She leaned against the mantleshelf and tried to disentangle the confusion.

'No. Papa persuaded me against rushing to conclusions. And, after all,' she said with a brittle laugh, 'he's the expert! Papa offered to go to Ireland to check the whole thing out on the quiet, to make sure it wasn't all some dreadful mistake. He telephoned me at the flat a few days ago. "Mrs Pendlebury" was a regular it seems. The manager described her to a T. "A very charming lady," he assured Papa. I haven't confronted Victor yet. I just can't take it in. It alters everything, you see...'

'And you wanted Pixie's advice?'

Madeleine slumped on the sofa, pushing back her long fair hair in a weary gesture. 'You must think I'm a selfish cow to pile my worries on Pixie, especially just now. But I've never *had* to make any important decisions, Judy. It never occurred to me that Victor had been in love with someone else all this time.

It's been going on for ages apparently. Papa made quite certain there could be no misunderstanding.' She was trembling, her cup rattled in the saucer as she replaced it on the table.

'Would you like something stronger?'

Madeleine shook her head. 'May I smoke?'

Judy went to the kitchen to fetch an ashtray while Madeleine scrabbled in her bag; she then produced some matches, observing Maddy's inexpert handling of the business of lighting up with considerable interest. Madeleine *never* smoked. In fact, she could be quite waspish about the habit. Victor's little romantic excursion must have knocked her totally off balance.

Madeleine leaned back and smoked in silence for a bit, deep in thought. Judith waited, wondering how Claire had managed to exacerbate the situation. Victor's affair hardly seemed the sort of thing to shock the unshockable Claire Pullen. Why attack Madeleine, for heaven's sake? Presumably, the strain of maintaining Pixie in a bubble of peace and quiet was proving too much. But surely, taking it out on Maddy was going too far?

Madeleine tapped the ash from her Gauloise and took up the story again. 'I told Pixie all this about Victor on the quiet, after tea, mentioning no names, of course – the last thing I wanted was to get Pixie so riled up she'd insist on bombing back to London and bounce Victor's stuff into the street.'

Judith's imagination went into overdrive, wondering what on earth had put Maddy's discovery in such a dramatic context that she imagined Pixie, normally so level-headed, playing avenging angel. Madeleine continued, her voice hoarse with emotion.

'It was all such a shock, Judy, I felt I must talk to someone close but in her present fragile state of mind Pixie's not the one to turn to. Usually, Pixie would have been the perfect confidante; so sensible, so practical, but just now...' Her hands opened in a gesture of despair.

'You told her the woman's name – Victor's mistress?'

'No, I edited out the sordid details, realizing too late that Pixie was too feverish to deal with my problems on top of her own. It seemed better to backtrack, and, to be honest, I wished I'd stayed in London and kept the whole thing under wraps for the present. Claire had gone to her office to sort out some bills. Pixie was in a funny mood, not herself at all and not really interested and I can't say I blame her, looking back on it. Adultery's a pretty banal story these days and Pixie's naturally upset just now, bursting to get well enough to join Tom in Zambia. But, suddenly, she took off at a tangent, started saying these horrible things about

Papa, nasty remarks about his having abandoned me all those years and how could we just take things up again as if nothing had happened.'

'But Alain always kept in touch, didn't he? It wasn't as if he's just popped up out of the blue.'

'Pixie couldn't see it. Papa spending Christmas with me in London rubbed salt in the wound, God knows why. She railed on and on about his "flexible relationships", as she called it. Poor man. Why he's become the focus of Pixie's witch-hunt beats me. She's only met him once or twice. If I didn't know Pixie to be the most generous and sweetest person, I'd say she was jealous. Papa's not the most wonderful man in the world but he's all I've got just now. Pixie's got you and Claire and probably a whole raft of relatives for all I know!'

Madeleine stubbed out her cigarette and immediately lit another.

Judith tried to smooth things over. 'Pixie's bonkers at the moment. Feverish in turns, sleeping badly. Take no notice. She spent Christmas trying to force Claire to cough up information about our family tree which seems not to exist according to our scatty mother. You're right. Pixie's probably envious of your closeness with Alain. Being cooped up in the cottage doesn't help.'

Madeleine looked unconvinced. 'Claire

came in when Pixie was railing on about Papa. She had become quite hysterical. Tearful, in fact. Claire fairly flew at my throat! Accused me of winding Pixie up, egging her on in this mad investigation of hers. I ask you? *Me*, leading *Pixie* on!'

'Then she showed you the door, I guess. Oh, Maddy what a to-do! I'm glad I wasn't there.' Judith laughed, stifling her image of the two women ganging up on poor Madeleine. 'Sorry, sweetie, it's no joke. It's just that I've seen Claire's tantrums so often I don't take them seriously any more. She's got a vile temper.'

'It's not Claire I'm worried about. Do you think I've upset Pixie? Rows are the last thing she needs. I'd never forgive myself if I'd precipitated a relapse. The local GP thinks Pixie's suffering from some sort of tropical bug she picked up on her travels. You've heard nothing?'

'Nobody's phoned. I'm certain everything's perfectly fine. It'll soon blow over. You've led a sheltered life, Maddy, I'm used to these family eruptions. Claire's accustomed to living alone and Pixie's campaign has put her on edge. Claire's always refused to discuss relationships and she's not going to drag any skeletons out of the closet at this stage of our lives even to placate Pixie. Forget it. I'll give them a ring this evening and call you back.'

'You won't say I've put you up to it?'

Judith patted her hand. 'Look here, juggins, if I'd wanted to join the bandwaggon I could have formed a grand inquisition with Pixie and forced Claire to come clean. For all we know, Claire doesn't even actually *know* who Pixie's father is and she ditched her own family when she joined the hippy trail. She chooses to be a private person and Pixie's sudden yearning for roots is a lot of sentimental hot air. Goading Claire will only end in tears.'

Madeleine absorbed this assurance with apparent gratitude and rose to leave. Judith couldn't help but feel sorry for her. Why should Pixie and Claire drag Maddy into their private squabble when she obviously had enough on her plate already? Judy promised to ring later so Madeleine could at least rest easy she had not abandoned Pixie to a maelstrom of family strife.

A lingering impression of things unsaid left Judith confused. Would Madeleine's distress merely be caused by a spat with Pixie? Victor's unfaithfulness had hardly been touched upon but must surely be the real reason for Maddy's cry for help. And what comfort had the poor woman received? Perhaps when it came down to it she had realized that Judy was just not close enough or even mature enough to help and the emphasis had shifted to that overblown set-to at Pike End.

She closed the door with one intriguing question still poised in her mind. Madeleine had recognized the charm bracelet belonging to Victor's paramour. But who was she? Judy absentmindedly straightened the cushions on the sofa and Madeleine's lingering fragrance hung in the air like the breath of disaster.

Eight

Chiaroscuro's open night was deliberately scheduled eight days prior to the Bath weekend. Sophie had advertised it as an introductory evening, hoping to tempt new members and augment the tour bookings. A slide lecture on 'Spa Towns in the Eighteenth Century' by William Haydock-Smith was to be followed by an informal buffet party during which, according to the bumph, 'Dr Kenneth Tyler will answer questions about his private collection of jade and Eastern art'.

Both staff lecturers were popular speakers, a perfect foil to each other, Will Smith disguising his considerable expertise under the jokey manner of an enthusiastic under-graduate and Ken Tyler coming into his own in the intimate circle he gathered round him to handle the oriental porcelain which was his special field. There was a latent sexiness in the way Tyler caressed the delicate objects, fingers briefly touching as the treasures were passed from hand to hand. He was a New Zealander and spare-time judo expert, his stylishness reminiscent of a young Cary Grant. Bruce Foxton chose his staff with care, confident that Chiaroscuro's art groupies would form the nucleus of a successful enterprise.

Judith drove to Old Chelsea with a sinking heart. She idled past the club premises now illuminated like a cruise liner. Bruce had combined two Victorian artists' studios, fitting out a flat for himself and converting the largest studio to a lecture room. A sign indicated a private car park situated at the rear and Judith steered the VW down the narrow side entrance, following the arrows.

The access was dark and the cars jammed into a tarmac area which had previously been gardens. A new minibus was parked in a corner, classic lettering on the black paintwork proclaiming, 'CHIAROSCURO – Fine Art Tours'. A six foot boundary wall had been breached to make a rear exit into Goff Street but Bruce's car park was unlit and almost full. Judith drove with care, cruising between a dozen vehicles before deciding to leave the VW in a back street. A discreet breakaway at half-time might be called for and extracting herself from a tight parking space could prove impossible.

Having found a slot in Goff Street, she returned via the back entrance, limousines parked close as bumper cars, the only illumination falling from the uncurtained studio window which shone directly into the yard. A black youth in denims and a multi-coloured bobble hat lounged in the shadow of the high wall and Judith nervously wondered if Sophie Neuman's security arrangements were even more lax than she seemed to appreciate.

Inside, the clubhouse was bright and very noisy. Sophie greeted members and guests in the hall, insisting they each sign in. Then Bruce took over, ushering them through to the lecture hall, the aisle between rows of seating offering plenty of space for chat. Cliques were already forming. Judy found herself swiftly taken in hand by Fenella Krantz, the dark-haired Canadian who had monopolized Erskine at Madeleine's party. Across the room Suki and Morton were chatting with friends. Things were looking up, Judy reflected. At least there were *some* familiar faces amid the alien corn.

'So you did come, after all. Sophie told me you would but I laid twelve to four against.'

Fenella drew her into the second row, where she had reserved four seats, one already occupied by a sulky girl in glasses.

'Let me introduce Lucienne de Blanc. Lucie's a chum of mine. She's really only here to see Ken Tyler's bits and bobs.'

Judy shook hands and said, 'You're not coming to Bath?'

The girl shrugged. 'Oh, yes, but oriental porcelain is my special interest. I hope to qualify this year and specialize in repair work. I don't care for the social aspect here but Dr Tyler is top in this field.'

After a further conversational skirmish, Judith was not surprised to be quizzed by Fenella about Laurence.

'He's been abroad. Damascus, I think.'

'He's not coming tonight by any chance?'

'No. Why should he?'

'No special reason,' Fenella countered defensively. 'He just said he might.'

Lucie cheered up, savouring the under-lying currents.

'It must have been Victor's champagne at the party. Or the after-effects of the bomb incident. Laurence isn't mad about joining things. Actually, neither am I.' Judy felt claustrophobic as the crowd started to bag their seats, pressing in all round, exuding overpowering waves of Femme and Jolie Madame.

'Fenella isn't interested in art either. She

96

only comes for what she can get out of it,' Lucie confided with a sly smile.

'Quite right.' Fenella missed nothing. 'The men have *their* clubs. Women have to make networks of their own. Sophie puts a lot of business my way. I scratch her back etcetera.'

Judith was surprised to see the coloured boy who had been lurking in the car park slink past and position himself by the projector. He was built like a weightlifter and moved as soundlessly as an exquisitely maintained piece of machinery.

'Who's that?'

Fenella glanced round. 'Oh, that's Brenton. Brenton George. He's Bruce's "heavy". Does all the humping.'

'He drives the minibus when we go on outings,' Lucie explained. 'Don't let Fenella fool you with that casual line. She adores Brenton's black muscles.'

Luckily, the blinds on the huge studio windows crashed down at that point, cutting short this incomprehensibly sharp exchange. Judith relaxed, a buzz of excitement passing through the audience as the lights dimmed and a fresh faced character wearing a sports coat with leather arm patches leaped on to the low staging where a lectern had been placed to one side of the screen. Bruce Foxton must have grabbed this one straight off the graduation line. He introduced his lecturer with a fanfare, listing his academic achievements including a veiled reference to Will Haydock Smith's unofficial attachment to the Wallace Collection, which startled the lad into a flushed acknowledgement of the muted applause.

In the darkness Judith glanced along the row of seating and wondered for whom Fenella's spare seat had been reserved. For Laurence? From the corner of her eye, as the speaker waited for silence, Judith glimpsed the pale head of Madeleine as she slid into a place at the end of a row.

There had been no contact since the telephone call reassuring her that Pixie's convalescence was back on an even keel. It crossed her mind that Madeleine must have come to some decision by now about Victor's defection. Judith got the distinct impression from the last brief conversation with her that her father, Alain Lambert, was pressing for legal action despite his initial caution and, although Maddy had refused to commit herself, the Frenchman's determination had been evident. His own complex love life made this attitude extraordinarily unyielding. But perhaps there was more to it. Paternal revenge? His dislike of Victor was no secret and this new starring role in Madeleine's life was, as Pixie had unkindly pointed out, intriguing.

Judith had asked her sister straight out to identify Victor's alleged mistress but no joy.

If it was a long-standing relationship, as Maddy had insisted, the woman in question was probably someone they both knew. Madeleine had always trusted her best friend absolutely but tact was not one of Pixie's strong points. She blamed Alain Lambert for all this secrecy.

These tantalizing conjectures had obliterated Haydock-Smith's introductory remarks. But once he had gained her attention, Judy was, as she admitted later, as hooked as the rest.

Will Smith's delivery was informative, quirky and amusing. His choice of slides, interspersed with excerpts from eighteenth-century jigs and dance tunes, struck just the right note. The audience was delighted with this show of calculated simplicity and when the lights went up after nearly an hour, the enthusiastic applause was music to Sophie's ears. The speaker nodded in shy response, a floppy forelock brushed aside in a gauche gesture at odds with his professionalism. William Haydock-Smith was worth his weight in gold, notwithstanding the perceptible cockney inflection which, to the girls present, seemed merely to add piquancy. During the interval Sophie Neuman's desk was beseiged with eager new takers for the Bath tour.

Judith crept out intending to slip away but a disquieting conversation overheard in the women's room made her change her mind. Afterwards she wandered back to the crowd and was pounced on by an earnest young man all set to make an evening of it. She made her excuses and found herself cornered by the Canadian girl once again.

Fenella impatiently thrust Judith ahead towards the coffee room, where a buffet table had been laid out and Bruce, assisted by the urbane Dr Tyler, proferred wine or coffee. Madeleine, looking subdued, eventually sidled in, deep in conversation with Will Smith. Catching her eye, Judith waved, expecting Madeleine to join them, but, after signalling a distracted response, she resumed her intense conversation and Judith lost sight of them in the crush.

'And what are you scowling about, miss?' The robust Yorkshire accent could only be Arnott's. Judy spun round, delighted to see his beefy chops amid all this sophistication.

'Arnott! What on earth—?'

'A drop of culture's just the job,' he said, tapping his temple in a clumsy bid for discretion. 'Grand talker that Lancashire bloke. Where do you think he left his bike?'

Judy laughed. 'What Lancashire bloke?'

'Bill Haydock-Smith. Never been to Haydock Park, lass? Don't know what you've missed, Pullen. Near St Helens. A bloody fine racecourse even if it's not Yorkshire.'

'William Haydock-Smith's a Londoner,'

Fenella retorted, somewhat taken aback by the riff-raff Sophie's open evening had attracted. Ralph Arnott did look a bit odd and Judith regarded his appearance at Sophie's club with glee. Arnott's idea of 'an arty do' had led him well up the sartorial garden path. His navy blazer with its anonymous club badge was one thing and the lovat green slacks, argyll socks and suede moccasins might have got him across the threshold without much more than a blink. But the final touch was the pink shirt and spotted bow tie. Arnott looked like a cross between a representative from the Gay Liberation Front and a double-glazing salesman.

He beamed, his Mr Punch nose dipping frequently into the goblet of red wine. Sophie bustled up, all smiles, and took his arm.

'Have you introduced Mr Arnott to Fenella and Lucienne, Judith? Our newest member, girls. Ralph Arnott. He will be with us at Bath. He's travelling down on the coach with Captain Devereux and the ladies from the embassy. Won't you join him, Judith? We still have two spare seats. Driving in January is pure misery. Why don't you relax and let Brenton deal with the motorway traffic? I'm trying to persuade some of the younger members to travel by coach, to even up the party,' she explained. 'Madeleine's leaving her car in London.'

'Suki would liven up any party,' Fenella said sweetly, indicating the Lebanese girl's noisy coterie at the centre of which Ken Tyler held court. Sophie let this pass, well acquainted with Fenella's tongue, and led Arnott off to meet more members. Judith sipped her wine, finding the evening much more fun than she could possibly have anticipated.

Bruce Foxton circulated, greeting familiar and unfamiliar faces with equal warmth. His languid public-school tones could clearly be heard above the chatter and Judith had to admit Bruce and his partner, Sophie Neuman, were pulling out all the stops.

The crowd had thinned out considerably. Judith seemed to be stuck with Fenella though the poisonous Belgian, Lucienne, was now deeply focussed on Ken Tyler as he weighed the merits of his jade objets d'art.

Fenella Krantz was, in fact, the perfect commentator, dispensing a good deal of biographical nonsense in a very short time. But Judith found herself unceremoniously dumped with Morton Playle when the Canadian suddenly dragged Suki away from him on a muttered excuse about 'some stuff in the locker room'.

Morton recovered smoothly and Judith finished her wine as he pontificated about Laurence's tour in the Middle East, where their paths had intermittently crossed.

Judith, bored with all this old history, idly observed Will Smith pick up a box and disappear into the lecture hall, presumably to pack up his slides. Madeleine had vanished and neither was Arnott in evidence.

Lucie abruptly cut away from her hypnotic attention to Dr Tyler and, at a distance, followed Suki and Fenella outside. Morton said he had to make a telephone call and sauntered off leaving Judith with a group of people who were anxious to include her in their plans for the Bath weekend. Judy began to feel distinctly trapped.

Suddenly, the door burst open, knocking two middle-aged members aside, and Brenton George exploded into the room. Bruce moved forward to intercept him, his face dark with rage.

Brenton's loud West Indian voice shrilled in the instantly hushed company.

'Someone's been killed out there! Her head's bashed in!'

Bruce held his arm. 'Quiet! For God's sake, Brenton, compose yourself!' He tried to pull the boy outside but he was obdurate, dangerous as a maddened bull.

Judith moved forward, finding herself beside Arnott and Sophie, who had rushed in to investigate the commotion.

Brenton shook himself free. 'I tell you, man. It's murder. She's dead as a chicken. Out there in the car park. By that big red sports car.'

Bruce told Sophie to keep everyone calm and bundled the coloured boy outside. Arnott brusquely insisted everyone stayed put, grabbed Judy and chased after the two men.

Sophie hastened to assure everyone there was obviously some sort of mistake which would clearly be sorted out straight away. 'Someone's fainted, I imagine. Hit her head as she fell. Brenton gets overexcited...' she finished lamely. The shocked faces regarded her blankly and in the silence a motorbike revved up in the street.

The freezing air hung in the yard like a curtain of icicles and Brenton, closely followed by the others, plunged into the dark. Bruce Foxton shouted hoarsely, 'Some lights, for God's sake!' as he crouched between two cars, where a girl lay spread-eagled, her head a dark blur in the shadows. Arnott produced a torch and bent down, not touching the body, urging the others to stand back. The studio blinds flew up in the lecture room and light surged into the yard.

'It's not Madeleine,' Judy whispered as the bloodstained head was revealed, the ghastly premonition surfacing and submerging like a drowned corpse. Having conquered this appalling supposition, her heart stopped thudding and sense prevailed. She and Arnott exchanged glances, instantly transported to their old roles of inspector and detective sergeant. Arnott's torch played about the long dark hair which clung wetly to the victim's face. Everything was soaked in blood, which glimmered blackly on the tarmac like a patch of oil.

Bruce gasped. 'It's Suki Nadhouri! She's been mugged. Her head's beaten to a pulp.'

'Get the police,' Arnott demanded. 'And take this lad with you. No one, no one at all is to leave.' They hurried off.

Judith and Arnott swung into their old routine, Arnott barking out orders, she sniffing round the scene like an alley cat. She circled the car, searching the ground and peering inside the vehicle. The driver's door was ajar, the key in the ignition. Suki's handbag lay on the seat and a scattering of shredded plastic littered the foot well. Judy walked round to the front and, glancing at the wide windscreen, realized that some of the letters of SUKI and KILROY had been ripped away, leaving the edges of the plastic strip jagged as if attacked with a penknife or a nail file. Surely Suki hadn't been clearing the windscreen when the blow fell? She borrowed Arnott's torch but could see no bloodstains inside the car. The remaining letters were SU KIL. She was about to comment when Arnott's bulk loomed round the long bonnet of the Ferrari.

'I've been taking a dekko at her 'ead,

Pullen. She's dead all right but the sick bugger who killed her took a souvenir.'

'What are you talking about? Her bag's on the seat.'

'It's no bleeding mugging, woman. Those head wounds... By 'eck, I've seen nowt like it. Like one of them horror flicks I've seen on the telly. Some pervert's sliced the top off her 'ead just like it was his boiled egg. The poor little cow's been scalped!'

Nine

The police arrived like an invasion force, blocking off the car parking area with swift efficiency.

Arnott and Judith stayed by the body, caught in the floodlights of the police emergency system like specimens under a microscope. Judith, chilled to the bone, felt herself at one with the corpse, both victims of the lumbering juggernaut of a police investigation bearing down on them.

Detective Chief Inspector Charlie Flood was well acquainted with Ralph Arnott and viewed the astonishing attendance of the ex-DI and his former sergeant at the scene of the murder with considerable irritation. Poaching on his old patch? What was the old fox playing at?

Without any polite preliminaries he called Arnott aside and they moved out of earshot. Judith stamped her feet, wishing she had a coat, not altogether sure of her role now the official contingent had moved in. Several private cars remained in the car park, presumably those of Chiaroscuro members detained inside. The other coppers kept their distance, equally uncertain of the status of Arnott's sidekick. She glanced into the Ferrari, now clearly illuminated, and questioned the assumption of a mugging. Why leave the handbag? Arnott's voice was raised in the familiar bullying tone all too familiar to Judith and she exchanged a wry smile with the constable guarding the corpse, who was also an old soldier from Arnott's former Chelsea squad.

It was all too close for comfort for Chief Inspector Flood, now audibly in dispute with Arnott and only too well aware of the watching eyes of his men, avid for any kind of internecine warfare. Arnott's early retirement from the Force, a gesture of protest against the interference in his last case by Special Branch in general and Inspector Laurence Erskine in particular, had placed Arnott in the annals of police folklore on the Chelsea beat.

Judith watched Arnott abruptly turn away from the DCI and curtly beckon her to follow him to the back entrance of the club premises. Taking her arm, he muttered, 'Listen here, Pullen. Button up about the head injuries. I've persuaded Charlie Flood to keep the details under his 'at for now. You and me'll go inside and make our statements like responsible citizens, but mum's the word about the scalping. Right?'

She shivered, clasping her arms to her chest, nodding like a rag doll, too cold to argue.

His eyes gleamed under the shaggy brows. 'You're bloody perished, lass. Get yourself indoors. We'll squeeze some hot toddy out of that poncey twerp Foxton. And to think, I only came on this charabanc club caper to check the locks.' Arnott rubbed his hands together briskly, evidently enjoying himself.

The warmth of the clubhouse defrosted her sense of humour.

'Arnott, it's not a charabanc club. It's called Chiaroscuro. That's an art term. It means the balance of light and dark. You can't go about calling it the Charabanc Club! Makes it sound like a seaside trippers' knees-up.'

'When you blow the froth off, woman, that's all it bloody well is.'

Judith laughed. Poor Sophie. She was going to have her work cut out fitting Arnott into the culture belt.

Those unfortunates who had stayed on to the bitter end of the Chiaroscuro open evening were herded into the coffee room and looked decidedly haunted. In an effort to lighten the tension, Sophie produced more coffee and put on some cheerful background music. The glum faces of the members were a poor reward for her efforts and in desperation Bruce Foxton offered tots of brandy to those who had decided to make the best of it. Two uniformed men guarded the exits.

Fenella Krantz was helping with the coffee and the Belgian girl had grabbed the opportunity to corner Dr Tyler, her captive orientalist. Half a dozen women huddled in a corner, whispering together and casting furtive glances at the men. They were subdued and suspicious, by no means convinced the danger had passed. A detective was going through the membership book with Foxton, preparing an attendance list. Sophie suggested Bruce brought the sergeant into her office and, sweeping aside all the papers from her desk, offered the use of it as an interview room.

She said, 'Is it really necessary to detain the ladies? You have their names and addresses, Sergeant. The accident was clearly nothing to do with anyone here.'

'We have to wait for the Chief Inspector, madam. The doctor's arrived,' he conceded, 'he won't be long.'

Sophie's ragged nerve ends sparked like exposed wires and she rounded on Foxton.

'Do something, Bruce! Don't just let them walk all over you, man. Scandal's the last thing we need. A mugging in a car park's not exactly news in this neighbourhood, for chrissake.'

Bruce wearily shook his head. 'It's not that simple, Sophie. The girl is dead. It's more than a question of damage limitation.'

Madeleine appeared in the doorway, pale as death.

'It's Suki, isn't it? The boy said "the red sports car". The F-Ferrari?'

Sophie nodded and hurried across to her. Then, addressing the policeman, she urged, 'Surely Mrs Pendlebury can go home? She's obviously got nothing to do with any attack.'

The man regarded the frail-looking female in the doorway and was inclined to agree but was not to be browbeaten. He started to reiterate the official procedure but, before Sophie could continue the argument, Detective Chief Inspector Flood breezed in and took over.

Sophie Neuman turned the full force of her complaints on the senior man. 'It's late. Surely, you can't prevent them from phoning home? Their families will be worried.'

The American's shrill summary of the dire

consequences of delaying all these important people stung Flood with its unstated threat and he flushed angrily, a man unused to having his orders questioned. He ignored Sophie, addressing himself formally to Bruce Foxton.

'The sooner we get started, sir, the sooner we can finish. No phone calls will be necessary. I must interview every person on the premises – including staff – to establish their movements this evening. We can then eliminate any who had no connection with the deceased after she left the coffee room. We may have witnesses here. This is a murder inquiry. Any small observation could be of the utmost importance.'

He took the handwritten list from his sergeant and ticked off several names, seating himself at Sophie's desk without further preamble. 'I want to go over the boy's story in detail. He found the body, I understand. Then we can get the ladies in here and they can get off home as soon as we have made quite sure nothing's been overlooked.'

Sophie flounced out and Bruce Foxton sank into a chair in front of the desk, defeated by the inexorable progress of the police machinery in motion.

'Before I take statements, Mr Foxton, I would like some information from you about the victim.' He produced an international driving permit and passed it over. Bruce accepted the document with distaste, confirming the identity of the girl in the photograph.

'That's Suki. I had no idea her real name was Saba. Extraordinary ... Twenty-eight years old. I would have thought her much younger.'

'And how long have you known Miss Nadhouri?'

Bruce frowned, anxious to be accurate, fully aware of the inspector's perspicacity.

'About three years. I knew her brother before that through dealings at the bank. Before leaving the City I was employed in investment banking. The Nadhouri family were respected customers.'

'And the brother lives in London?'

'With Suki. Cadogan Gardens. Sophie has the full address. Hammad is the head of the family, the parents were killed in Beirut. There is another brother attending university in the States, I believe, but Suki and Hammad have been established in London for at least ten years. Has anyone informed him of his sister's death?'

'He's in Paris. Been there since Christmas, I'm told. A message has gone through. Mr Nadhouri will be here in the morning to make a formal identification. The family is wealthy, I assume?'

Bruce allowed himself a brief smile. 'You could say that. Hammad is a cosmopolitan, well liked in London and with many friends in America and Europe. A very successful businessman. He also runs a newspaper – not commercially, you understand, more of a newsletter and public relations exercise. Hammad Nadhouri promotes the Palestinian cause in a decent civilized fashion. He has the ear of many international politicians and has entertained them here in England. Mostly at race meetings. He has horse-racing interests and a house near Cheltenham with a stud farm and training stables. He must be devastated by Suki's death, as indeed we all are. As Hammad's kid sister she was totally indulged. Rather a spoilt brat to be honest, but utterly charming...'

'And interested in art.'

'Not really.' Bruce decided not to beat about the bush. 'Chiaroscuro is primarily a social venue. We employ top class lecturers and provide deluxe touring opportunities but frankly few of our members are serious students. Suki enjoyed the social side of things and encouraged many of her friends to come along. Despite being spoilt she was nevertheless kept on a silken cord by her brother, not allowed to stray too far, if you take my meaning. Hammad and his crowd kept a close eye on little Suki – but coming here and joining our weekend art tours was considered harmless. After all, the people who join are all very respectable and because several of the diplomatic clique are touchy about security Sophie and I take infinite pains to treat our activities like well-guarded school trips.'

'I understand, sir.'

Flood stared at the photograph in the driving permit. A dark-eyed girl, very pretty, her mouth lifted in a mischievous grin. It was a funny set-up and no mistake. Chiaroscuro was little more than a gold-plated playpen if Foxton could be believed. And where was the motive for murder? No apparent theft. No disarranged underwear. No screams. But perhaps there had been something else in the girl's handbag before the killing? Maybe the killer wasn't out for money or sex. Flood was seriously worried: the case was taking on an ugly mysteriousness. Rich kids were always trouble.

The Chief Inspector rose and asked his sergeant to accompany Foxton back to the coffee room after he had taken a statement from him.

'Keep the lid on things out there, Browning. I'll have the black guy in now.'

After grilling Brenton George, it took Flood an hour to eliminate the innocent bystanders caught up in the net of Suki Nadhouri's death like minnows in pike-infested waters. Eventually, he had whittled down the cast list to Foxton and Sophie, their two lecturers – Will Haydock-Smith and Dr Tyler

– Arnott and Judith, the odd-job man, Brenton George, and three women: Madeleine, Fenella and Lucienne de Blanc. Morton Playle, the middle-aged lothario who had accompanied Suki, was put on ice in a separate room. He refused to answer any questions until his solicitor was present. He was permitted one telephone call.

Morton Playle's silence was a facer. The IRA training manual put it in a nutshell: 'The best anti-interrogation method is to say nothing'. The man obviously had something to hide. At least the fingerprint blokes had been all over the Ferrari but what would that prove? Playle had been seen driving the powerful sports car on more than one occasion and had been the victim's constant companion for weeks according to Foxton. And the black guy admitted touching the car as he bent over the body. Bruce Foxton and his American partner were the only two principals in this little drama who had never left the public rooms and had dozens of witnesses to back up their alibis. Flood was willing to put his money on his first suspect: Brenton George, the man who had discovered the body.

A tap on the door interrupted these conjectures and the police surgeon entered, throwing his considerable bulk into the empty chair. A young man, Richard Crane was built like a rugby player who had cheerfully abandoned the scrum but continued with the beer and singsong. Flood leaned across the desk, eyeing the doctor's baggy tweed jacket and polo shirt with amused tolerance. They were lucky to have Dick Crane – his sloppy appearance was a blind. His work was prompt, accurate and solid as a rock. With verdicts being overturned right and left, Flood wanted no slipups when it came to scientific evidence.

'Well, Dick, what's your first impression?'

Crane relaxed, propping his trainers on the bulky medical bag at his feet.

'One deep cut to the throat. Left to right, probably struck from behind. With such an efficient slash the victim would have had no chance to scream. No broken fingernails or signs of a struggle. Clothing intact. No obvious bruising. The killer may have grabbed her hair but that's conjecture, of course. The extensive injuries to the head will have to be examined at the post-mortem but the main blood flow was from the neck. It would be safe to assume at this stage that she was scalped after death. Grisly souvenir to take! Didn't think they were playing cowboys and indians on your patch, Charlie. I'll have to make some calculations before giving a time of death – it's pretty cold out there – but no more than a couple of hours ago at a guess.'

'Witnesses saw her after a lecture which finished about eight thirty. The guy who found the body blew the whistle at nine thirty-five. We have a clock watcher on the scene – and old mate of yours – Ralph Arnott.'

'Well, blow me down.' Crane grinned widely, slapping his massive thigh.

Flood straightened the papers on the desk and shot a further fusillade of questions before the police doctor could expand the joke.

'Brenton George is a sort of "odd-job" character here. His story is he was stacking chairs on to the path behind the lecture room fire exit ready for collection next day. Apparently, tonight's do was an open meeting and Foxton had hired extra seating which was due to go back in the morning. One of the lecturers was packing up his slides while George was humping the furniture. He can more or less back him up so far. George reckoned he noticed the lights of the Ferrari left on in the car park and mentioned it to Haydock-Smith, who didn't seem interested. George says he finished stacking the chairs outside and took another dekko at the Ferrari before locking the doors. He said he saw someone sitting in the passenger seat picking bits off the sticker pasted along the top of the windscreen. It spelt out the girl's name and the name of her dog, I'm told, but it's been torn up.'

'I noticed the names had been half

stripped away. Funny time to spring clean. Got bored hanging about, maybe?'

'George thought it was someone waiting for the Nadhouri woman to come out and took no notice. But later he saw the lights were still on and no one was sitting in the car, so he walked over to take a closer look. That's when he found the body.'

'Sounds reasonable. Poor mutt was worried about an expensive heap of metal like that being broken into. He was supposed to keep an eye on the car park as part of the job, supposedly?'

Flood shrugged. 'Have you seen him?'

'Should I?'

'I'd like you to have a quiet look at him before you leave. Don't give anything away but I'd swear he's on cannabis. Browning's got him siphoned off in a side room. I've seen dozens of these blokes with their red eyes and funny smell. I can't swallow this fairy story about him seeing someone in the Ferrari from the fire exit door. The car park's lit up like a bloody fairground now but before we set up our own lighting out there it was like the black hole of Calcutta. You'd be hard pressed to see your hand in front of your face let alone the inside of a car in the pitch dark fifty yards away. And the young lecturer, Smith, says he can't remember George saying anything about car lights being left on.'

'And you're pretty sure this chap's on cannabis?'

'I'm no mug on that score, Dick.'

'In that case his night vision's like an owl's.'

'Don't give me that!' Flood let out a snort of laughter, pointing a derisory finger at the young man sprawled on the other side of the desk.

'No kidding, Charlie. A pharmacologist discovered that Jamaican fishermen who drink a white rum extract of cannabis are able to steer a safe course between coral reefs even on a moonless night. He experimented with them and concluded their astonishing ability to see in the dark was due to the cannabis, not the rum.'

'You're pulling my leg.'

'It was published in the *Lancet* – straight up! It markedly affects the incidence of glaucoma in heavy cannabis users. Anyhow, this doctor in the West Indies has treated patients with an extract of cannabis which is non-psychoactive and many of them have remarked on the additional side benefit of wonderful night vision. So don't rubbish George on that score.'

Flood looked squarely at his medical expert and recognized all too clearly the word of a professional never known to fool about on the job.

'I still think he did it,' he said at last. 'Brenton George has got the strength and the opportunity. And he's the sort to carry a knife as an insurance policy. An umbrella in case it rains.'

'Found the weapon?'

Flood looked away.

The doctor hauled himself out of the chair and shambled to the door.

'Well, don't say I didn't warn you, chum.'

The Chief Inspector leaned back and lit a small cigar, confident of his hunches, more at ease knowing the bulk of the interviews were out of the way and the investigation had taken on a more manageable shape. He sent his sergeant off to get some coffee and studied his notes. Flood was a stickler for detail. Fifty-something, grey-haired and with a stern expression which lent his lantern-jawed face the cast of a Roman senator not given to jokes.

A knock preceded the readmittance of the DS.

'What's up now? Not more fall-out from that bloody American woman?'

Browning placed a miniature plastic bag on the table, a carrier from an expensive boutique used for packaging small purchases of perfume or earrings.

Flood fixed his sergeant with a hard stare and shook out the contents. Several paper sachets lay on the desk. He carefully un-folded one and tested the white powder on his tongue.

'Coke?'

'Locked in the glove compartment of the Ferrari. Too many, I thought. Do you think she was dealing?'

Ten

Charlie Flood decided to stretch his legs and strolled through to the coffee room, where the dregs of the audience and the staff of Chiaroscuro waited for him to pull the plug and let them all go home.

He drew Arnott to the deserted end of the room, wishing to make their talk seem informal. He knew Ralph Arnott from way back and calculated the man's propensity for non-cooperation if he felt Flood was pulling rank. They spoke in undertones, a feat of considerable self-control for the Yorkshire ex-copper, whose style was never discreet.

'Look here, Ralph, we'll have to take a proper statement from you later but just fill me in with a rough outline. Did you notice anyone slope off after the girl left? According to Browning, who interviewed this Neuman woman, she says she started making the coffee at the end of the lecture. The kitchen overlooks the car parking area. She corroborates Brenton George's claim that the kid had left the car lights on, she could see the Ferrari from the window. That fits. Browning checked it out and even in the dark the shape of the Ferrari is obvious and it was facing the back of the building. She told the Nadhouri female to slip out and turn them off before her battery went flat. The American's a bossy cow and used to issuing the orders round here. Foxton seems a bit of a wet nelly to me, lets her run the show.'

'My first time here, mate. All my dealings have been through Mrs Neuman. She hired me, like I said, to check the security. Some stuff had gone missing from the lockers. The victim, Nadhouri, claimed her car keys had been nicked some time before Christmas while she was here but the boss lady wasn't impressed. She said the girl was vague about the whole thing and I was not to waste too much time over it.'

'Security's a special feature here, then?'

Arnott nodded, drawing deeply on his cigarette, showing signs of strain. It had been a long night and Flood was picking over every loose fibre of this bundle of dirty washing.

'My problem is, Ralph, Neuman's evidence puts a slant on George's story. He *says* he went out there to check the car lights but they were off when we got here. You didn't turn them off by any chance? Or Pullen?'

Arnott scowled, underlining in no uncertain terms that he and Judith Pullen had touched nothing. 'Strikes me,' he said, 'the girl rushed outside, opened up the Ferrari, leaned in to reach across, switched off the lights and this bloke jumped her. Brenton George could be lying about the lights. P'raps he was just nosing round and got caught with his hands under the dashboard.'

'You could be right. He said he saw a man sitting in the Ferrari but he would, wouldn't he? You didn't notice any funny business before this? None of the other men here giving the Lebanese girl the eye? Following her about?'

Arnott shook his head.

'What about the staff?'

'They wouldn't tamper with the paying customers. Though now you mention it, the Haydock-Smith character was probably having it off with one of them. Just my fancy, nothing to do with this lot, one of the other women. But I suppose it does go on. But from what Pullen says, the dead girl was cheek to cheek with the ex-army type you've got banged up in Foxton's flat.'

'Morton Playle. He's waiting for his solicitor to turn up before saying a dicky bird. He telephoned. Someone's on the way now. A lawyer called Laurence Erskine.'

Arnott's reaction was almost comical, his

eyebrows flying up like furry caterpillars. He stubbed out his half-spent cigarette. Flood watched his former colleague's nervous response at the mention of Erskine with deep suspicion. 'You know this legal minder of his?'

'Erskine's no solicitor, Charlie. He's Special Branch and don't I know it! Judy Pullen's boyfriend. She's hugger-mugger with all this art club lot here an' all. But if your Laurence Erskine's the same slimy bugger I think he is, you're in for a big shock, mate.'

As if on cue the doors swung open and Erskine walked in, closely followed by another plain-clothes man. From the deference shown by the constable who brought them over, the newcomers had not come to read the meter.

Arnott had rallied before the Chief Inspector had put two and two together and, much to everyone's embarrassment, the Yorkshireman threw back his head and laughed fit to burst. His eyes streamed, his normally florid complexion flushing dangerously magenta as he tried to speak. Erskine was equally shocked. Judith Pullen hurried over, eyeing Erskine with dismay.

He introduced himself to Flood and said, 'This is Inspector Turner from the anti-terrorist squad. If you don't mind we must speak privately. You've set up an interview room, I take it?'

Flood shook hands, still shell-shocked but, struggling to retain the initiative, led the two men back to Sophie's office, all too well aware from Arnott's performance that the postman had indeed knocked twice on the Chelsea beat. Laurence Erskine was making another takeover bid.

Twenty minutes later, Flood returned and after a brief consultation with Bruce Foxton made an announcement.

'In view of further developments we have decided to postpone the rest of the interviews until the morning. Please make arrangements with Sergeant Browning on your way out, ladies and gentlemen. The car park has been cleared. You may remove your vehicles. However, I would like to ask all staff members to assemble in Mr Foxton's flat before leaving to clear up a few outstanding details.'

Charlie Flood's normally staid features were now positively haggard. A mugging escalated into an anti-terrorist inquiry? Special Branch shoving in and two former officers from his own manor prime witnesses? It was all too much. A sergeant approached and touched his cap. He quietly informed his superior that a second set of car keys belonging to the Ferrari had been found under the corpse when it had been lifted into the mortuary van. With one set of

keys in the ignition and the other presumably belonging to the victim, Brenton
George's insistence that a man was already
sitting in the parked car before Suki Nadhouri went out to douse the lights was now
emerging as more than a tall story. And then
there was this suggestion that keys had been
stolen from the dead girl before Christmas
while she was here on the premises. An
inside job? Or, at best, a thief who passed the
keys to the murderer?

Flood signalled to Arnott and Judith Pullen to follow him upstairs to Foxton's private
apartment. Erskine and the anti-terrorist
squad officer had taken over Sophie's office
and were now closeted with Morton Playle.

Flood was totally at sea, normal procedure
seeming to have flown out of the window. He
stared balefully into the knowing eye of
Arnott as they faced each other across Foxton's coffee table, both aware of an unprece-
dented empathy. Ex-Inspector Ralph
Arnott's retirement had been precipitated by
a very similar Erskine coup. Flood was
determined to keep hold of the reins and
struggled to bring the investigation back into
line. He closed the door and took out his
notebook. 'Now, Pullen. I'll take your statement. Tell me what happened here when the
lecture finished.'

Judith coughed and when she spoke the
words came hoarsely. She started again, this

time choosing her words carefully before putting her recollections on record. After describing the discovery of the body and filling in some details about the Chiaroscuro members who were particularly friendly with the Lebanese girl, she recounted a small incident which was still bugging her.

'Just a silly thing really, sir. More embarrassing than anything else. When the lecture ended I went to the women's room, which has three cubicles and a coat rail, plus the usual basins and mirrors and so on. While I was in one of the cubicles, two people came in and began arguing in French. At least, I think they were arguing. You know how it is when a conversation in a foreign language is really fluent – it always sounds like a row even if they're only discussing the menu.'

Charlie Flood looked bone weary, his mind fizzing with superfluous detail like a dose of salts. Arnott would have shut her up but Flood, a patient man, heard her out, jotting notes in a pad on his knee.

'You speak French?' he asked.

'Sort of. Not well and not if it's too fast. I wouldn't have given it a second thought but one of the women turned out to be Suki.'

'Was anyone else in the cubicles?'

'No. All the doors indicated "Vacant" when I walked in – I half expected a queue during the coffee interval bearing in mind the number of people at the lecture. And I would have heard footsteps if anyone else had come through. I heard the other two as soon as they entered. I think they were bickering about skiing conditions, one of them complaining about "poudre" – powder snow, you know,' she added.

Flood remained impassive, pen poised.

She continued at a rush, Arnott's obvious irritation with this useless chit-chat all too evident. 'Yes. I heard that very distinctly. A disappointing holiday, I suppose. A waste of money if the snow isn't perfect, especially if you're an expert. I reckon they had just got back from a chalet party which had turned out badly, the weather had been against them and, boxed up together in a small party, it's easy to get quarrelsome. "Off-piste" cropped up once or twice, I seem to remember, so they were both pretty expert, I imagine. One seemed more annoyed about the cost of it all but I guess that wasn't Suki. I can't say I recognized the voices but after a few minutes one walked out, slamming the door. I felt a bit embarrassed but decided to brazen it out and when I emerged I wasn't altogether surprised to see Suki. She had taken her coat from the rail and was putting it on. I asked her if she was leaving early but she said no, just going to the car to fetch something.'

'Did she seem upset?'

'Not particularly. A bit cross and in a

hurry. Probably anxious to get back to the party. She spoke to me in French initially – it's what she speaks at home, I think – so her mind must have been still on the previous conversation. But as soon as she realized her mistake she switched to English.'

'She assumed you hadn't understood?'

'Most likely. She's not too interested in those outside her own circle if you know what I mean.' Judith felt the need to elaborate. 'Suki didn't waste time on ordinary girls like me. I couldn't pinpoint the voice of the other woman. It could have been almost anybody. It's a cosmopolitan membership and there were strangers here for the open meeting. I'm new myself but I was friendly with many of them through my sister. I was surprised to see so many young professionals here tonight. I thought it would be more of a leisure group for the over-fifties as a matter of fact. Actually, it was rather fun.'

The door tentatively opened and Bruce Foxton's head appeared. 'OK if we join you? Madeleine's feeling a little seedy. I wondered if Judith could take her home?' He opened the door wider and Flood closed his notebook in a gesture of finality and said, 'Come in by all means. Is Inspector Erskine still interviewing Mr Playle?'

'He's just on his way. He's sent everyone home. The other officer has driven off with Morton. The press are outside. They want an interview, Chief Inspector. I'm not sure what's going on.'

'Join the club,' Flood sourly retorted.

Judith left, gently propelling Madeleine ahead. Madeleine had the dazed look of a sleepwalker, allowing herself to be shepherded through the now almost deserted rooms, not uttering a word.

Arnott rose to go, promising to be back next morning to liaise with Bruce Foxton about security measures.

'How about more coffee?' Foxton suggested. 'Or something stronger?'

Arnott shook his head and Flood stiffly responded.

'I'll leave you in peace, Mr Foxton. I must consult Inspector Erskine about issuing a press statement.'

'I'll come down with you if I may, Chief Inspector. Any media coverage is of the utmost importance to my business. I would like to hear the official version before the hacks start knocking at my door.'

The three men followed Judith and Madeleine downstairs. Sophie had been sent home with the rest of the staff, including Brenton George, much to Flood's irritation. His temper was rising, a man slow to rile but now on the verge of flashpoint. He burst into Sophie's office ready for a showdown.

Arnott decided to tag along, bewitched by the prospect of being a fly on the wall in what was shaping up into a bitter replay of his own pre-retirement drama. Bruce Foxton was too anxious to care about any police protocol in such a situation: he needed to find out whether blame would be sticking to Chiaroscuro once the news broke. He had been meaning to install proper lighting in the car park. It was only one of Sophie's many complaints. The wretched woman was always bobbing up with 'I told you so' like some shock-headed jack-in-the-box.

They surprised Erskine alone at Sophie's desk studying a sheaf of statements spread out before him. He stood politely, waving vaguely at a couple of chairs. Arnott hovered in the doorway trying to look like a neutral observer. Flood fired the first salvo.

'What's all this about, Erskine?'

Laurence sat down again, balancing his options. The silence was electric. At last he said, 'The fact is, Chief Inspector, the murder of Nadhouri was a terrorist reprisal. For this reason everything I say now is top secret. My colleague, Inspector Turner from the anti-terrorist squad, received a message from an organization calling itself the Sioux, which ties up with the shredded strip on the windscreen of the Ferrari which now reads SU KIL. This killer has a perverted identity crisis, he likes to leave a calling card to claim all the credit, you might say. The Sioux eliminated the girl for reasons I am not at liberty to divulge at present. A general threat to the Nadhouris was made a few weeks ago but little was known about this splinter group calling itself after a native American tribe and no one took the matter seriously. Morton Playle alerted me directly about the tragedy tonight because we have a professional interest in common. I immediately consulted Inspector Turner, who was in fact already on his way here. Unofficially, the case is now to be quietly taken out of the CID jurisdiction and you need only go through the motions of an investigation, Flood. An arrest of two members of this group is imminent and it is imperative the operation is not hampered by counter-inquiries from the CID. If diplomatic immunity is at stake, the investigation will inevitably get complicated. I regret the necessity to be elliptical about all this but, to add to our troubles, there is also a drug-dealing connection. The official scenario is this: as far as the public is concerned, a girl has been knifed in the car park but absolutely no details of the exact nature of her head wounds will be given. The coroner will be advised.'

Foxton butted in. 'What about our West Country tour next week? Do we have to cancel?'

'Not at all. Go ahead as usual.'

Flood was flabbergasted. 'Your lot may

have decided this murder was a matter of political diplomacy, Erskine, but a killer is still at large. Who's to say he wasn't present at the club tonight? A member even? It could have been an inside job. Are you suggesting all these people are re-exposed to a madman who not only cuts throats but takes scalps like a savage?'

'The scalping was a sadistic flourish which would only inflame a gutter-press manhunt and from an intelligence angle it is imperative we keep the matter as uninteresting as possible. A mugging. International cooperation is at stake here, other agencies must be consulted. The scalping, gentlemen, is—'

Arnott suddenly swivelled round and lunged into the corridor, precipitating himself into a ferocious scramble just outside the door. Erskine flew from behind the desk, shoving Flood aside, to join in. He collared Arnott's quarry and pulled him into the room.

'Will Smith!' Bruce gasped. 'You still here?'

'You know this man?' Erskine pinned the struggling lecturer to the wall.

'One of my staff. William Haydock-Smith. For God's sake let him go, you'll break his arm.'

Arnott bundled into the room, straightening his bow tie, looking re-energized by the unforeseen scrap and cocky as a bantam.

They all stood round a sweating young

man now wearing jogging kit and an anorak.

'I had a burst tyre,' he gasped, dabbing at a rapidly swelling lower lip. 'I came back to get the puncture kit from my locker.'

'You overheard all this?'

'Regrettably, yes.' Will Smith drew himself up, cold anger underlying the formal response.

'No help for it now.' Erskine buttoned his jacket and put the full force of official muscle behind the call for secrecy, which now included not only Flood and Arnott – who were at least professionals in his book – but two loose-lipped academics. His direct gaze was chillingly effective. Flood was impressed and even Arnott reduced in size. Bruce Foxton and his young art historian looked as if they were being skewered for a barbecue. Apart from putting them in mortal fear of the Official Secrets Act, Erskine threw in his own personal warning for good measure. They trooped out in silence, each man considerably chastened by this unexpected turn of events.

Not one gave a thought to the mutilated body of the young girl now laid out on the mortuary slab.

Eleven

Four days later Arnott was not surprised to have a telephone call from Chief Inspector Flood. But Flood's suggestion that they meet for a drink knocked him back and Arnott astonished himself by inviting him to the house in Mortlake. But what really bowled him over was seeing Charlie Flood on his doorstep proferring a bottle of Bell's.

'Come inside, Charlie. Looks bloody foggy out there.'

'Smog. Freezing over. You should see the silly buggers leapfrogging on the flyover. Traffic's terrible. You're well out of it, Ralph, takes a bloody fortnight to get anywhere these days. Total gridlock before long, you mark my words.'

Arnott led him through to the overheated little sitting room which was as foggy as the atmosphere outside after a packet of cork tips and an evening of *Sports Highlights of the Year*. The tolling bell of *News at Ten* filled the room and Arnott switched off, turning back to confront Charlie Flood, who, still nursing the whisky bottle, now sat in the Parker

Knoll looking decidedly ill at ease.

'Surprise visit, Charlie. What brought this on? New Year resolution? Visiting the pensioners?' Arnott's eyes glittered under the shaggy brows, ramming home Flood's discomfiture.

'Get some glasses, Ralph, and cut the cackle.'

After a couple of stiff ones they relaxed and got down to business. Arnott and Charlie Flood had never been mates after hours. It was not their style. Not like the young officers who seemed in no hurry to get home. But these two men were out of the same stable, needing no spurious friendship to understand each other.

Flood put his cards on the table. 'It's this bloody art club killing.'

Arnott knew it would be that. It could be nothing less to drag Charlie Flood across the river on a freezing January night.

'I saw your bit in the evening paper. Tied up with bows on, I thought.'

Arnott rifled through the accumulation of newspapers on the coffee table and pounced on a marked page, the small news item tucked away on page three, the quote ringed with biro. He savoured the pleasure of reading it aloud. 'Chief Inspector Charles Flood of Chelsea police said: "It's a full murder inquiry. There are marks on the young woman but I am not prepared to say

136

what they are yet." Sticking your neck out a bit, ain't you, Charlie? Thought Erskine told you to soft-peddle this job?' He grinned, shaking the newspaper like a chequered flag.

Flood scowled and waved it aside. 'I'm no rubber stamp for Special Branch.'

Arnott sobered. 'Joking apart, Charlie, I'd go easy if I was you. They play dirty in that mob. And they harbour grudges. Don't I know it! Anyway, you don't hear half the bleeding story your side of the counter. Did that Morton Playle bloke cough?'

'I've been warned off by the Commander. "Out of our hands, Flood. Nasty business," he says and then shoves me back on the chain gang wading through a million break-ins.'

Arnott refilled the glasses. 'Who cares, mate? Barmy, the lot of 'em. If Special Branch want to handle it, it's no skin off your nose.' Arnott didn't believe a word of this but felt he owed it to Charlie to offer a dignified let-out. It was true, nevertheless. Flood could break his neck chasing clues but he was a long way off retirement and there was no mileage in upsetting the Commander over a chit of a girl who probably had it coming to her. 'What about the cocaine they found in the car? You think she could have been trying to muscle in on a dealing cartel?'

'I got nowhere much with that line of inquiry. Mostly because I was elbowed out of interviewing the staff. I could have shaken down that black boy, Brenton George, in half an hour, given a clear run. If the girl was supplying – and the stuff we found was quality merchandise, make no mistake about it, Ralph – I never got the chance to chase it up. This Nadhouri family's got Erskine by the balls. The so-called terrorist mob calling itself the Sioux is just a smokescreen, if you ask me. Whoever heard of a bloody terrorist taking scalps? My guess is we've got a real nutter at work here and once he's got the taste for it he'll slice the top off someone else's head just to add to his collection.'

'You don't believe it's political then? A diplomatic cover up?'

'I know sod all about politics but a girl cut up in a car park is something you and me have seen before often enough without Special Branch taking over. I still reckon it was an inside job.'

'That club's as tight as a drum, Charlie. Doors locked, identities checked, not any old Tom or Dick gets inside. It's very exclusive. Mrs Neuman'd soon kick out any suspicious character. But, if it *was* an inside job you could be right and some other dolly's going to need an Easter bonnet.'

Charlie Flood had to laugh. The sarky devil hadn't changed much. He'd heard most of Arnott's unvarnished versions of murder cases over the years and the cunning old bugger was often nearer the bullseye than any of the young detectives with all their computer know-how and forensic gadgets.

'Tell me about this Chiaroscuro caper of yours, Ralph. You still on this West Country tour Foxton was on about?'

Arnott nodded. 'Next weekend. Mrs Neuman thought she could pass me off as a new member originally – she didn't want anyone to suss out they was worried about security. But after the murder it was obvious that Pullen and I were not kosher art fanciers. Sophie Neuman can't afford to cancel the tour. Between you an' me, I'd bet my bottom dollar the whole circus would pack up if they had to refund this tour. Several punters took fright after the Nadhouri killing and pulled out. It's lucky for Foxton that Special Branch put up the shutters on the murder inquiry and hushed everything up. Without their interference the scalping of a rich girl with a drug connection would dish the Salvation Army let alone a daft bloody art club.'

They sat in silence, sipping their whisky, two cunning old hounds sniffing out the quarry. Charlie Flood tilted the half-empty bottle and said, 'Well, how about it, mate? My hands are tied. Are you on?'

Arnott knew what he was after. And he understood the obstinacy which prevented

Charlie Flood from letting go: it went against his nature to let sleeping dogs lie. Ralph Arnott knew the feeling.

'OK, lad. I'll keep you posted strictly on the q.t. You help me out if I need any background.'

They clinked glasses, eyeing each other with the solemn regard befitting a gentleman's agreement.

Charlie produced photocopies of statements and a list of the Chiaroscuro membership with names ticked and crossed out with reference to the open meeting. The staff had separate dossiers, the only one of professional interest being that of Brenton George, showing an official caution in respect of joyriding when he was a teenager. It was all pretty insubstantial. Arnott sighed, anticipating a lot of leg work.

'Anything on the grapevine about the coke dealing? No whispers about this Nadhouri tart muscling in? She was loaded, Charlie. I can't see her sidestepping the drug boys even for kicks. These rich kids shove stuff up their noses just to get into the party mood. Why should she try to make money out of it?'

'Murky waters, Ralph. These foreign types keep their women in gold birdcages. She could have been blackmailed by somebody who knew about her party poppers and decided to come clean with her brother herself. Let him deal with it. Strikes me the

Nadhouris could settle something like that with no problem at all.'

'More likely she was just dishing out freebies to her best mates. You know how open-handed these middle-easterners are and buying friendship ain't new. She mixed mostly with the Europeans as far as I could see. Not the sort of girl to stay at home hiding behind the veil. Could the murder have been some sort of religious execution? Are these Nadhouris on their knees five times a day?'

Charlie Flood spread his hands in incomprehension. 'Search me. But surely the brother would have locked her up at home before it got to that? She had a free run of it, even had a British boyfriend. Playle never let her out of his sight, so I'm told.'

'Pity he didn't shut off the car lights for her then! No other reason for the kid to rush out to the car park in the dark, was there?'

Charlie shrugged, increasingly worried. Arnott lit another cigarette, unhappy at the maze into which their exploration was leading. He threw out another suggestion.

'The dead girl was putting on her coat after that little eavesdropping episode Judy Pullen was telling us about and—'

'Pullen listening in on the French tarts talking while she was in the bog, d'you mean?'

Arnott nodded. 'Nadhouri could have

been going outside to fetch something from the car like she said, not to cut the lights after all. Meeting someone on the quiet, maybe? P'raps she didn't want the Playle bloke on her tail every minute...' He paused, letting his mind wander and then raised his head, looking directly across at his old sparring partner with a sly smile. 'Pullen said one of the women was complaining about the "poudre". Said they was chewing on about their rotten skiing holiday. I know sweet f-all about that winter sports lark but Pullen could have got the wrong end of the stick. How about it not being a general moan about the snow at all?'

Flood started up, spilling ash down his jacket. 'The powder! They were arguing about the quality of the cocaine! The other bird was banging on about her supply, not bloody skiing holidays. Why didn't we think of that before? We've let ourselves get bamboozled by all their bloody smart talk, Ralph.'

'Pity it was all in French. Pullen could have picked up the whole story. Dangerous though. She only got away with it because Nadhouri thought she was too dumb to have understood a word of it. But who was the other woman?'

'That's what I want you to ask Pullen to chase up when you're in Bath. Could she put a name to the voice if she heard it again?'

'You're asking a lot, Charlie. Bloody unlikely if you ask me. And, anyway, what would that prove? Never stand up in court, mate.'

'Who says only men are capable of cutting throats? You should see my old lady slice up the Christmas turkey.'

Charlie Flood struggled out of Arnott's only comfortable chair and put on his overcoat, casting a bloodshot eye over the spartan conditions in which his old colleague now chose to live. He had never visited Mortlake before but guessed the late Mrs Arnott, whom he had met on rare police social occasions, had not shared such a pared-down existence. Charlie Flood suffered a moment's remorse at the indifference which had been shown at Arnott's departure. Maybe his own professional predicament, very similar to the crisis which had propelled Arnott to request early retirement, was rough justice. Perhaps he should ask Sheila about inviting Arnott round for supper ... Though, on reflection, he doubted whether the crusty old sod would come. It was too late to pick up the pieces.

They walked through the narrow hall.

'You still follow the gee-gees, Charlie?'

'When I can afford it. Do you have a flutter now you've got more time on your hands?'

'Not my idea of fun, Charlie. Never liked

143

horses. Wouldn't trust a horse with my hard-earned brass. I've bought meself a boat. Keep it near Rye. Needs a lot of work though. The reason I asked about the racing was a floater in connection with Hammad Nadhouri. He's got a lot of fans in the betting shops. Plenty of winners and his trainer's Farley Prestcott, no slouch in the turf game.'

'For a non-betting man, Ralph, you keep your ear to the ground.'

Arnott opened the door, waiting for Charlie to button his overcoat. He was not surprised to see a car nose up to the gate, Browning at the wheel.

'I thought this was a family visit, Charlie? On the side, you said.' Arnott grinned, enjoying the satisfaction of putting his former sparring partner on the spot.

'Browning's deaf and dumb if he needs to be. Can't have a Detective Chief Inspector driving over the limit, can we?'

'I heard about your promotion after I left you with a clear field. Congratulations, Charlie. You deserve it.'

Arnott's genuine approval caught Flood off balance and his awkward half-salute as he made his way back up the path was an acknowledgement of many things left unsaid.

Arnott's shout carried clearly on the still night air. 'Hang about, Charlie!'

Flood swivelled on the icy path, his hand on the gate, and for a split second Arnott had a lurching sensation of *déjà vu*. Luckily Flood was light on his feet and there was no repeat showing of Pullen's arse-over-tip. Why was it, all of a sudden, everything had to happen twice?

'Charlie, it's just occurred to me – you would know with all your racecourse info. Had Hammad Nadhouri got in anyone's black books over his horses? The race gangs can play just as wicked as the drug boys. D'you think his sister's murder was a revenge attack in lieu of Nadhouri himself?'

Flood's shoulders sagged and he absorbed this eager proposition with disbelief. He picked his words with tired deliberation.

'Ralph, all we've got here is a kid knifed in a car park. It happens all the time. Suddenly, Special Branch bundle in saying it's a political crime. Narcotics are sniffing round in case it's the first round in a war to snuff out the amateurs. And now you say it might be some Dick Francis lark connected with the Arab infiltration of the racing game. Give me a break, mate! I only came here to ask you keep an eye on the arty mob while they're off on this club weekend. There's no need to stir up the entire CID here. Just do what I ask, Ralph. As a personal favour. Just keep your eyes skinned and keep me posted.'

He climbed into the car and it disappeared in the dark.

Arnott stood at the gate, suddenly deflated, feeling his age.

Twelve

The day following Suki's murder, Judith drove down to spend the weekend with Claire and Pixie at Pike End. It seemed the least she could do to allay their fears following the lurid press speculation, which, despite Erskine's best efforts, was unstoppable. At least the scalping aspect of the case remained under wraps. She arrived Friday night, exhausted and with no energy to spare to palliate the ongoing froideur towards Madeleine, which Claire unaccountably seemed determined to sustain. Between her mother's moodiness and her sister's helter-skelter temperature, Judy negotiated a mine-field.

In fact, Suki's death had swept away their neurotic preoccupations. Both were avid for the unexpurgated version with full background music. It was well past midnight before Judith was allowed to crawl into bed. Far from being gripped with terror at a first-hand account from the scene of the grisly crime, they were absolutely delighted to have access to the finer details. She omitted any mention of the scalping, for which professional discretion she knew they would never forgive her once the facts eventually emerged.

The rest of the weekend passed pleasantly. The weather was good and Claire allowed Pixie out for a short stroll with Judith in the afternoon sunshine. Each carefully avoided any mention of Madeleine. Judith made no attempt to smooth over the contretemps which had given Maddy such a fright and of which Pixie assumed her sister had no knowledge. It was better left unsaid. And Pixie, who in normal circumstances was a byword for unflappability, has put us all on the spot here, Judith irritably concluded. We indulge her every whim and in three weeks this sensible mature woman has regressed into a spoilt child. When all this is over I'll make them both apologize to Madeleine.

Claire and Pixie, individually strong characters, were a bit out of poor hesitant Madeleine's league but as a combined force there was absolutely no contest. Madeleine, shocked and depressed by Victor's affair, had turned to Pixie only to get a bloody nose as the innocent bystander in a mother and daughter bout which had reached its final round. Judith had to smile at this whimsical idea of the three of them embattled over – of all mythical beings! – a non-existent family circle.

She got home to Kensington about nine o'clock on Sunday night. As she ran upstairs, Craig Thomas's door opened and they almost collided on the landing. He carried a huge bag of rubbish.

'Judy, my only love! Where have you been? I had a farewell party here last night. You were badly missed.'

Judith giggled, hugging her overnight bag to her chest, delighted to be home.

'You off to New York so soon, Craig?'

'Might as well. I think I've found an apartment. A SoHo loft. A pal of mine gave me a buzz. I'm flying out tomorrow before I lose it.'

'Sounds wonderful. Pity I missed the party. Fun?'

'There's still a bottle of bubbly in the sink. Come in and share it with me.'

Judith hesitated only for a moment. Craig Lomas was just what she needed after a weekend on Romney Marsh. He dumped the black plastic bag on the landing and they went inside.

The flat was in chaos. Piles of books and clothing littered the living room and half-sorted debris was all too visible in the kitchen. Paper plates, cigarette ends and dozens of bottles had been shoved into boxes

148

but the entire apartment was redolent of stale smoke and curry.

'Wow!' Judith was considerably impressed. 'And you've been clearing this *all day?*'

He laughed, crossing the room to slam the kitchen door on the worst of the shambles before fetching an unopened bottle of Dom Perignon from the bathroom. Judith cocked an eyebrow. Such extravagance had not been reserved for a casual passerby. She guessed his first choice had chickened out – doubtless appalled at the prospect of having to clear up first.

He poured the wine. 'I didn't surface till noon. Then a crowd of us went out to lunch in Fulham. I only got back an hour ago.'

'Some lunch! You could do with some help here.'

'Forget it, love. Just wish me luck.'

They clinked glasses and he tossed some laundry on a chair so they could sit down. She shuffled about to make room for her feet on the littered floor.

Craig would be a great success in the Big Apple. The English social circuit was too precious for this wild colonial boy. She grinned, glad to be celebrating his good fortune. It was a wonderful time to escape from recessionary London, plastered all over with 'Closing Down Sale' and 'Final Bargains' posters.

He quizzed her about the Chiaroscuro

murder and her sister's involvement with Suki through Madeleine Pendlebury.

'Craig, last time we met you hinted something about the Pendleburys which caught my fancy. About Victor's father retiring to breed snowdrops.'

'Peter Bloch? A fascinating man. Can't think why nobody's ever published a biography. Might even get down to tackling it myself one of these days. Don't pretend you never heard that old story? And you with the SFO? It's a classic. Predates all the current financial scandals by twenty years and made one hell of a splash at the time. We got used to mega-fraud in the 'nineties. His name wasn't Pendlebury, of course. His wife reverted to her maiden name after the divorce and changed the kids' surnames while she was about it. She skipped to the Argentine when he was convicted. Theft, fraud and cutting a swathe through the reputations of city institutions from here to Wall Street. Peter Bloch was tap dancing through company balance sheets years before boardroom fraud became an all too-frequent banking hazard.'

'Good Lord. I knew Victor and Genny had been living in South America but nobody breathed a word to me about all this. I'm certain Madeleine doesn't know.'

'Your friend Madeleine's not noted for her financial nous, dear. And it *was* a long time ago. Victor's mother suffered from a rheumatic heart and died young, still bitterly unforgiving by all accounts. Not a pretty story. Luckily, her own money must have been secured because Victor brought his sister back to live in England at the Pendlebury family seat, which is where Genista keeps her horses. I heard on the grapevine Genny was hoping to supply Hammad Nadhouri's stud farm but Suki scotched that one, can't think why.'

'Genista's stables are at a place called Finings?'

Craig nodded, refilling the champagne flutes. 'I got my nose into all this old history by accident when I was researching a spread about the Chelsea Flower Show last year. Peter Pendlebury's name cropped up as still being the Last Word in snowdrops. Funny old world, isn't it? The old scoundrel dropped the Bloch tag when Victor and Genny welcomed him back to the family homestead after he had served his sentence. An open prison, pretty cushy. He must have had an untapped flair for plant breeding and prison gave him the time to specialize which he never would have had without the financial scandal.'

'Is he still alive?'

'Died years ago, before Victor's marriage. Pushing up the snowdrops himself now, poor bugger.'

'It sounds so romantic, doesn't it? An old lag rescued by his children and making a name for himself in an entirely new field.'

Craig choked on his wine, slopping the carpet, rocking with laughter.

'Romantic? That double-twister? He didn't screw pension funds but he came bloody near it. You ask the shareholders if the name Bloch strikes a sentimental chord.'

'Apart from all that, Craig, you must admit it's a touching example of family loyalty. Victor's a real gentleman, of course. Terribly soft-hearted.'

They agreed to differ and after a genuine show of affection Judith grabbed her bags and left Craig to finish his mammoth clearance operation.

Her own flat seemed chillingly uncluttered after that. Flinging her coat on the sofa, she switched on all the lamps, pulled the curtains and lit the gas log fire. The answerphone provided the final touch of welcome: a message from Laurence.

'I *must* see you tomorrow, Judy. I've been ringing all weekend. I've got to go off on Tuesday. Can you take a day off? Meet me at my flat in the morning? This is vital, darling. I must speak with you before I go.'

In the event Judith was unable to get away from the office until half past eleven. He picked her up in his car, dressed casually and flatteringly attentive. The sun shone winter bright, glittering on the river as they made their way towards Richmond and his flat. Between the bridges at Battersea a cormorant driven inland by the weather perched on the rusting wheels of a half-submerged supermarket trolley wedged in the shallows amid the flotsam of low tide. Its mate persisted with its fishing, diving and resurfacing with patient deliberation, floating low on the surface like a boat holed below the water line.

Judith touched his arm. 'Laurence, let's get some air. I was jammed in the cottage with Pixie most of the weekend.'

'How did you sister get such a stupid nickname?'

'Pixie? Oh, at school. Madeleine formed a fairy ring, you know what little girls are. Only those with lobeless ears could belong. Maddy was Queen Mab, of course, and the rest of them had names like Elfin, Imp, Sprite and so on. A soppy game. Pixie's was the only name that stuck. They wouldn't let me join, the rotton lot.'

'Wrong sort of ears,' he said with a chuckle.

'The sunshine's wonderful today. Let's get out and walk. How about Richmond Park?'

Laurence parried, anxious to get her back to the flat. 'It's deceptive, darling. It's bloody cold out there.'

'Don't be wet, Laurence.'

'OK. But don't say I didn't warn you.'

He took her to Kew Gardens and they scurried down avenues of leafless trees to the haven of the Palm House. The heat was sublime, the sunshine twice as sparkling and robbed of its winter chill. They strolled under the high glass roof, giggling at the notion of wandering hand in hand under banana trees on a freezing January morning. The place was practically empty.

'Laurence, it was a stroke of genius coming here. But why the urgency? Damascus again?'

'Damascus? What *are* you talking about, girl?'

'Your postcard over New Year. Damascus...?'

'Was the card from – oh, that! I didn't say I was *in* Damascus, did I? No, it's just Paris but I'm not sure for how long this time. That's what I have to speak to you about. It's in connection with Morton Playle. You *are* still going on this Bath weekend, I take it?'

'I'm not sure I want to after Suki's death. It will be a bit maudlin, I imagine. I was pinned to the wall discussing it endlessly with Pixie and Claire all weekend. Sophie's trying to gloss it over, she wants me to go down in the minibus with Madeleine and the others. Arnott's still on the payroll as a temporary security guard.'

'There's no danger, you know. It's all perfectly safe, honestly Judith. It was a political killing – there's absolutely no chance of any murderer on the loose in Bath. You might as well go ahead with it. There's no point in throwing away Pixie's generosity when it's all paid for, is it? You'll love it. I'm told these weekend jaunts are terribly well organized.'

Judith drew away, pretending to smell an exotic flower, which was, in fact, scentless, of course. She didn't trust Laurence's enthusiasm, his words totally at odds with his usual jibes about any sort of cultural excursion. It was also quite unlike Laurence to force an urgent meeting just to reassure her about Chiaroscuro. But perhaps he was more concerned for her than she gave him credit? This alluring possibility made her smile. She turned to face him, his anxiety suddenly very attractive.

A gardener approached and started trimming dead blooms. Laurence pulled her on to an iron bench in an arbour and they leaned together under the branching palms like Victorian lovers on a valentine card.

'Laurence, what *are* you up to?'

He frowned, balancing his options, then decided to come clean. Judith well understood the terms of Erskine's confidences. He stroked her hand.

'It's like this, sweetheart. Morton Playle

has been persuaded, much against his will I might add, to go back on this art club case. He's running scared but that doesn't mean that anyone else is at risk. It goes back to the day of Madeleine's party. I asked him for extra info about the Kilburn set-up. He contacted me in Tignes and later faxed a letter of introduction to Hammad Nadhouri. I flew to Paris to meet Hammad just after Christmas.'

'Morton was in love with Suki. It must be terrible for him to have to go back to Chiaroscuro on his own.'

Laurence looked startled, then laughed, affectionately squeezing her arm. 'You couldn't be more wrong, you sweet romantic soul! Morton had been employed by Hammad as a low-profile bodyguard. The Nadhouris didn't want to curtail Suki's fun too obviously – after all, she had been at a girls' boarding school here – and Morton as a minder was acceptable on both sides. There was no love affair – they would have cut his balls off if there had been. Suki and Morton were inseparable for practical reasons.'

'But why did you want to meet Hammad *before* Suki's murder?'

'Morton was worried. Hammad had received some nebulous threat. The tip-off I got about the house in Kilburn was, wrongly as it happened, accredited to one of Nadhouri's staff reporters and Hammad was given a final warning. When I saw Hammad in Paris he was seriously concerned. He wanted an intermediary to put his case to the Foreign Office in London. He was offering information in exchange for a deal on security. He needed protection for his family.'

'I thought he was already on the diplomatic list? His news sheet was very frank about Islamic militants. A journalist was telling me all about it. Hammad was far from sympathetic with the foreign troublemakers for a start.'

'Since when have you got so matey with newshounds?' he quipped.

'Just chit-chat. We got talking at one of the Fraud Office press conferences.'

He shrugged. 'Well, he's right. Hammad is a moderate. He uses his wealth to promote peace in the Middle East through legal and diplomatic channels. Hammad feels that terrorism can only destroy world sympathy.'

'The destruction of the twin towers certainly did that. And the escape of the embassy bombers in Kenya was a hard pill to swallow.'

'Morton doesn't know everything about Nadhouri's political manoeuvres but he was the one who tipped me off initially and Hammad was sufficiently impressed by the threats to take me into his confidence. In a nutshell, Hammad knows the identities of the kidnappers who beat and tortured those Western aid workers. To protect these thugs from reprisals they have been given sanctuary in one of the sympathetic countries – more than twenty of them, all minor associates of one of the most fearsome terrorist gangs in the world.'

'And Hammad was passing information to British Intelligence?'

'Considering it. But he obviously has spies in his own network. Hammad is treading eggshells.'

'Did Suki know any of this?'

'Hammad swears not and I believe him. It would not be in his nature to involve his womenfolk.'

'But the murder?'

'Hammad put Morton through the mangle about that, of course. Morton's never heard of this splinter group calling itself the Sioux and refuses to consider it likely a political assassination would include scalping.'

'Mutilation like that would cause revulsion all round. Scupper any sympathetic hearings. Perhaps it was an anti-Palestinian organization wishing to start a conflict between the different factions? Revenge is an automatic response, isn't it?'

'Who knows? I'm not party to the finer points and I'm no expert on Middle Eastern affairs. That's why I have to rely on Morton Playle. But my boss had back-up information confirming Hammad's story. The threats were genuine. Chiaroscuro is perfectly safe. Morton is tagging along to Bath to placate Hammad on another front. Hammad wants to know who was supplying Suki with the joy dust. His own personal vendetta. He wants whoever it was put inside. You can get a decent stretch for dealing snow. I don't envy the poor sod when the Nadhouris get their hands on him.'

'Or her. Are you sure Nadhouri himself isn't involved in drug peddling?'

'Absolutely certain. Hammad's pure gold, believe me. He doesn't even drink, for God's sake.'

Judy shrugged, unconvinced, privately appalled at the extent of Laurence's familiarity with all these people.

He lowered his voice, giving her elbow a gentle shake just to emphasize the point.

'Keep an eye on Morton while he's in Bath, will you, Judy? For all I know he's been doublecrossing Hammad all down the line. I can't imagine the girl was boring holes in her nostrils and Morton didn't even notice. I don't trust him an inch.'

'But he evidently trusts you. You were the one he rang from Chiaroscuro when the police were trying to interview him about the murder. Flood thought he had phoned his solicitor.'

'Morton knew it was imperative to keep

the lid on the political threats to the Nadhouri family. He dare not say a word without consulting Hammad. He thought I could get him off the hook.'

'And you did.'

'Morton hasn't done anything illegal. He works for Hammad and the only qualification for that job is to keep your mouth shut.'

Judith raised her face to the sun, closing her eyes, absorbing the warmth in that gigantic glass palace, imagining herself in Paradise.

'You know, Laurence, all this place needs is birds. Parrots flying about in the palm trees. Humming birds in the blossom.'

'I was in the garden of a hotel in Tokyo once where they had that all worked out. I was sitting in this miniature Japanese landscape in the centre of a buzzing metropolis listening to what sounded like the dawn chorus in an English woodland. All on tape, of course. Loudspeakers hidden in the trees. But it did the trick. Do you think Kew Gardens would wear it?'

They drifted back outside. Then, galvanized by the bitter wind, hurried back to Laurence's flat.

Judith had been there before, so often in fact that there had been a time not so long ago when she had been tempted to accept his urge for her to move in. But Laurence blew in and out of her life too precipitously

160

to tip her over the edge, however enticing the prospect. His work took him abroad at a moment's notice, the exact nature of these forays inevitably secret. It made her nervous, unsure of any real future in a love affair in which she found herself continuously stumbling into black holes of misinformation, not all, she suspected, occasioned by professional necessity.

Thirteen

On Friday, after work, Judith drove to the West Country in the VW, the main party having departed in the minibus from Chiaroscuro that morning, the rest travelling in their own transport. The club members were all to stay at Chevenix Park, a country house about six miles from Bath, the home of their hosts, the Shaws.

Bruce's map and directions were excellent and, having left London when the mass exodus from the city had already thinned out, Judith enjoyed a straight run on the motorway, arriving in Chevenix village on the stroke of nine. The house suddenly appeared at a curve in the road like a miniature castle complete with crenellated stone walls surrounding a central courtyard. Sophie's effusive architectural notes in the club brochure rhapsodized on Chevenix Park, describing its medieval origins and its history under generations of the Shaw family. It all sounded very romantic and certainly Judith's first impression of the lighted gothic windows and floodlit archways rising from the mist was exciting.

She drove between twin towers flanking the gates and parked next to the minibus in the yard at the back. Garages had superceded what she assumed to have been stables and, from the heavy reggae beat issuing from the accommodation above, it would seem that Brenton George, Chiaroscuro's Man Friday, had settled in for an evening with his ghetto blaster. Judy was slightly surprised that there had been no check at the entrance and although the barking of a guard dog at the rear of the house sounded menacing, no one came to investigate.

The weather had turned mild, a slight drizzle augmenting the fog which hung about the honey-coloured stonework. Rows of mullioned windows, some with stained glass, glowed brightly through the murk, illuminated with sufficient wattage almost to warrant Chevenix Park running its own power station, Judy wryly concluded, she herself living in dread of the electricity bill plopping on her doormat.

She entered directly into a panelled entrance hall in which a massive log fire authentically leapt and smoked in an inglenook occupying one entire wall. Sounds of laughter and conversation filtered from a banqueting room leading from it and, dropping her weekend case by the door, Judith walked in just as Bruce was imploring the members to take their seats for the start of Dr Tyler's lecture.

There was no time to introduce herself. She slipped into the back row as the lights dimmed, the only witnesses to her arrival being Lucienne de Blanc, who gave an irritable nod of acknowledgement, and Arnott, occupying an aisle seat by the door, who missed nothing. He greeted Judith with a cheerful thumbs-up and everyone settled back for the evening's entertainment.

The lecture was a mini-tour of Far Eastern cultures illustrated by slides featuring textiles, painted scrolls and teapots. Ken Tyler's style was elegant, informative and utterly serious – in contrast to the badinage of Will Haydock-Smith – but was greeted with equally rapturous applause.

Having spent more than a month dissecting the Mickey Mouse accounts of a City mega-fraud case, Judy found herself, with increasing frequency, pondering the cost effectiveness of any sort of commercial enterprise. Balance sheets produced even by top-flight firms disclosed shortfalls which should have been foreseen. She glanced round at the audience, mentally assessing the number of bums on seats. It was a well-heeled crowd, the sort of folk who generously shelled out on their leisure pursuits, and Pixie had hinted that the Chiaroscuro junkets were far from cheap. Judy could well believe it.

Even so, the overheads must be considerable. Apart from the cost of running the club premises in London, the Shaw family presumably charged a fat fee for the use of their country house and the outlay for staff and lecturers was clearly no small item. Will Haydock-Smith was new to the game and probably well down on the salary scale but, taking in Dr Tyler's accomplished performance and his experience – not to mention his valuable jade collection – Judith guessed that the senior lecturer swallowed the lion's share of the takings. Sophie and Bruce could hardly subsidize the club activities for ever ... For how long could they hold out?

The lights went up and Sophie announced coffee would be served in the library. Her exit in the wake of the Shaws, plus an eager following from the body of the hall, gave the impression of a royal progress.

Arnott joined Judith and they stood waiting for the audience to disperse. Their voices echoed in the loftiness of the vaulted ceiling.

'Good run down, lass?'

'Great! You came with the charabanc outing?' she asked with a grin.

'By 'eck, Pullen, that driver of theirs, Brenton George, thinks he's steering a bloody sputnik. We rocketed down the M4 so quick no one had the chance to use the sick bags.'

'I expect Brenton was glad to escape from the murder investigation. I hear the CID had him in overnight for questioning.'

'Charlie Flood's got a bee in his bonnet about that case. Busting a gut to nail him. I think he's wrong. They had to let him go, of course. Not a shred of evidence.'

'No weapon?'

Arnott shook his head.

Judith lowered her voice, repeating Erskine's assurances that Suki's killing had been politically motivated but economical with the truth about Hammad Nadhouri's diplomatic involvement. 'Laurence says it's nothing whatsoever to do with Chiaroscuro. There's absolutely no possibility of further violence.'

Arnott shrugged, unwilling to touch wood on that score.

'Who came down in the bus with you?' she asked.

'The usual lot. Mrs Neuman and the Canadian woman – Fenella something or other – and her sidekick with the sour face.'

'Lucie.'

'That's her. Curdle milk she would. Erskine's ex-army pal, Morton Playle, made up for her miseries though. Right as ninepence. Never thought *he'd* show up. Wasn't he sweet on the Nadhouri kid?'

'Just looking for a rich wife, I think.'

'So's the Boy Wonder, Will Smith, if you ask me. All over your friend Mrs Pendlebury and wasn't she loving every minute?'

'Madeleine? Oh, good. She looked utterly wretched last time I saw her. Her husband's been straying.'

'And what's sauce for the gander...?' Arnott tapped his beaky nose.

'With Will Smith? He's years younger than Madeleine. It's just a bit of fun.'

'You 'avn't forgot we saw the two of them before, have you Pullen? Outside the pie and mash shop? When we was driving back from Romney Marsh after Christmas? Gordon Bennett, Pullen, don't you use your eyes?'

Judy's jaw dropped. 'The chap in the cycle gear, do you mean? That wasn't Will Smith!'

He nodded.

The picture in her mind re-formed, of Madeleine laughing up at a young man leading her into the working-class nosherie on the rim of central London.

She shook her head in disbelief but had to concede the point. 'You're right, Arnott, now

166

you come to mention it. I should have twigged right away.'

'Mrs Neuman looked worried on the way down. Your mate made no bones about nabbing the seat next to Foxton's new attraction. Smith's the club's biggest draw if you ask me. Puts his other star turn well in the shade. All that blue-eyed magic had the old hens at the back of the bus on the edge of their seats all right. Him and his tight little bum. Cut no ice with the new couple, though. A Major Herbert and his snotty missus, Lady Harriet. Mrs Neuman was turning somersaults buttering *them* up.'

'Sounds quite a trip.'

'We got here in time for a sandwich lunch affair with Foxton and the owners here, Shaw and his wife, doing the honours with that other teacher, the bloke who did the talk just now—'

'Dr Tyler.'

'Yes, well, them two was here ahead of the main party, smoothing out the Shaws and bagging the best digs for themselves. Tyler and Foxton are staying in the private wing with the lord and lady of the manor. The rest of us are bedded out on the top two floors, Smith and yours truly in the attics like frigging bats. Nice rooms though, I'll give them that.'

'And warm! I can't believe how comfortable it is here. Sophie must have laid the ground rules about keeping the heating at full blast.'

'The Yanks can't stand the cold like we can. Most of these old places are bloody freezing. Must cost a ruddy fortune to run – no wonder they have to take in lodgers.'

Judy snorted, imagining the Shaws' reaction to Arnott's gritty assessment of their conference facilities.

A door opened behind them and Madeleine appeared, the glint of her hair bright as the gilt mouldings framing the ancestral portraits which lined the walls. She wore a loose black crêpe trouser suit, hand-painted with a splashy poppy design, eye-catching but with a restrained exotic glamour, deceptively informal.

'Judith! I've been looking everywhere for you. Why don't you join us in the library? You must be gasping for some coffee after driving down. Sophie thought you might need a sandwich.'

'Thanks, Maddy, but no. It's awfully kind of Sophie but I'll be in later. I'd like to unpack first. Mr Arnott and I were just catching up on the day's events. I hear Brenton gave you all an exciting drive down.'

'And how! My guess he's practising for the Monte Carlo Rally. Why don't you let me show you your room? It's next to mine. I expect you'd like to freshen up.'

They left Arnott to trundle into the library

on his own and, after reclaiming Judy's suitcase, hurried upstairs. The house was lovely. Madeleine muttered apologetically about the smallness of Judith's bedroom, originally a dressing room, but then showed her the connecting bathroom with a flourish. It was large and luxurious. Twin hand basins stood under mirrors lit by spotlights under which a wide glass shelf was already set out with Madeleine's make-up jars and perfume bottles. The bath and lavatory occupied an alcove and a door at each end gave access from both bedrooms to complete the suite.

'I'm next door, through there,' she said, indicating the other door, which led into a double bedroom where lamps threw a soft glow over flowery chintz. Each of the bathroom doors sported a narrow glazed window like an arrow slit, presumably to check occupancy as there were no keys.

'You don't mind sharing a bathroom, do you, Judy? These rooms are normally used as a family unit. Sophie spent hours juggling with the allocation of rooms. She thought, as we're chums, we could cope with one bathroom between us. The Shaws have done a wonderful job with the layout, carving bathrooms from all sorts of unlikely cupboards and storerooms. But it is a bit topsy turvy. Victor supplied all the light fittings, so I saw the redecoration before the Shaws went in for all this conference entertaining. In fact, it

was I who persuaded them to give Chiaroscuro a try. Finings is only ten miles away.
Victor's family has known the Shaws for
simply yonks. This house was used as a film
location last summer – a TV series set in the
thirties called *Gilded Edge*. It's supposed to
be very glamorous.' She made a comic
grimace, looping strands of hair behind her
ears in a schoolgirlish gesture which Judy
had seen often before but which always
struck her as being appealingly gauche in a
woman of such studied elegance. Madeleine's stutter had entirely evaporated during
this exchange and, with a jolt, Judith recognized another change.

'Your nails, Maddy! What happened to
your wonderful long scarlet talons?'

Madeleine laughed, fluttering her hands.
'They weren't real, darling. Didn't you
guess? I got fed up with all the palaver. It
seemed such a waste of time.'

Judith was confused. Was this new Madeleine a Born Again nature girl? Hardly that,
she thought, casting an eye over the flawless
turn-out. But a move in the right direction.
Pixie always maintained that Madeleine's
beauty schedule occupied every moment of
her waking hours and that she was as busy as
any working girl fitting everything in. What
with her health club, the hairdresser, a
weekly manicure, aromatherapy, indoor
tennis and workouts, Victor's wife had had

no time for naughtiness. Perhaps this little flutter with Will Haydock-Smith had played havoc with her routine as well as her heart. Madeleine certainly hadn't suffered by the rescheduling: she seemed to have shed years despite the anxiety of Victor's unfaithfulness, not to mention her quarrel with Pixie and Claire. Judith privately applauded the courage of this woman who, manipulated all her life, seemed suddenly to have broken out. Bully for you, Madeleine Pendlebury.

Judy took advantage of the lighthearted atmosphere to ask a personal question.

'Have you changed your mind about confronting Victor?'

Madeleine sobered and, perching on the edge of the bed, looked directly at Judith before answering.

'Victor and I met last week to talk it over. I told him about the delivery of the gold charm bracelet and Papa checking it out at the hotel in Ireland. There's clear evidence. It wasn't a mistake. Victor denies nothing. We've agreed on a divorce straight away. I shall need nothing from him, of course. But the woman's name will have to come out – I've no alternative short of waiting years to finish things quietly and Victor's in no position to argue about terms. After all, it's been going on for years. Much better if we cut loose before bitterness sets in. Victor intends to sell up the business and live quietly at Finings. I shall remain at the flat in London. I've already changed the locks.'

This last remark struck Judith with icy finality. Surely Madeleine had nothing to fear from Victor? A more sensitive, gentle man would be hard to imagine.

'I'm so sorry, Maddy.' It was true. Madeleine's unemotional account of the end of her marriage made it seem as prosaic as the rolling up of a carpet. Judith had never seen this side of her before. Such assurance. And everything so neatly determined. Perhaps Madeleine was more than a match for Pixie and Claire after all.

Madeleine rose, smoothing the counterpane, examining the framed silhouettes hanging above the bedhead.

'Shall we join the others?' she said at last.

Judy glanced at her watch. 'I'm feeling pretty tired, Maddy. I think I'll have a bath and turn in early. We'll have to come to an arrangement about sharing the bathroom,' she added with comic emphasis.

'I shan't be coming up for ages, Judy. You go ahead. I'll see you at breakfast. Will's taking some of us on a walk round the city in the morning. Sophie's organized an expedition round the antique shops but I think you'll probably enjoy it more with us. We're seeing the Abbey and the Pump Room and an eighteenth-century house furnished in period. Just a few people, no more than eight or ten.'

'Sounds great.'

'Oh, by the way. There are no bolts on any of the doors here. Sophie's appalled but the Shaws can't do much about it now. It would ruin the old doors to insert modern locks. It's probably a hangover from the days when house parties were really sporting.'

Judith laughed. 'I could always wedge my door with a chair. Pity Brenton's been pushed into the staff flat above the old stables.'

'Tut tut. I had no idea you were secretly hankering after a bit of rough, Judith Pullen.'

Madeleine crossed to the dressing-table to check her lipstick before going downstairs to rejoin the party. Judith withdrew to her own room via their shared bathroom and unpacked her night things with more than a fleeting regret that Laurence had been unable to come. Despite her worst misgivings, the weekend with Arnott's Charabanc Club, as he persisted in calling it, looked like being a whole lot of fun. She turned back the counterpane on her single bed and resigned herself to a quiet night's sleep.

Fourteen

Judith jerked out of a deep slumber, instantly aware that someone was creeping about in the next room. She put on the bedside light. Three a.m. The arrow slit in the bathroom door shone bright as a neon strip. With a sigh she turned out the light, realizing it was, after all, only Madeleine coming to bed.

She lay in the dark mocking her own nervousness. Not normally a light sleeper, Judy wondered if Laurence's overblown reassurances had had the opposite effect: sensitizing her nerve endings to every unexpected movement. Now she was jumping at her own shadow.

Madeleine's bedtime ritual took a very long time. Much running of water seemed involved and at one point a lid dropped, the sound of it rolling across the bathroom floor exaggerated in the small hours, even Madeleine's muttered exclamation clearly audible in the silent house. Judith hoped Madeleine's tiptoed descent – presumably from Will's attic – had been accomplished with less rigmarole than these unending ablutions. Judy pulled the bedclothes over her head, shivering despite the heat of the room, and hoped she wasn't starting a cold.

Next morning she woke late, surfacing with a jolt to discover it was already after eight. Leaping into the bathroom, she peeped into Madeleine's room, already empty, fresh air blowing the curtains, obviously yet another requirement in Maddy's health programme. Knees-bend at an open window before breakfast? Judy went in and shut it with an irritable flourish and re-entered their bathroom, sourly surveying the cluttered glass shelf above Madeleine's basin. Apart from cleansing cream, toners and make-up there was an atomizer, vitamin pills, throat lozenges, Evian water, an electric toothbrush with a fearsome number of attachments, not to mention herbal sleeping tablets and witchhazel. The most puzzling items were slices of lemon and cucumber individually wrapped in clingfilm. Hardly a midnight feast.

She washed her face and, climbing into leggings and an oversize sweater, flew downstairs to catch up on the day.

The refectory was still half full, one large circular table accommodating a noisy party comprising Morton Playle and Fenella, Dr Tyler, Madeleine, Will Smith and three middle-aged ladies bathing in the sparkling repartee of Chiaroscuro's younger element. Sophie Neuman held court at another table with a bevy of Americans discussing the morning's shopping potential.

Judith was never at her best first thing. She saw Arnott across the room, seated at a small table with Lucienne de Blanc, tucking into his plate of eggs and bacon. The Belgian girl was just leaving, getting to her feet as Judith approached, looking as discontented as ever.

'May I join you?'

Lucienne shrugged, gathering her bag and jacket, leaving Arnott to choke down a mouthful as he nodded vehemently at the empty seat, pointing with his knife. Judith dropped her satchel on the floor and went off to fetch fruit and coffee from the buffet table.

She slid into the chair opposite Arnott. He had dressed formally in a dark suit. She eyed him critically.

'What happened to the arty get-up, Arnott? The bow tie? The pink shirt? Lose your nerve?'

'You get out on the wrong side this morning, Pullen? As it happens, I don't have to make out I'm a paying customer no more. Mrs Neuman's taking her ladies round the shops this morning. I'm looking after them. Bloody pickpockets roaming this town are just as bad as the dips in Oxford Street, I'm told. May look like a picture postcard but these tourist watering holes are a magnet to all the villains. Do you know, a poor little Nip got beaten up walking round the Royal Crescent after dark only last weekend? He should have let go his camera first off and no messing. Not worth getting no black eye over.'

'Well, I never!'

Arnott looked at her sharply but she kept a straight face and attacked her grapefruit. She tried to imagine Arnott tailoring his rumbustious style to Sophie's notion of a discreet detective but was unconvinced.

She said, 'I'm going on the walkabout with Will Smith.'

Arnott pushed away his empty plate, burped with satisfaction and poured himself a cup of strong tea, liberally sweetened. 'You're on a better road than me then, lass. Beautiful city. Never been here before myself. Nothing like retirement to broaden the mind. Seriously, Pullen, thanks for putting me on to this caper. It's a right doddle. Mrs Neuman says she'll probably want me on all these trips. It's Harrogate next, by 'eck. And they're going to Scotland for Easter.'

'I can't see you in the kilt, Arnott.' Judy giggled.

'Saucy trollop!'

'Mind you, you're full of surprises these days. I never imagined you latching on to

Lucienne at the breakfast table. I thought she was your least favourite here.'

'Our Lucie? Oh, she's not so hard-nosed as she makes out. She can't really afford it, that's the problem. It gets up her nose seeing all these silly old cows not even bothering to take notes. She wants to train to be a proper pot-mender, she was telling me. Antiques. Riveting china, like.'

'Fenella mentioned it. I suppose you can see Lucie's point. But she's a malicious little vixen all the same.'

'Tells me your friend's causing comment. Cuddling up to young Smith on the side ain't gone unnoticed. The squire's wife here knows the husband, you know. Victor Pendlebury. Lucie tells me Mrs Shaw's not well pleased with all the bed-hopping that's going on. You ought to tip Mrs P. the wink. Tell her to watch her step.'

'It's only gossip, Arnott. Take no notice.'

'Would I waste my time peddling cats' piss? I'm sleeping in the next room, Pullen! If I put me 'ead in a tea-cosy I couldn't miss hearing Smith and your mate jawing away half the bloody night.' He lit a cigarette, oblivious to Nancy Shaw's meaningful stare and unimpressed by the discreet 'No Smoking' sign.

'I got woken up myself, Arnott, you're not being exclusively picked on. But you're right. Madeleine's playing a dangerous game. It's gone to her head. She's never gone overboard for anyone before.'

'It's no joke, missy. I need my eight hours. Got to keep your wits about you here with all the old biddies flashing their diamonds about the place. None of the ruddy bedrooms 've got any locks. Can you believe it? Mrs Neuman's worried sick there'll be another bout of pilfering while we're out on the town. They've never cleared up that other trouble, you know. The stuff missing from the lockers. Lucie was telling me she lost a ring and the tart who got her throat cut had her car keys pinched. It might have some bearing on the murder. I told Charlie Flood about it. He still thinks it was an inside job, that killing.' Arnott lowered his voice, leaning over the table, spilling ash on the cloth. 'Your boyfriend, Erskine, tried shutting him up the same as he did me on that Swayne case, you know. But Charlie won't wear it. He's still making his own enquiries. He reckons our Brenton's got something up his jumper he's not too proud of. If the thieving starts up again I reckon it's Brenton bloody George who's head's going to be on the block.'

'Well, don't go looking for trouble, Arnott. It's all going nicely so far. Let Flood worry about all that in London. Enjoy the break. And don't let Lucienne get you off on any wild goose chase looking for her ring. Sophie said it wasn't very valuable anyway. Madeleine lost her wallet, credit cards, the lot – and she's not bawling from the rooftops. Lucie's just trying to stir up trouble. Probably thinks if she shouts loud enough Sophie will recompense her in some way. Offer a free weekend maybe?'

'Don't run away with the idea I'm a silly old sod taken in by a pretty girl with a hard luck story, Pullen. I know Lucie Longface is a spiteful little madam but she's useful. She's the only one here who fills me in with all the juicy bits. One of the little tasters she passed over before you struggled out of bed this morning was she heard a couple in the room next to hers last night.'

'Not another wicked pair playing Postman's Knock? Poor Nancy Shaw. She'll have to boil up all the sheets after this little weekend.'

Arnott glared, eyebrows lowering over the broken nose, a dangerous flush staining his jowls. No wonder their nicknames at the station had been Punch and Judy. She stifled a grin. All they needed now was the dog and a string of sausages.

'Listen to me for a change, Miss Cleverclogs. You might learn something if you shut up for a minute. Lucie's room is next to that Canadian's. Vanilla.'

'Fenella,' Judy corrected.

'Right, monkey. Well, after lights-out last

180

night this Fenella was entertaining the other lecturer, Dr Tyler, in her room. And Lucie tells me they was having a right old barney.'

'What about?'

'She couldn't say. Or won't.'

'Mind you, Arnott, Lucie's a funny girl. She's very possessive with Fenella, doesn't like her having other friends. Do you think she's a lesbian? On the other hand, Lucie's one of Tyler's fan club. Might be jealous. A woman scorned and all that...'

Arnott stubbed out his cigarette in the saucer, deep in thought. 'It reminded me of that business you overheard in London the night of the murder.'

'When I was in the loo?'

'You said you caught someone talking to Suki Nadhouri. Could it have been Lucie?'

Judith thought for a moment. 'Possibly. The tone was bitter enough. It must have been a French national, it was absolutely fluent. There's also Madeleine, of course,' she reluctantly added.

'Is she French?'

'Half. Her father is. She's bilingual. It would have been perfectly natural for her to speak to Suki in her own lingo. But now I think back, it couldn't have been Madeleine.'

'You would have recognized the voice?'

'It's not that. In fact, in French I doubt whether I would recognize my own mother's.

No, it's just a gut feeling. The woman with Suki was angry. That was pretty plain without knowing all that was being said. Maddy wouldn't use those swear words! She never raises her voice, she's much too timid.'

'How would you know? She might have a mean streak and she ain't so timid here with Will Smith.' He told her about the drug connection that he and Charlie Flood suspected was the real subject under discussion, not skiing in the Alps.

'And you reckon there was only three French-speaking women there that night.'

'Who knows? There were probably lots more. I only *know* of three: Suki, Lucienne and Madeleine. The three French hens.'

'What you on about now, Pullen? What bloody chickens?'

'Three French hens, two turtle doves and a partridge in a pear tree,' she sang softly across the table. 'Don't you remember the old Christmas song, Arnott? *You* were the one who first mentioned it. Driving past the pie and mash shop the day we spotted Madeleine and Will together.'

Arnott glowered, already fed up with Judy's larkiness. He missed the status of being a salaried detective inspector. No back-chat from Sergeant Pullen in those days. Not at everyone's beck and call either. Sophie Neuman was urgently signalling to him across the room, tapping her watch in a prompting gesture. He rose, shedding ash and crumbs on the cloth, and lumbered across the dining room to join her.

Bruce Foxton stepped on to the dais at the end of the room to make an announcement. The chattering hushed and he gave a run-down of the day's programme.

'Lunch back here at twelve thirty, ladies and gentlemen, and this afternoon we shall be visiting the American Museum, which I need hardly tell you is a truly wonderful experience. The coach will be departing promptly at two o'clock, so may I beg you all to be on time? We shall have tea at Claverton Manor and after dinner tonight we hope you will all join in a little lighthearted enter-tainment Sophie and I have devised. Will and Kenneth plus four other team members will be participating in an arts quiz which promises to be a lot of fun and will involve audience participation. So don't say I didn't warn you. The Chiaroscuro Mastermind Contest. Prizes will be awarded to members who outwit the quiz panel.'

Judith swallowed her coffee and was mov-ing towards the exit as Madeleine caught up with her, linking arms. She smiled, looking fresh as a daisy in a white sweater. Judith marvelled at the stamina of someone who had not only been up half the night but had spent a further half-hour priming her com-plexion before turning in. Judith herself felt slightly feverish. Perhaps she really was coming down with a cold.

'Judy, we're leaving almost straight away. OK? Meet by the gates in ten minutes. Will's got first go with the minibus. Brenton's dropping us off in the city and then coming back for Sophie's crowd so we mustn't keep them waiting.'

'Is Morton coming?'

Madeleine looked up sharply. 'I think so ... I'm not sure. He's with Fenella...' she finished lamely.

At that moment, breaking into Madeleine's confusion, Sophie hurried up to say there was a telephone call for her from London. 'You can take it in Nancy's office upstairs. There's a pay phone in the small study off the hall if you need to call back, Madeleine.'

Judith watched her rush off, all bright hair and spindly legs, the mohair sweater giving the impression of a fluffy wading bird. Judy's conversation with Arnott, reviving a muzzy recollection of the eavesdropping incident and the barely comprehended dialogue, bothered her. Could Madeleine really be involved in Suki's drug dealing? She had all the signs: reed thinness, mood swings, sleeplessness, little appetite, the overbright vitality of a firework which sparkles brilliantly before extinction.

Judith baulked at this bogey of Madeleine involved in a cocaine ring and tossed it aside.

Even if she had been tempted by Suki's joy dust she could never be a key member, let alone a dealer. No, there was someone else at the top. Neither Suki nor Madeleine was capable of organizing a chimpanzees' tea-party. Or were they? What about Lucienne? Certainly she had the temperament for it but did she have the money? Lucienne was stony broke. There must be a man involved some-where. Morton? Laurence had told her to keep her eye on Morton. He was the one closest to Suki after all...

Her throat was beginning to tighten up. She ran upstairs for her coat, snaffled a couple of Madeleine's lozenges and hurried outside to join the others waiting with Brenton by the minibus. The air was like champagne. It was the perfect day for a stroll round the elegant terraces and squares of Bath. A nice long walk would blow the cob-webs away, clear her head of all these night-marish conjectures.

The minibus dropped down into the city in a sweep which gave them all an enchanting panorama of serried ranks of Georgian houses laid out in geometric perfection. Brenton left them near the Abbey and they trooped off behind Will and Morton, eager not to waste a moment.

Judith counted eight in their party, Major Herbert and Lady Harriet, Morton and Fenella, the earnest young man with a camera and, of course, Maddy. Will was the perfect guide, enthusiastic and attentive, knowledgeable and with an all-embracing friendliness which warmed even the stony hearts of the Herberts. Madeleine linked up with the shy young man, leaving Judith free to tag along with Morton.

They crossed the square. In a restaurant doorway, an untidy pile of cardboard fell apart, revealing a scruffy youngster jammed in the entry. He clutched a small brown-and-white terrier, which escaped, ecstatically circling the pavement as the boy rose to fold the cardboard into a neat package, on top of which the words 'HOMELESS' and 'HUNGRY' crudely put his case. The door opened and a waiter appeared with a broom to sweep the forecourt, momentarily shocked to discover the teenage vagrant blocking his exit. The dog yapped defensively, snapping at the man with the broom.

Judith stopped speaking and she and Morton watched as they walked by, both mentally assessing the lad's chances. The waiter, signalling to him to wait, disappeared back inside while the youth, grabbing the dog, tucked it in his bomber jacket. He glanced across at Judith and her companion, nervously acknowledging their curiosity. The waiter returned with a plastic carrier bag and delved into his pocket for small change just as Will Smith shouted back at them not to drag behind the rest of the party. They hurried to catch up, the bloodshot eyes of the apprentice down-and-out haunting as a spectre at the feast.

After touring the Assembly Rooms they agreed on a coffee break and the Pump Room – as opposed to Sally Lunn's – won the vote. Will was keen to keep his small party together, using his charm to jolly them along. Judith studied him covertly, curious to discover the secret of Madeleine's fascination. Will Smith's unfeigned enthusiasm was appealing and, Madeleine herself being naturally naive, Peter Pan must seem an attractive contrast to dear old Victor. Perhaps she was tired of being protected so assiduously? According to Craig Thomas, she had passed directly from her grandmother's safekeeping to Victor's. And there was Genista. The brother and sister were mutually supportive. Powerfully so. Old man Bloch's disgrace and imprisonment must have set them apart in their teens. Nothing like a skeleton in the family closet to keep siblings close. Guarding a family secret was a lifetime's burden and their strong alliance had moved in to enclose Madeleine within its exclusive circle. It must have been stifling.

The Pump Room was busy, a buzz of conversation and the constant rattle of teacups almost obliterating the trio sawing away on the little platform surrounded by potted palms. The Chiaroscuro group had to split up, the Herberts commandeering a table for six and Madeleine and Judith cheerfully bagging a place by the windows.

Madeleine's pale skin looked almost translucent in the winter sunshine. A waitress took their order and after a few general remarks about Bath Madeleine launched into an intensive appeal to Judith's good nature. Judy wondered if being syphoned off to a table away from Will's tour party was entirely fortuituous.

'Judy, thank God we've got a moment to ourselves. I've got a problem.'

'Oh, yes?' Judith poured the coffee, avoiding her eye.

'Papa phoned me from London just before we left. He's driving back to France today to join up with a film company who are testing locations in Morocco. I told him about my talk with Victor and that he's agreed to the divorce. I told Papa I was going to a solicitor straight away.'

'Madeleine, I really don't want to hear all this. Your private life is strictly between you and Victor. *Please* leave me out of it.'

Madeleine touched her arm, her eyes brimming.

'Bear with me for a moment, darling. We only have a few minutes. Papa says I *must* assemble *all* the evidence before I take any legal steps.'

There was silence and Madeleine forced herself to continue.

'The gold charm bracelet and wrapping – the package I told you about when I came to your flat – it's still in the desk at Finings. Papa insists I retrieve it to back up the letter from the Irish hotel manager which he took away with him.'

A fearful supposition surfaced in Judy's mind. 'You're not asking me to go to Finings for you, surely? To ask Victor to hand over this bracelet thing?'

'No, of course not! All I'm asking is that you come with me this afternoon. Victor and Genny are not even there. He told me they had to go to Newmarket this weekend. There's only Mrs Hatton, who looks after the house. There will be no problem, no confrontation, if that's what's bothering you. I promise. It's just that I haven't a car and this afternoon may be my last chance to collect all my personal things from the house. Victor took a dim view of me changing the locks at the flat.'

'I can't say I blame him. It's all a bit sudden, isn't it? Locking him out was a funny thing to do. He'll have to rent somewhere near his office, I suppose ... Honestly, Maddy, I don't want to get involved. You can borrow the VW if you like. I'm going on the coach trip to the American Museum.'

Will's group was breaking up and Morton

was signalling for the bill. Madeleine became desperate.

'Judith, please, I beg of you, come with me. I *can't* go there on my own. I've never liked Finings. It's a gloomy old house and I've always been "de trop". Victor's housekeeper is his old nanny and the stables are run by an irrascible toad of a man called Paddy Frith who has been with the family for years and years. He's always despised me because I'm frightened of the horses. I can't explain it. Victor thinks I hate going there because it's so isolated but it's not that. Finings gives me the creeps, the place itself, not just the horsey set-up. Do come with me, love. I won't ask anything else, cross my heart.'

Will joined them before she could answer but she nodded and Madeleine's anxiety lifted like a lark on the wing.

Fifteen

After lunch Madeleine and Judith slipped away to drive to Finings. The VW was jammed between the minibus and a huge luxury coach which had been hired for the visit to Claverton Manor. Bruce and Ken Tyler stood with the driver checking the paperwork, absorbed in the timing of the afternoon's events. They looked up in surprise as the VW emerged, startled by Madeleine's obvious defection. Judith irritably clashed the gears, wishing she could have evaded this dubious expedition. Madeleine waved to Bruce in mute apology and the car accelerated through the gates, scattering gravel.

The sight of Will Smith waiting at the next bend in the road was the last straw as far as Judy was concerned. She braked hard and Madeleine let him in, saying, 'Judy, don't scowl, love. I mentioned to Will we would be skiving off this afternoon and thought he might like to see the house. There are some fine watercolours. And I might never go there again.' This last admission seemed the crux of it and it flashed into Judith's mind that there was still time for her to back out and join Bruce's coach party. She suggested Madeleine and Will took the VW after all. 'Three's a crowd,' she snapped.

They wouldn't hear of it, insisting she came along, Madeleine, as persuasive as ever, putting the case that Finings would be much more interesting than Claverton Manor, especially with Will along for the ride, able to explain the architectural merits and so forth. Judith, mollified, allowed herself to be drawn into their conspiracy and resigned herself to it.

They approached the house from the east and it emerged from thick woodland like a theatre backdrop, the winter sun a ball of fire silhouetting jagged rooflines.

Madeleine directed her to drive to the back. In the shadow of a belt of trees the stonework was dank and mossy but as they turned off the drive the vista suddenly opened up on to a magnificent new stable block, sparkling with fresh paintwork and oiled timbering.

'Genista's,' Maddy unnecessarily explained. 'The house hasn't seen a lick of paint for years but nothing's too good for the horses.'

No one was in the yard but three steeple-chasers peered over stable doors as they passed, watchful as sentries.

'Leave the car by the conservatory. I always go in the back this time of year. Victor only heats the west wing in the winter, the main part of the house is as cold as charity. He even has the shutters bolted to keep out the damp but in an old ruin like this it's a losing battle.'

They marched through an enormous cast-iron conservatory where the empty staging was relieved by a dozen pots of early snow-drops and freesias wafting a fugitive sweetness on the air. An old office desk had been dumped between two garden doors leading into the house, its metal handles rusty. Madeleine went ahead, stepping straight into the morning room, the fading Victorian wallpaper defiantly robust in the greenish light filtering through the glasshouse. Judith recognized the antique desk she had last seen in the hall at Madeleine's flat, its over-decorated surfaces entirely at home in this lady's bolthole. The room was unheated, its chill shockingly in contrast to the Shaws' management of Chevenix Park. She was about to comment when the door from the next room burst open and the three were suddenly faced with a cheerful young woman with red hair.

'Tricia! What on earth—?'

'I *thought* I heard a car,' the girl replied, opening the door wide, smiling warmly. 'Victor had a bout of indigestion last night so he and Genny decided to cancel New-market.'

'Victor's here?' Madeleine's dismay was embarrassing.

Judy leapt into the breach, holding out her hand to Victor's secretary. 'We didn't have a chance to meet at the party, Tricia, but I'm Judith Pullen. I can't tell you how much I admired your playing. Absolutely wonderful.'

'Thanks. Victor's Bechstein would fossilize if I didn't give it a bash occasionally. You must be Pixie's sister. How is she? Oh, do come in. Victor's having forty winks. I'll tell him you're all here.'

Tricia Carroll ushered them into the next room, every inch the hostess. Judith could understand Madeleine's remark about being 'de trop' at Finings, not that Tricia's manner was unwelcoming. Quite the reverse. Will shambled in behind, obviously ill at ease, his cocksure manner entirely deserting him. Coming here was turning out to be a terrible idea.

The morning room led into a small sitting room in which a log fire leapt and crackled in the grate, brightening the dimness of the room shadowed, like the other, by the conservatory which ran along the back of the house. It was comfortably furnished with leather chairs and well worn Persian rugs, the maroon walls giving the ambiance of a gentleman's club. Double doors in the French style presumably led to yet another room. Judy could understand Victor's desire to shut off the rest of the house in winter, reserving this cosy set of rooms as a warm retreat. It was really a summer house, she imagined. In its heyday the conservatory must have been charming but its dank emptiness now attached itself to the house like a reproach, the pair of garden doors linking it to the morning room and to the winter sitting room a constant source of draughts. A third door stood open on to a passage. Tricia waved her hands towards this passage, Indian bangles clashing on her wrists as she said, 'I was just going to make some tea. I'll put out some extra cups and call Genny.'

'Oh, please don't bother her. We were just p-passing,' Madeleine stuttered. 'Don't wake Victor if he's not well. We'll come back another t-time. W-Will Smith is an art historian. He's interested in the w-water-colours.'

'Ah, yes.' Tricia stared at him with undisguised curiosity but, before they could withdraw, the double doors opened and Victor emerged from the adjoining room. Judith was shocked by his appearance. He looked drained, papery skin drawn tight across his cheekbones, his sunken eyes boring into Madeleine like a man unsure if he is alive or dead.

'Victor, we woke you. I am so sorry. We

called on the off-chance. You s-said you might go to Newmarket for the weekend. I – er – w-wondered if I could pack a few things.'

'Victor and Genny had to cancel,' Tricia explained, leading Madeleine's husband to a chair and smoothly introducing Will. 'I'll fetch the tea.'

She disappeared, leaving Judith to fill the conversational gulf, both Madeleine and Victor raw with the shock of this unexpected meeting. Judith, acutely uncomfortable in the presence of Will, was unsure if Victor suspected anything. It seemed highly unlikely but it was just as well she had been badgered to come along; nothing like a third party to cloud the issue.

Judith prattled on about Bath and Victor rallied, pulling together his natural courtesy like a man swiftly donning his clothes on a beach after a swim. Madeleine remained totally subdued, mesmerized as a rabbit in a snare. Could she be *afraid* of Victor? Judy shrugged aside this preposterous idea and was more than glad when Genista put in an appearance. Victor repeated the introductions, reminding his sister of Judith's part in the general picture of Madeleine's friends.

Genista was dressed as at the party and Judy wondered if riding clothes were her only attire. The woman's eyes, pale as a shallow rock pool, flickered with recognition as she entered the room and a meaningful glance passed between herself and her brother. The penny dropped in Judy's mind: Victor's secret had been blown – Tricia Carroll had been caught on the nest. No wonder Victor had looked so shattered by their arrival.

'We'll go and see the horses,' Genista announced briskly, pushing Will and Judy ahead the way they had entered, back through Madeleine's morning room and into the unkempt garden via the conservatory. Let's leave husband and wife to sort it out on their own was Genista's unspoken message. And why not? Judy walked across the grass behind them, 'gobsmacked' by the revelation which Madeleine had never shared. Tricia Carroll of all people! How Pixie would be amazed. Victor and his secretary. Come to think of it, what could be more obvious?

'We try to keep this part of the house sealed off in the winter,' Genny explained. 'The rooms at the back are easy to keep warm and Victor sleeps in his study off the little sitting room these days. It's more convenient all round. He had a touch of indigestion at the office on Friday, felt nauseous and faint. Gastric 'flu I expect. Tricia drove him down. She's staying over, helping out with things. A super girl!'

They trudged to the stables, a surly-looking elderly man in mud-spattered breeches turning a beady eye on the group as they approached. She called him over.

'Paddy, these people are friends of Madeleine's down from London. Miss Pullen and Mr Haydock-Smith.'

Without replying he turned on his heel and walked off, slamming the door of his office.

'Take no notice of Paddy,' Genista said with a chuckle. 'Social graces don't feature with him, he's a rude beggar at the best of times. He's got the hump because Victor missed out on Newmarket. Paddy's got his eye on a two-year-old we are thinking of buying for one of our clients. The stupid man thinks Victor's backing off.'

Will had perked up once outside, fascinated by the immaculate operation which was obviously Genista's pride. 'Do you breed here?' he asked.

'No such luck. Stud farms are for millionaires. Victor and I do a little horse trading. We are hoping to set up as bloodstock managers once Victor gets shot of the firm.'

'What exactly are bloodstock managers?'

'We advise clients. It involves a lot of travelling, mostly to America and Ireland, buying yearlings at the top sales throughout the world. Paddy's got a natural eye and Victor's shrewd. We make a great team, the three of us. We've already got some deals lined up. Useful contacts are the key. We have been trading in a small way for years, of course. We've never liked London, Victor and I.'

'Expensive, I imagine, in air fares alone. Or do you work on expenses and commissions, working directly for each owner?'

'It varies. Sometimes we operate independently but it's like any other business. Capital's vital. These new buildings alone set us back thousands of pounds. Luckily, Paddy concocts his own horse potions so vets' bills rarely feature to any great extent.'

Judith tagged along, not wildly comfortable with the skittish mare Genista led out from one of the stables for them to admire.

'This is Farouche, our white hope. We have a Saudi buyer in the offing.'

Judith was impressed – thought it looked like being Genny's show judging by the unhealthy look of her brother. 'Is Victor up to all the travelling?' she asked.

Genny's pale eyes focussed with intensity. 'Of course he is! It's only 'flu. He's off colour at the moment but he's as tough as old boots.'

'What about his heart condition?'

'Stress. Nothing more. As soon as he's away from London he's a different man. Victor was never meant to toil away in a bloody lampshade factory. My mother's family has lived here for generations. We're country folk.'

Her tone was dismissive. Will jumped in

with a whistle of admiration as he pointed to a cycle leaning against the wall.

'A Star Ride! The stainless-steel version, too. Wow!'

He spoke with boyish enthusiasm. 'The Rolls of folding bikes. I got a cheap imitation through mail order but it's nothing like this. Use it all the time though and it hasn't quite dropped to bits. I brought mine down here in the back of the minibus so I don't feel totally trapped. Knowing I've got my bike keeps me sane even if I don't use it.'

He walked over to take a closer look, bending down to touch the mud-caked wheels and the zig-zag rods and diagonal braces which made up the frame.

'Yours, Genista?' he asked, smiling over his shoulder.

'Victor's actually. Madeleine bought it for his birthday last February. She thought the exercise would do him good. In fact, the stable lads get most use out of it nipping down to the village for their fags.'

The awkward moment had passed and Genny was off again about the horses. Unstoppable.

Judith sneezed, wrapping her coat closer against the chill of the late afternoon. 'I think I'm getting a cold.'

Will said, 'We had better push off.'

Genista led the mare back to the stable and excused herself to speak to Paddy, leaving

Will and Judy to find their own way back.

Madeleine greeted their return with saucer eyes, aghast at having been abandoned to Victor. It would seem that her newly acquired confidence had shrivelled on home ground. Perhaps finding Tricia and Victor so comfy together had been a shock after all, Judy guessed. While they had been touring the stables, Madeleine had packed some clothes and now sat on the edge of a chair, her suitcase at her feet, looking like some sort of evacuee.

Tricia had set herself up at a table in Madeleine's morning room and could be heard typing. She joined them for tea, a larking jolly schoolgirl character, difficult to dislike though Judith resented, on Maddy's behalf, the ease with which she had taken over the reins. Tricia poured tea, passed round cakes, made small talk. You had to hand it to the girl: she had style, carrying off an impossible situation with aplomb.

Madeleine seemed hardly to notice, nervously accepting her cup without a word, almost dropping it in shock as Tricia suddenly leapt away to fetch Victor's tablets, passing them to him with a teasing admonition. He seemed to have recovered himself and politely asked about Will's work with Chiaroscuro, joking about the efforts of Sophie Neuman to keep the show on the road.

The three eventually escaped in the VW, anxious to leave Finings and its self-sufficient household. Madeleine sat beside Judith trembling with nervous reaction. The trick had not been pulled off: the charm bracelet remained in the fancy little desk. Madeleine's lawyer would have to do without it.

Will said, 'Bad luck, Maddy. Never mind. I enjoyed seeing the bloodstock. Genista's project sounds absolutely gold-plated to me. Is this Paddy Frith really a wizard at judging horseflesh?'

Madeleine nodded, stiff with fright either from being so close to being caught with her hand metaphorically in Victor's back pocket or from her own terror at the realization that she really was out on her own. The gauntlet had been thrown down on each side. There was no going back on it. Divorce was a foregone conclusion.

Judith privately thought Madeleine well out of it. Finings struck her as a funny set-up: the brass effrontery of Victor establishing his mistress in his house almost before Madeleine's bed was cold took a lot of beating. One supposed, having agreed not to contest the case, he had nothing to lose. But that Madeleine should be made to feel like excess baggage in what was still technically her own home was ironic. Tricia Carroll should have been the one to feel embarrassment at their surprise visit. Surely,

Madeleine had not known the woman would be there, insisting she and Will witness the real situation at Finings in order for them to accept that Victor's unfaithfulness was no figment of her imagination? No, Maddy had been truly appalled to find Victor at home.

Judy shook her head and pressed the accelerator, determined to shake off the miasma of conjecture clouding her thinking. It must be her cold, making her feverish, constructing ghoulish fancies out of thin air.

Dinner at Chevenix Park that night had been hyped up by Sophie to a gala occasion, giving her ladies the chance to put on their glad-rags. Bruce had tricked out Brenton George in a waiter's white jacket and bow tie and the boy was enjoying his new role. The Shaws had set up a bar in the library and Brenton was discovered to be a whizz with the cocktail shaker, his gleaming smile in the black moon of a face lending a touch of exoticism to an evening which might easily turn out to be a flop.

Bruce had worked hard on the quiz, expertly mixing simple and erudite questions to keep his audience on the ball. As coffee and liqueurs were being served, Ken Tyler and Will took their places at the high table and with a stroke of genius invited Teddy Shaw and Major Herbert to join the panel plus two others who actually knew their onions.

Everyone settled back to enjoy the fun, obviously taken with Bruce's insistence on having a glamorous female from the audience to keep score. The Chiaroscuro members had shed their reservations in the course of a gourmet meal plus plenty of wine and loudly insisted that Madeleine be urged on to the platform to fulfil this important role. Judith grinned, wondering if Bruce guessed what he had let himself in for: Maddy's arithmetic was as imaginative as her spelling.

The lights dimmed, the candlelight lending a romantic atmosphere. Bruce was an excellent compère, putting in his own pithy remarks to mitigate the pregnant pauses, juggling the questions when Teddy Shaw or Major Herbert were in the hot seat and generally making the whole thing go with a swing. Questions remaining unanswered by the panel were thrown open to the audience and this generated a raucous response which only added to the excitement. It was all becoming quite noisy. Judith caught sight of Sophie slumped in her seat next to Lady Harriet, stupified with relief that the Bath weekend had managed to erase the memory of the distressing business of Suki's murder, which had almost scuppered the entire enterprise.

After ten minutes, Judith slipped out to the

bar, determined to shake off the shivers which confirmed her worst fears about the cold that had been threatening all day.

Brenton was still on duty, his only customer Arnott, who had made himself comfortable with a whisky by the fire and, having drawn up a seat for Bruce's temporary barman, was deep in conversation. As she entered, Brenton jumped to his feet, then, recognizing her, delivered the full power of a hundred-watt grin.

'A brandy please, Brenton. You couldn't top it up with a little hot water and lemon, could you? I've got the shakes.'

He scuttled off to the kitchen.

Arnott patted the empty chair and they settled down for a natter. Arnott was as pleased as Sophie Neuman at the smooth way the Bath weekend had gone and filled in Judith about his day. The morning's shopping trip around the antiques quarter had been dicky but, apart from the bona fide fleecing by the dealers, Sophie's ladies had been unscathed.

'The American Museum was a treat, lass. You should have come. I never knew all that stuff about the settlers and the Shakers. All I ever sussed out about the Wild West was from Gary Cooper. I thought Mrs Neuman would skip round the bloodthirsty bits but you can bet how the Yanks all lapped it up. Where did you get to? I heard you bunked off with your girlfriend.'

Judith told him about their nerve-racking visit to Finings and shared her disquiet about the whole situation.

'It's a weird set-up, Arnott. Victor's as nice as pie to Madeleine apart from shoving his girlfriend under her nose, of course. He's such an upright sort of man, everyone's idea of a real gent, it's difficult to understand why Madeleine is so wary of him. She's quite skittish when she's here but at Finings she's a different person. If I didn't know them so well, I would say she was terrified of Victor.'

Arnott sipped his whisky, contemplating the complicated lives these folks led. He and Peg had had none of that. Being like a frightened rabbit with your own husband took some beating. It wasn't as if the Pendlebury woman was short of cash. According to Judy, it was the wife who had all the lolly, getting divorced wasn't going to put her on the dole. He shook his head, puzzled, and changed the subject, asking Judy if she had any news from Erskine about the murder.

'He's in Paris just now following up a lead Morton Playle put him on to. Suki was definitely a victim of this Sioux political group, Arab in-fighting of some sort, Laurence thinks.'

'Funny sort of code name, ain't it?'

'The Sioux? Weird. Perhaps they're spaghetti western fans.'

'A bloke at this American Museum this afternoon reckoned those poor bloody Indians got the blame for every kind of torture, took the can back for a lot of blood-letting which was nothing to do with 'em.'

'Scalping, do you mean?'

'Sometimes. He said they was all at it, whites an' all. Anyone who wanted to lay off the blame sliced off the victim's topknot and nobody give it a second thought, automatically put it down to the redskins.'

'Any evidence?'

Arnott shrugged, perplexed by the age-old cruelties of man against man. 'What bothers me about the Suki Nadhouri killing is the drugs. Who was supplying the girl?'

'Perhaps *she* was dealing.'

'No way. Why should she? Got all the pocket money she needed.'

'Who knows? Perhaps she just did it for kicks. A little power maybe. Having people at *her* beck and call for a change. From what I hear, the brother calls all the shots at home and Suki was given very little leeway. Don't you think she was killed by terrorists then?'

'No, I don't. I don't care what Erskine says. It's a cover up. Got to be. Think I'll get your friend Mrs Pendlebury to one side in the morning. She knew the dead girl, didn't she? There's a few questions I'd like to put to her about the goings-on backstage at this club of theirs. What about Foxton? He could have been supplying Nadhouri and half a dozen others for all we know. Needs the money, I hear. Just got back from Thailand after Christmas, didn't he? Could've easily got a connection there.'

'You're just blowing bubbles, Arnott. Let Flood sort it out. I thought you liked the nice little earner you've got here with Chiaroscuro. Sophie won't thank you for questioning the clientele, not to mention casting suspicion on her partner. Laurence assured me, no one at the club is involved. He wouldn't lie to me, Arnott. The Sioux is entirely responsible for Suki's death.'

'Never done no scalping before though, had they? Who's ever heard of any Arab tit for tat like that? Suki didn't have her hand cut off for thieving, did she, lassie?'

There was no answer to that.

Brenton returned with a hot toddy for Judith and she excused herself to Arnott. 'I'm just going to put through a call to Pixie, see how she is. And then I'm getting an early night. You haven't any aspirins by any chance? Madeleine has everything bar the kitchen sink on her bathroom shelf but she seems to have a horror of the pharmaceutical industry. Everything's herbal or chemical-free. Aspirins don't seem to pass the test.'

Arnott shook his head and Brenton looked nonplussed as if his own problems never weighed sufficiently to need headache pills.

Judith made her way to the small study off the entrance hall and called Pike End. Pixie was on her own and feeling a lot better for it.

'Yes, darling, can you believe it? Claire's gone off to Dover on a date, the old hussy. Wouldn't say who, just an old flame from her art student days. But she certainly pulled out all the stops. Went off looking a million dollars. Quite a goer, isn't she?'

They giggled, constructing a picture of Claire's ex-hippy date, wondering if he had become disappointingly bourgeois in the intervening years. Judith confided her fears about Madeleine and their absurd visit to Finings that afternoon and was relieved to find Pixie's reactions were back on course, her neurotic behaviour reduced to normality since their sisterly set-to the previous weekend. Perhaps Claire was the catalyst in all this? Left on her own, Pixie reverted to her nice sensible self.

Judith put down the phone with a sigh of satisfaction. She felt better for sharing her worries over Madeleine. It was none of their business, after all. She went up to her room and lay on the bed in the dark, sipping her brandy and thinking about Laurence Erskine.

She awoke with a jolt. Scrabbling sounds from the next room just like last night. She relaxed – Madeleine's bedtime routine was well under way. Judy pressed the little light on the alarm clock and was astonished to discover it was only just after nine thirty. She must have just dropped off for ten minutes. Whoever was in the next room was not Madeleine, she was still totting up the quiz score in the dining room.

Judy sat bolt upright listening to bouts of applause filtering upstairs from the party, wondering if the phantom pilferer had grabbed this opportunity to fleece Sophie's well-heeled guests.

Sixteen

Judith slid off the bed and, barefoot, crept through the bathroom to the light glimmering through the glass slit in Madeleine's door. She peered in, her vision limited by the narrowness of the aperture. It was like trying to squint into a letterbox set sideways on.

Inside, only the dim wattage of a bedside lamp illuminated the room but by pressing her face against the door she could make out Madeleine's open suitcase on the bed and fingers sifting the contents. A box lay on its side, jewellery spilling on to the counterpane. A fitted leather dressing case was also upended and a plastic toilet pouch rifled,

210

tissues and balls of cotton wool scattered in all directions.

Judith's rage erupted. She burst in, launching herself into the unarmed combat routine which her new job with the Serious Fraud Office had no call for. The woman, knocked to the floor in the attack, lay gasping, her arm pinned behind her.

'*Merde*!'

The expletive hit Judith with such force that she momentarily let go and the victim swivelled to face her, glaring balefully at her assailant. The third French hen had come home to roost and it wasn't the Belgian girl after all.

'Fenella! What the hell do you think you're playing at? No, don't try to give me any old rubbish, I *know* what you're looking for. The moment you swore so effectively I recognized your voice. It was *you* arguing with Suki just before she died. I was in one of the cubicles. I heard every word. You're searching Madeleine's room for coke. Don't try to deny it.' Judy mentally crossed her fingers as she spoke, in no position to claim any real comprehension of the French conversation but, taking a leaf from Arnott's book, hoped for the best.

Fenella's eyes narrowed as she assimilated the extent of the evidence against her.

'You can't implicate me in Suki's murder. I never left the clubhouse that night.'

Judith let her rise while maintaining the painful armlock, then pushed Fenella to the bed and backed off, positioning herself by the door. The Canadian sat amid the ransacked contents of Maddy's suitcase, her eyes fixed on Judy in shrewd calculation. After a full minute's silence she said, 'OK. What next? You can see I found no snow. I could argue I was looking for something for my headache. Aspirins? Madeleine's the last person to squawk about it, you know. It's not as if I had stolen anything.' She looked with contempt at the inexpensive necklaces and bangles spilled from the jewel box.

Judy leaned against the door, aware of the continuing sounds of applause and laughter filtering from the refectory. She weighed her options, suddenly confused. Anyone but Fenella caught red-handed like this would have reacted with at least a flicker of guilt.

Fenella pushed home her advantage. 'I don't deny I got stuff from Suki but so did your spotless friend Madeleine and one or two others at Chiaroscuro. Bruce cottoned on but it was no big deal as far as he was concerned. He turned a blind eye. It pepped up the atmosphere at the club and no harm done. Just a bit of fun.'

'And who supplied Suki?'

Fenella shrugged. 'That I'm still working on. Suki left us high and dry you see. Suddenly being cut off like that poses a problem. It occurred to me Madeleine had found another source, that Boy Wonder of hers, Will Smith, seemed likely – a common little runt like that would have his finger in every pie. But Madeleine was a novice, never into freebasing. I decided the new boyfriend was weaning her off it, not supplying. No, between you and me, Judy Pullen, I'm certain Ken Tyler is the pusher. How else could he finance that jade collection of his? And he travels all the time, to all the right places. It would be easy for him to import small quantities, just enough to tide him over, to sweeten the cash flow.'

'Why don't you tackle him direct?'

'I did. Our Dr Tyler denied everything, so I took a gamble and lied. I said I had a witness willing to testify if necessary. Brenton *had* mentioned he had seen Tyler passing stuff to Suki but Brenton's a chum of mine, no friend of the police and in no hurry to blow the whistle. I threatened Tyler I'd turn him in myself and force Brenton to sing – after all, Ken Tyler couldn't prove Suki was sharing her own stuff with me. But Tyler pointed out what it would do to the club if he was charged. He hinted someone else was involved. Brucie? Personally I doubt that but I need hardly remind you of the penalties of allowing premises to be used for the dealing or supply of cocaine. Ken Tyler was scared witless when the police flooded in after

213

Suki's death and has "ceased trading" as they say. I doubt he wastes the coke up his own nose, his obsession is with the oriental collection and the money to finance it. Drugs are not the only driving force to criminality, you know. The police think being hooked on the habit is the key to everything. Don't you believe it. Evil flourishes on obsession.'

She paused, sure of her advantage, and waited for the other girl to make the next move. Judy tried to evaluate all this new information, far from certain which part was true and which part a clever ploy by the Canadian to extract herself from a damning situation. She was clearly not a person to be fazed by an emergency and bringing Tyler into the calculations was an interesting idea, especially on the spur of the moment.

Judy cleared her throat. 'I'll have to speak to Arnott about all this. He's in charge of security here. Then there's Madeleine, she must be told you were rifling through her things looking for cocaine.'

An unspoken ceasefire had been agreed and they tidied the room, repacking Madeleine's suitcase and placing it back beside the wardrobe. Fenella walked out, quietly closing the door behind her, leaving Judith standing in the reconstructed tidiness, her mind fuzzy with indecision. It was this bloody cold of hers, she decided, thickening

214

her head, clouding the issues. Tomorrow she would see things clearly. After a decent night's sleep and once she had spoken to Arnott, they could decide what to do.

She turned off Madeleine's bedside lamp and entered their shared bathroom, flooding its sterile interior with light as she searched Madeleine's shelf for the herbal sleeping tablets. Judy was utterly determined to put up the shutters for the night and 'knit up the ravell'd sleeve of care' or however it was the wretched Bard put it. Maddy's 'Natural Balm' pills worked a treat; she was asleep in minutes.

She dreamed of woodlands peopled by fairies flitting in the treetops like fireflies, the dark oaks magically dissolving into coconut palms. Birds revealed themselves to be parrots, then owls and finally woodpeckers boring holes in the trunks of jungle trees. The rapid machine-gun fire of their activity was making her head swim and she writhed under the bedclothes, trying to shut out the insistent tap, tap, tap.

Voices filtered into the dream. A single human voice, shrill with anxiety, penetrated her unconsciousness and, surfacing, she realized that the tapping was real, the urgent rapping on a door accompanied by increasingly loud admonitions. The name brought her to her senses. Madeleine. Judith recognized the irritated squawk of Nancy Shaw trying to rouse Madeleine. It seemed all too evident that Madeleine was not at home.

Judy slipped out of bed and into the bathroom, listening at the door, hoping the Shaw woman would give up and go back to bed. But as she was about to return to her own room she heard Madeleine's voice and then both women whispering together. Isolated words struck home: 'hospital', 'an emergency'. Judith panicked. Pixie? Was Nancy Shaw waking Maddy to act as intermediary? To break the bad news to her about her sister?

She barged in, white-faced, confronting them, Nancy massive in a cashmere dressing gown, Madeleine looking frailer than ever, the pale hair hanging limply over her narrow shoulderblades. They both stared at Judith for a moment but the older woman was unstoppable.

'You must get dressed immediately, Madeleine. The doctor said a hire car had been ordered from Finings for you. It should be here any time now. I suggest you wait at the gates, dear. We don't want to rouse the entire household at three in the morning. Oh, my dear, I am so sorry. I do hope the news is hopeful.'

Madeleine was dazed with shock, her fingers pressing against her temple as if the message must be forced into her brain.

'It's Victor,' she explained. 'He's been

taken ill...'

'A heart attack,' Nancy intervened. 'The poor brave man's been rushed to the Infirmary. It really is too tragic for words. Poor Victor.'

'Would you like me to go with you, Maddy?'

'N-no. Please!' She seemed almost frightened by this suggestion, queerly afraid that her meeting with her husband would be witnessed. 'I have to speak to Victor alone. There are things I must s-say ... N-no one else need know...' Her voice petered out on a vague note and then, as if gaining strength from her decision, Madeleine gently pushed Nancy outside and closed the door, turning to Judith, suddenly calm and decisive. She stripped off her pyjamas and rapidly got dressed.

After she had gone, Judith went back to bed, but lay wide awake, the effect of Madeleine's sleeping tablets now extinguished. She lay in the darkness and explored the possibility that Victor would die.

To put it bluntly, Victor's death would certainly simplify Madeleine's situation. The break with the Pendleburys would be instantly executed, legally painless and erase any necessity to expose a scandal. Perhaps the prospect of a court case held particular terror for a man whose adolescence had been blighted by the public prosecution of his father. For a reserved man like Victor Pendlebury, the stress of an impending divorce could well have triggered the coronary.

Hours later, her mind was still in turmoil, the wretched business of Fenella Krantz still unresolved. She waylaid Arnott going in to breakfast and steered him to a quiet table. The Sunday morning diners were sparse at eight thirty, a few nursing thick heads after the quiz night and even the abstainers taking advantage of a lie-in. There was to be a later start to the day's programme. A select party had been invited to attend Morning Prayer at the Abbey with the Shaws followed by lunch with the bishop. Bruce had organized a coach outing for the hoi polloi, which promised to be a lot more fun: a tour of the countryside around Glastonbury and lunch at a hotel on the way back.

Judith waited for Arnott to begin dissecting his kipper before telling her story about overhearing someone in Madeleine's room during the quiz game. Arnott tersely butted in.

'You spend all your bloody time with your ear to the keyhole, Pullen?'

She bridled. 'No more than you, sir.' The 'sir' had accidentally popped out as she felt herself slipping back into her old slot in Arnott's mind: the unasked-for female assistant.

'Out with it then, woman!'

Judy took a breath and launched into a rapid summary of her confrontation with Fenella and the light it had shed on Suki Nadhouri's cocaine operation.

Arnott wiped his mouth and took a swig of tea, his formidable intelligence ticking away behind the Mr Punch disguise.

'I told Fenella I had to speak to you about it, Arnott. We must tell Sophie, of course, but it puts us in an awful situation, especially as Fenella's convinced Ken Tyler's at the root of it and says Bruce knew what was going on. *He* kept a low profile after the murder, didn't he? Said nothing about Suki's coke habit. Did Charlie Flood know any of this?'

Arnott shook his head. 'No way. Me and Charlie had a deal going. He wouldn't have let me walk into a mess like this if he'd known the extent of it.'

'What shall we do?'

Arnott lit a cigarette and stared gloomily at the tablecloth.

'Leave it to me, lass. No point in raising the dust straight off. Let them get this show off the road. I'll tackle Foxton on his own when we get back to London. You and the Canadian woman found nothing in Mrs Pendlebury's suitcase?'

'Not so much as a tin of talc. Fenella had already done a pretty efficient search when I burst in and we both repacked everything. I'd swear there was nothing there. I even checked the lining. It was the bag she packed yesterday afternoon at Finings. Fenella saw her bring it back here, we all met in the hall on the way in. Perhaps she thought Maddy had collected a few grammes from home.'

'Your mate Mrs Pendlebury's in deep shit over this and no mistake. I'll have to talk to her before I get on to Foxton.'

'That's not possible, Arnott. Madeleine was called away in the night. Her husband's had a massive coronary. He's in intensive care.'

Arnott leaned back, shaken by this additional turn of events. 'Bloody 'ell, Pullen, you and this art fancying lot live dangerously one way and another.'

Judith filled in the details and watched Nancy Shaw enter the refectory chatting with the Herberts. She wondered if she had any news about Victor but decided to leave it until after breakfast.

She felt much better this morning and despite the broken night her cold was lifting, now merely a miserable sniffle. Just a sudden squall more threatening than real – perhaps something to do with overanxiety not to be the party pooper on this cultural foray.

She glanced around the refectory, spotting Ken Tyler making a thin repast of black coffee and a cigarette. He looked glum, gazing out at the rain blowing fitfully against the long window, his attention entirely absent from the shy young man sharing his table, whose confidence had bloomed since Will's city walking tour the morning before. Tyler's new companion rattled on, his words muted but, even from across the room, seemingly intimate.

Could Fenella's indictment be the whole story? Was Chiaroscuro's senior lecturer peddling cocaine? If so, there was only the Canadian's word for it that Tyler was not the only one involved and if her hunch hung on Tyler's opportunity to buy drugs during his travels, Foxton was no stay-at-home either – he'd been in Bankok for Christmas for starters. Recreational drugs were not unknown in City dealing rooms in the nineties before Foxton 'retired'. Judith determined to make some discreet enquiries with Bruce's former employers when she got back to her SFO desk. Perhaps the loss of his banking career had not been just another failure to blame on recessionary trends in the world of high finance. And perhaps, knowing the ropes as a user, Bruce Foxton had turned to another type of dealing now the going was getting rough in the art club business.

She pushed away these fascinating conjectures and decided to order a full breakfast – feed a cold and starve a fever, wasn't that what they said? Having tossed the bad news to Arnott, who was, after all, being paid to shoulder the problems here, she felt more than ready for a day out. The people on the Bath jaunt were now well acquainted with each other and several of them had turned out to be a lot of fun. Judy's apprehension about this weekend had been largely unfounded: no wonder Madeleine had taken on a new lease of life since joining. Her previous lifestyle had, in its way, been arid. After all, for whom had Maddy been nourishing that beautiful body? Guiltily, she thrust aside the thought of Victor Pendlebury in his hospital cot, plugged in to all that medical engineering, fighting for his life.

Arnott sloped off to buttonhole Will Haydock-Smith before he pitched into his scrambled eggs, leaving Judith to immerse herself in the Sunday newspapers and finish her coffee. She kept an eye on Nancy Shaw and, as she slipped behind the buffet table to enter the kitchen, Judy hurried after her, catching her arm as she passed through the green baize door.

'Mrs Shaw. I wondered if you had heard anything about Victor this morning?'

'Two minds with but a single thought, my dear. I didn't mention it to the others. Teddy and I thought it best to wait for news before spreading alarm. Several other people here are friends of the Pendleburys from London, I understand. It would be a pity to worry folk unnecessarily. I'll telephone Finings from my office. Why don't you come along?'

She got through and spoke to the Pendleburys' housekeeper, who was dispatched to fetch Genista. Nancy's voice assumed a softer, sympathetic timbre as she was connected and Judith, rigid with apprehension, was nevertheless shocked by the woman's dramatic reaction.

'What's that you're saying, Genny? It's just a terrible jape? Victor's perfectly well? I don't believe it! Oh, my dear, do forgive me. Yes, of course I'm relieved to hear it was some sort of mistake but, Genista, please listen to me for a moment ... Yes, that's right. I spoke to someone at the hospital myself. Good grief, Genny, *I* took the message. It was all perfectly plain. Madeleine went off in a taxi which had been sent to collect her.'

Victor came on the line, his curt phrases clearly audible to Judith, who had moved in beside Nancy, now gripping the telephone in a state of total incomprehension. Judy took the receiver from her and confirmed the facts. Victor was completely at sea with all this, had absolutely no idea what all the fuss was about. They agreed to wait and see. Madeleine was sure to turn up soon. Judith suggested that Maddy, having discovered she had been sent on a wild goose chase, had decided to stay put in Bath rather than disturb Chevenix by rousing the Shaws yet again in the small hours. It did cross her mind that Madeleine might have been too shattered to come back and had hired a car to take her straight home to London. Knowing that someone hated her enough to play a sick joke like that must have been a bitter pill to swallow, as obviously the perpetrator was aware of her movements and was, in all probability, a fellow guest here. Judith shivered. The spiral of spitefulness in which Madeleine had been caught up seemed unending.

Nancy Shaw repeated her insistence that the wicked trick be a secret between them and grudgingly Judith agreed. Even so, she broke her promise and shared the mystery with Arnott – after all, he already knew half the story. He decided to stay at the house and keep an eye on things, especially on Brenton George, whose duties as a driver were not required until after tea when the London members would be taken home. Arnott was not going to give his Brixton globetrotter free run of the place while the paying customers were exploring the district.

He wasted no time worrying about Madeleine Pendlebury's temporary disappearance. The trouble was he was at a loss to understand these people. The rich had the world at their feet. Why make their lives so bloody complicated? Practical jokes were not funny in Arnott's book. They ranked on a par with throwing bread rolls in restaurants; upper-class antics ordinary folk could never grasp.

The discovery of Madeleine's body in the unlocked boot of a rusting Nissan saloon car hidden in a private woodland fifteen miles away brought Chiaroscuro full circle. Madeleine Pendlebury had been scalped and the killer had, as before, retained his trophy.

Seventeen

The news broke at teatime.

A lively clique occupying the library were exchanging addresses and trying to organize a repeat performance at the Chiaroscuro Easter tour. Some members who had arrived in their own transport had already left, the London group forming an enthusiastic nucleus which had warmed the cockles of Sophie Neuman's fluttering heart. Against all the odds the Bath weekend had been a huge success. Until now.

The arrival of the CID officers was as devastating to the art club as Suki's murder. Even before the terrible details of the second killing were divulged Sophie knew Chiaroscuro was finished. Nothing would be salvaged from this repeat catastrophe.

Arnott burst in on the initial police proceedings, introducing himself to the man in charge, an Inspector Peter Palmer, a clever young officer of the CID new wave. Bruce Foxton stood by, utterly stunned by the appalling news, and allowed Arnott to put the local bobbies in the picture. Arnott was insisting on a police link-up with Charlie Flood, still struggling in London with the Nadhouri case despite the Special Branch cover-up. The DI listened to all this with icy politeness, saying nothing. Judith stood at Arnott's shoulder, her face crumpled with shock, wishing Laurence were here.

The facts were plain. Madeleine had been abducted by the practical joker posing as a driver, the elaborate deception corroborated by Nancy Shaw between bouts of hysterical sobbing. Judith was not at all clear whether the woman's grief was for Madeleine or for herself at the prospect of being caught up in the crossfire of publicity the murder would engender. Sophie Neuman's life savings invested in Chiaroscuro was not the only financial penalty involved.

Inspector Palmer cleared the room and conducted a long telephone conversation with his boss, who was not best pleased to have his Sunday afternoon shattered. But the mention of Special Branch involvement

226

brought him up short, the prospect aggravated by hints about the additional interest of the anti-terrorist boys. The unwelcome information that Chiaroscuro had its own private detective on hand, an ex-CID inspector also flexing his muscles in the case, was the last straw. The Superintendent swiftly decided to get his act together and drove to his office to put through a call putting Charlie Flood's hat on straight before the investigation got entirely out of hand.

There was no help for it, Special Branch would be sending their own man and Charlie Flood was already on his way, tipped off by that fly in the ointment, Arnott. The dead woman's injuries were almost identical to those inflicted on the Lebanese girl. Who would have thought a terrorist gang would pursue a fancy art club down here? And why? Was Chiaroscuro a front for a group of politicos?

Superintendent Ross was floundering, out of his depth with all this conspiracy nonsense. In Bath of all places! Was it possible Mrs Pendlebury had evidence about the Nadhouri murder which she was threatening to divulge? After all, the Nadhouri's stud farm was no more than fifty miles away and rich Arabs were quite capable of protecting their own interests in their own way, he supposed. Had this Special Branch man

Erskine's conviction that the first killing was a political assasination clouded the issue? If Erskine had been misled and had deflected a full-scale police manhunt, it was entirely possible that the copper from London, DCI Flood, was on the right track after all...

And apart from all this political claptrap there were local problems in this case. The latest victim, Madeleine Pendlebury, was a member of a family long established in the area. The widower enjoyed the esteem of the county set, his generous support for local wildlife charities much publicized, not to mention the sister's high standing with the horsey crowd. This all only added to Ross's problems. Admittedly, Pendlebury's wife had been a Londoner, an unknown quantity and apparently rarely seen at local events. Something of a 'townie' by all accounts. She could have got herself embroiled in a political skirmish for all Ross knew. He sighed, glad Palmer was running the show. That young man had his head screwed on. Palmer would stand for no bulldozing from Special Branch.

Ross was wrong, of course. The first person to be snatched off to London by Special Branch was Morton Playle.

A faxed copy of the pathology report on Suki Nadhouri was put under scrutiny by the police medico, who conducted his examination with extreme attention to detail. The injuries were not the same, the fatal stab wounds being to the woman's chest. But the scalping was identical, neat and precise as a surgeon's.

If this mad brigade, the Sioux, *had* struck again – and for the Superintendent's money a coincidental repetition of such bizarre mutilations was inconceivable – the motive was unclear. This Middle Eastern assassination group had felt no need to confirm its actions a second time. There had been no claim for the murder received by Scotland Yard as in the Nadhouri case and no clumsy attempt to leave a calling card such as the half-stripped letters SU KIL on the windscreen of the Ferrari. But what other motive was there? The scalping of the Nadhouri woman had never been publicly disclosed by the Chelsea police, so there was no question of a copy-cat killing. Erskine must be right, the Sioux was conducting a carefully thought out programme of retribution. Or a serial killer at large? That possibility struck fear in the Superintendent's gut, literally churning his Sunday roast beef. He had never been faced with a maniac on the loose before...

He instructed Inspector Palmer to put aside the political considerations until the Special Branch supercop arrived and to concentrate on what he was good at: stolen cars. At least this line of enquiry was on familiar ground, the Nissan was well cordoned off.

Brenton George was immediately singled out for interview. A man with a record, albeit a minor one, was always cooperative. And the murder weapon had yet to be discovered. While Palmer was questioning the Chiaroscuro driver, two officers made a thorough search of the minibus. Two bank cheque cards were found hidden under the rubber matting in the footwell and one of these bore the name Mrs M. A. Pendlebury. After that, uncovering a small quantity of cannabis in Brenton's room above the garage was almost an anti-climax. Palmer packed him off to the station and Bruce Foxton was informed George was 'helping the police with their inquiries'.

The Shaws came up trumps, sending out for a scratch supper from a local Chinese takeaway for the rump of the party detained for questioning. Arnott was deeply despondent, all too well aware he had been down this road before and that his vigilance at the art club 'jolly' had been totally in vain.

Nobody blamed him, not even Sophie Neuman, drowning her sorrows in the makeshift bar re-established in the library. Arnott's association with the enterprise had been dogged by double vision from the start: two murders, both girls scalped in almost identical circumstances having been lured to a car. And then there was also the wholesale involvement of innocent people whose only mistake was joining an exclusive art club which had attracted a cold-blooded killer. Arnott felt himself to be walking down a hall of mirrors, the repetition of events reflecting ad infinitum into the distance.

He shambled into the library, where a few subdued members huddled in corners waiting to be interviewed. He brought a couple of whiskies to a table by the window where Judith Pullen sat gazing sightlessly into the darkness.

'Sup up, lass. No good moping.'

'Any news?'

'Nowt fresh, any road. Charlie Flood's on his way. He and the locals seem to have their hooks into poor old Brenton. I got something out of Palmer about the Nissan though. It's been traced to a bloke living on a council estate in Keynsham.'

'A minicab driver?'

'No. The motor was nicked from outside a pub disco Saturday night. He reported it missing about one o'clock in the morning. It was likely driven straight down here and dumped in the woods not long after.'

'No witnesses?'

'Not so far.'

'So whoever made the telephone call here was capable of breaking into a car and conning Madeleine into driving off with him to the hospital?'

'That's about the size of it.'

'Cuts out everyone here then, doesn't it? Maddy's not known for her high IQ but even in a state of panic over Victor it would strike her as odd if the cab driver was a man she recognized.'

'He could have been well wrapped up. It was dark. Pouring with rain. A cold night. Who looks at drivers anyway? Could *you* pick out a taxi driver on an identity parade?'

'No, I suppose not.' Judith sipped her whisky, aware of Arnott's studied patience. He just sat there watching for a reaction like an examiner waiting for the right answer. She knew the crafty devil of old. He was keeping something back, hoping she would confirm his own hunches without prompting, uncover the truth for herself.

Desperately casting about for anything remotely relevant she said, 'There is one thing you should know, Arnott. Madeleine mentioned it to me ages ago. I thought it very philanthropic of Victor at the time, a really charitable gesture. Victor takes on stable lads straight from young offenders' training from time to time. Gives them a fresh start. One or two have turned out to have a real flair for horses, apparently. If one of them had seen Madeleine at Finings and fancied her, stealing a car would be no problem. Joyriding's about GCSE level for these boys, isn't it? And in a place like

Finings gossip about the family is normal. It was well known she was staying with the Shaws this weekend. The stable manager, Paddy something or other, saw us there on Saturday afternoon. It could have started off as a prank that went tragically wrong. Two lads looking for a bit of excitement after the pubs turned out. Boys like that might well carry knives.'

'To get the stones out of the horses' hoofs?' Arnott dryly retorted. 'You and this arty-farty lot seem to kick out at these bad lads as a knee-jerk reaction. That poor bugger Brenton was pulled down the nick in a flash once the local bobbies knew he'd got some form. Talk about give a dog a bad name! I finally got them to let me have a "fatherly chat" with the boy. He's not much of a villain, Pullen, just dead unlucky. They'll have to beef up the cannabis and bank card charges to keep him banged up. Brenton's got an alibi for last night.'

'Really?'

'One of the girls from the kitchen here went round to his place after the party last night. They had a few smokes, listened to his jungle music and were still balling the jack when the girl hears someone running on the gravel outside. Poor kid's scared stiff – thinks Mrs Shaw is coming to catch her with the sambo. They look outside and see a woman with an umbrella jumping into a Nissan. The

233

driver didn't get out which rings true: it was pissing down. They asked him the colour. He got it off pat: a white Nissan with a bloody great bash on the offside wing.'

'In the dark at *that* distance and from behind a curtain! Brenton got 20/20 vision all of a sudden?'

'Take it from me, weed gives the black boys telephoto lenses for eyes at night. Charlie Flood had it on oath from that police quack in Chelsea. You remember the bloke – Dick Crane. He wouldn't pull the wool. Try harder, Pullen.'

Judy's brief flash of confidence fizzled out like a spent firework in the bucket of Arnott's contempt and, dispirited, she fell back on small talk.

'Nancy Shaw was terribly upset about sending Madeleine off on that fool's errand to the hospital. Blames herself. She thought it was a doctor who phoned. That's what he told her. Do you think it was just a practical joke that went wrong? Having driven poor Maddy off to the hospital the guy, whoever he was, made advances which accidentally turned into murder? She *was* beautiful.'

'Your friend wasn't raped. Or robbed, apparently. And I don't think she was bundled in no red indian ambush neither. Any chance Mrs Pendlebury knew more than was good for her? Something to do with the Nadhouri killing?'

'You mean she only realized the significance of what she knew when she got down here? Seeing all the same faces again in similar circumstances to the pre-course open meeting in London and it jogged her memory? Maddy was never quick off the mark.'

'What about this drug business she was supposed to be involved in? D'you think the Canadian's in deeper water than you guessed? Reckon she was searching the suitcase for something which tied her in on the Nadhouri murder, Pullen?'

Her scalp started to tingle. 'Funny you should say that. I've been thinking it over. It didn't add up, all that stuff Fenella was saying about Madeleine using coke. Maddy treated her body like some sort of holy sepulchre. She didn't even take aspirins, let alone drugs or alcohol. Madeleine just wasn't the addictive type. Why would she play about with cocaine? Ask Will Smith, he would know.'

Arnott hunched over the table wreathed in cigarette smoke, his smile dangerous as an alligator's. 'I wondered how long it would take you to work that out, lass.'

Her eyes widened in slow recognition.

'I jumped to the wrong conclusions, didn't I, Arnott? Handed Fenella an excuse on a plate. How bloody stupid! She wasn't looking for a few grammes of coke at all. What *was* she looking for?'

The door flew open and a lantern-jawed stranger wearing a long black coat burst in. The quiet conversations of the few people present broke off and several pairs of eyes regarded the man standing in the doorway. He looked like an undertaker who had lost his way.

Arnott jumped up, raising a hand in greeting.

'Charlie! Charlie Flood. Never thought I'd get you off your backside so quick on a wet Sunday night.'

A constable standing by the door was instantly on the alert.

Judith sat tight. Being observed in cahoots with a private detective whose unwelcome interference had already aroused the ire of the local superintendent was bad enough, to be seen plotting with a CID officer from London would go down like a lead balloon with the current investigative team. All that the three interlopers on this case needed to make their presence totally unacceptable would be the arrival of Laurence Erskine. From Inspector Palmer's point of view there were already too many cooks spoiling what was an increasingly murky broth.

She vacated her chair for Inspector Flood and glanced at her watch.

'If you'll excuse me, Arnott, I have to telephone Pixie. I've put it off too long already. God knows how she will take the news about poor Madeleine.'

Arnott bought a whisky for Charlie and persuaded him to shed the overcoat and take a breather. The two grey heads bent over their drinks could have been discussing the weather for all the emotion their subdued talk engendered. But Arnott had his strategy all mapped out. All he needed was to persuade Charlie Flood in his capacity as a serving officer to lead the attack. Two old soldiers like Arnott and Flood were not easy to keep in line.

Eighteen

Arnott had a few more whiskies while the remaining club members were sifted through the police dragnet, the library gradually emptying. Charlie Flood had managed to infiltrate the murder squad and did not appear again that evening.

Arnott grew impatient, cursing the difficulties under which he was forced to operate. It was only the fact that Charlie had promised to fill him in later that prevented him from barging into the temporary interview room set up in the small study off the entrance hall. Unfortunately, it was this room which harboured the only pay phone which left Arnott feeling totally impotent. Perhaps Pullen would lend him the VW and he could nip down to the village? He hated the country – he felt tied hand and foot.

He wandered around the house looking for Judy Pullen, wondering if she had been in contact with Erskine since the news broke. The whole place had a curiously abandoned air, the sound of his footsteps on the waxed floorboards echoing down empty passages. He opened doors, hoping to discover other castaways but those who had already been questioned had made a quick getaway and the rest were keeping their heads down. Even the Shaws had withdrawn to their own quarters, the lady of the house reportedly still in a state of hysteria. The staff had jumped ship, leaving dirty glasses and plates littering empty rooms. It gave the impression of a beached *Marie Celeste* with not a living soul on board.

It was getting late. Those still being interviewed would have to stay overnight and Arnott vaguely assumed that included himself. Somewhat unsteadily he climbed to his attic bedroom, the whiskies having swapped his shoes for lead-lined spaceman's boots, the final steep staircase to the garret reducing him to a gasping, red-faced gargoyle. Arnott decided to give up this private detective lark: he was getting too old for it.

As he reached the door to his room the one next to it opened and Will Haydock-Smith appeared. He was dressed in cycling gear with a sports bag slung over one shoulder. He looked shocked by the unexpected encounter and drew back.

'You off then, lad?'

He nodded. 'Some of the staff are staying on an extra night. Ken's driving the minibus back with Sophie and the others in the morning.'

'That poor bugger Brenton still down at the station?'

'Suppose so. Bruce is staying on with the Shaws. I can't stand another night here. I've got myself a room at the pub.'

'Just the one night?'

'No. I told Bruce I'm quitting. I'm stopping in Bath till they clear up this mess.'

Arnott was curious. He examined the man with renewed interest. 'Is that so? Can't say I blame you. Why don't you come in my room and have a smoke?'

'You staying on here with Bruce?'

'No one's let me into the secret of what *I'm* supposed to be doing. Mrs Neuman hired me and I'm the least of her worries now. Can't see myself having a job after this little lot and the local bobbies want no interference. I'll doss down here for now and probably go back to London with an old pal of mine, Chief Inspector Flood.'

Will Smith followed Arnott into his room and dumped his bag on the floor. He looked terrible. Never particularly robust, the catastrophe had fallen on Madeleine's romeo like a vampire, sucking every ounce of energy. In the few hours since the police arrived he had lost the bloom which had so beguiled Sophie's ladies. His eyes, dark with despair, bore into Arnott as if the shambling figure could supply some explanation for this latest tragedy.

Arnott offered him a cigarette and they sat either side of the empty grate, an unlikely pair in an unlikely setting, the attic room prettily decorated with sprigged wallpaper, the nursery windows barred. Will Smith leaned forward on his elbows staring at the rug under his feet, the floppy fair hair thinning at the crown.

Arnott regarded him with undisguised curiosity. 'Why don't you go back on the bus with the other lot in the morning, lad? A murder investigation could drag out for weeks.'

His reply was bitter. 'I can't put up with these people another minute. Not one of them cares twopence about Madeleine. All they're worried about is their jobs and the effect of the publicity. She hadn't a single decent friend.'

'You forget Judy Pullen. She's pretty cut up about all this. Not to mention Mrs Pendlebury's family...' Arnott ventured, testing the water.

'Victor? That's a laugh. Victor's counting his lucky stars. And that so-called secretary of his, Tricia Carroll, probably opened a bottle to celebrate.'

'You didn't know them that long, mate. Families can give a funny impression to outsiders.'

'Oh, yeah!'

Will's fingers shook as he drew strongly on his cigarette. 'I'm waiting to see what the Coroner has to say. They're all trying to throw mud at her. You can't libel the dead, eh? That girl had a heart of gold, Arnott. The police are already saying she was some sort of junkie.'

'That's rubbish. Pullen will settle that one, don't lose any sleep over it. Mind you, cocaine's difficult to spot if you're not looking. You sure she was clean?'

'I would stake my life on it.'

Arnott prided himself on spotting a liar a mile off and tried another tack. 'What about her dad? In the film business I heard. Anyone told him the bad news?'

'Victor wouldn't know how even if he had the inclination. They didn't get on. Alain Lambert's buzzing round Morocco somewhere, looking at location sites Maddy said. He hated what the Pendleburys had done to Madeleine.'

'She was hardly on the breadline last time I saw her, chum.'

'Not materially. Victor puts up a good front. But they kept her in a sort of cage, sapped her confidence. Made her out to be some sort of dumb blonde. Until I came on the scene Madeleine was frightened of her own shadow. That's why she spent all her time trying to make herself perfect. Alain begged her to leave Victor. She had money of her own, she didn't need Victor to support her.'

'Lucky lady. And what about you? How are you going to support yourself now you've quit the art club caper?'

'Chiaroscuro will never survive this, I'd be out on my ear anyhow. Maddy told me on the quiet that I should look around for another job. She lent Sophie five thousand quid after Suki's murder to shore things up until the heat died down. The bank was threatening to close in. This weekend was a make or break situation for Chiaroscuro.'

'Have you got anything else lined up?'

'Oh, I don't just rely on this. I have consultancy work for a couple of the top auction houses which is very well paid. Attributions. Research for a publisher sometimes. This and that. And there's an extra-mural university course which keeps me busy teaching one evening a week. I get by.'

Arnott relaxed. Will Smith was not such a

flopsy bunny after all. He checked his watch. 'Where are you staying tonight?'

'The Crown. It's in the next village. I was lucky to get a room, the first pub I tried was already filling up with the press. It's going to splash in all directions tomorrow. I'm going down to the mortuary in the morning. I've got to see Madeleine, see for myself what that bloody maniac did to her.'

Arnott tried to argue him out of it but Will Smith was adamant.

'Look here, Will, you don't know what you're letting yourself in for. Why don't you let me tag on? I might be able to swing it for you. They won't let you in without proper authority. And there's her husband...'

'I loved her, Arnott.'

Arnott let it go at that and they shook hands. Arnott closing the door and hearing Will's trainers bouncing down the steep stairs. He lit another fag and wished he could catch the late news. But the prospect of prowling about downstairs looking for a TV set in that maze of empty rooms was more than he could stomach. Time enough in the morning. Where was that bloody girl, Pullen, hiding herself?

Arnott, the last man one could call a worryguts, pulled up the drawbridge and went to bed.

Arnott had opted out on the Chinese takeaway the previous evening, never having considered fried rice and noodles food for a Yorkshireman. He woke early with a howling void which cried out for bacon and eggs and which he guessed, in the light of the Shaws' problems, would remain unfilled.

He levered himself out of bed and prepared himself for the day, eventually descending at seven to an empty kitchen. Never one to suffer unnecessarily, he opened the fridge, found all that was needful and was soon seated at the big deal table tucking into a huge bacon sandwich and a cup of tea.

Ten minutes later Mrs Moss, the cook-housekeeper, blew in through the back door on the tail of a squally wind and zoomed in on Arnott with all the power of a cruise missile, her reluctant helpers in tow – Valerie, a jumpy teenager in a turquoise anorak, and a pimply youth known as Rambo. The girl swiftly changed into an overall and backed up to the draining board, all eyes. Mrs Moss was a woman with the build of a sumo wrestler and none of their fabled good nature. The two youngsters sniggered nervously, waiting for the fallout. But Arnott merely wiped his mouth, grinned with all the warmth of Father Christmas and offered them a cuppa from his teapot.

'You're a copper,' she said, sweeping his empty plate to the sink. 'Well, you listen here. This is *my* kitchen, not the police canteen. You and your lot can stay out.'

'Right old mess you've got here and no mistake, missus,' he replied with a flick of his head towards the service door into the refectory. 'You could do with some sensible help. You go and collect up all the empties chucked about the place, Rambo, while Mrs Moss and me make a start on the breakfasts. You know how many folk stayed over last night, lass?'

Mrs Moss shook her head, the iron-grey perm solid as corrugated roofing. Arnott bustled about, talking all the while, restoring a sense of order to the chaos that had overtaken Chevenix Park since the murder had broken up the house party. The cook was swiftly won over, dispatching the hapless Valerie to lay up tables while she prepared a tray for Mrs Shaw. 'The poor soul will want to stay in her room with these policemen crawling all over the place. Mr S. warned me last night there were guests staying over. What a terrible thing...'

Arnott slid off to give Valerie a hand and cornered her in the dining room. 'Just a mo, love. I've got a message for you from Brenton.'

The girl dropped the cutlery with a clatter and stepped back, visibly shocked.

'I ain't done nothing,' she muttered. 'What's he been saying about me?'

'I didn't want to drop you in it with the old

hag, but you *have* been naughty and no mistake. All that stuff you told Inspector Palmer about seeing the lady get into the Nissan was a load of bullshit. You would be a very silly girl if you made any mistakes.'

'I never!' The girl tried to pass the bulky figure blocking her escape and he suddenly relented, giving way like a rotten floorboard, throwing her off balance.

'No, of course you didn't, lass. Why should you? You didn't know Brenton before, did you, Valerie?' His tone had modified but the steel gleamed through, barely concealed. 'I've been down to the station to have a private word with your boyfriend. Me and Brenton are mates. I'm not with the police, Valerie, I'm just the poor old security man here. But you would be in deep trouble if I told the inspector the whole story, wouldn't you? Cannabis is against the law as you well know. I can guess what Mrs Shaw would have to say if your little night out come up in court. Think on, lass. Being stuck for pilfering on top would put you in the local papers in double quick time. This is a murder investigation, my girl, in case you've forgotten. And once the police start searching *everything* gets tipped out of the drawers.'

'I ain't done no pilfering. Who says so?'

'Only your word for that, Valerie.'

He paused, letting this all sink in, then resumed in a fatherly way. 'You should watch your step, Val. There are ladies here who got involved in drugs and look what happened.'

The girl shrank back, now thoroughly mixed up, mentally whirling from Arnott's alternate accusations and tender concern.

'Brenton tells me – and this can be our little secret, Val – that he gave you something special on Saturday night. Not for keeping your mouth shut about something, was it? Dangerous lot to mix it with. I don't have to spell it out to a sensible girl like you, do I?'

Arnott's amiable disguise was now brutally transparent and the girl thrust her hand in her pocket, her eyes flickering with fear. She didn't speak. Arnott moved in, lowering his voice to a whisper. 'No good holding out on me, Valerie love. Brenton told me all about giving you a sparkler but I shall have to have it back, shan't I? It wasn't Brenton's to give away. I think you knew that, didn't you?'

Slowly she drew out her hand and removed a ring from her finger, thrusting it at Arnott as if the dull red garnets in the ugly gold-coloured setting were hot coals.

'Sorry, duck. But you've done the right thing. Brenton told me you was a good kid. I'll return this to its owner and no harm's done. No need to bring your name into it with the inspector.'

Having relinquished her prize, Valerie found her voice and, truculent now, burst out, 'How was I to know it was pinched?

247

Bren said he got it off a mate of his. Crap jewellery. I'd hardly get myself in trouble over a few chips of glass, would I?'

'Course not. Let's forget all about it, shall we?'

Arnott patted her arm and sauntered off, pocketing the trinket, and went in search of Charlie Flood.

He homed in on the small study which had been commandeered as an interview room, hoping to use the payphone before Inspector Palmer moved back in. A pretty WPC had set up her machine at a side table and was busy typing up statements.

She looked up sharply as the untidy old party with the red face walked through the door.

'Hard at it, I see.'

'The inspector wants these ready for signature before they all go back to London this morning.'

'Soon as that? By gum, that boss of yours don't let the froth settle on his beer, do he? A good looker 'n all. Nice bloke, this Inspector Palmer of yours?'

She shrugged and the typewriter broke out again like a Liszt concerto.

'Mind if I use the blower?'

She nodded, barely pausing, and he rang Charlie Flood at the station, where he was already pitching into Brenton. Charlie was not pleased: Arnott's demands were bad

248

news all round. Charlie Flood had enough problems of his own, hopping between the local police and the confused signals issued by Special Branch. Arnott was getting the cold shoulder from all sides now the pace had quickened. Without giving any details he impressed on Charlie the necessity to stand together and badgered him into agreeing to a briefing. Flood reluctantly promised a meeting at Chevenix as soon as he had seen the Scotland Yard man, who was due in Bath about ten o'clock.

'Bloody 'ell, Charlie, the bird will have flown while you're billing and cooing with Erskine.'

'It's not Erskine. It's that other bloke he brought in after the Nadhouri business. The anti-terrorist geezer's coming an' all.'

'Fat lot of help he was! I thought you didn't buy this political claptrap, Charlie?' Arnott bellowed, ill-temper never far beneath the surface.

'Going through the motions, Ralph. Going through the motions. Keep your hair on, mate. I'll get back to you as soon as I can. By the way, that art teacher, Haydock-Smith's here raising the roof. Wants to view the bloody body if you please!'

He was called away and broke off, leaving Arnott impotently gripping the receiver, the familiar background music of a police station in full swing touching a raw nerve.

Being retired was like having his legs cut off. Arnott's money ran out and the line went dead. He swore, expletives banging off like firecrackers, causing the WPC to smile without slowing her assault on the keyboard.

Arnott slammed out of the room and ran straight into Judy Pullen.

'And where the bloody 'ell was you last night, miss? Too busy like every other bugger round here, I suppose.'

The bushy brows jutting over his beaky nose in the angry countenance projected such a caricature that Judith burst out laughing.

'Arnott, for God's sake, cool it,' she managed to say at last. 'You'll blow a fuse.'

'And no sodding wonder, trying to work in this Bedlam. Coppers pounding all over the shop, two murders, petty thieving, witnesses snorting themselves stupid and I can't even make a bloody phone call. I'm getting out of here! Drive me to the pub up the road, Pullen, and I'll book in. I'm not staying here another night and that's flat.'

'Hey, hold on. I haven't had my breakfast yet. And anyway, I'm expecting a call from Laurence about ten. He's ringing from Paris. The Shaws are letting me use their private line. I tried to speak to him last night but he was out. I left a message for him to call back this morning. I'll drive you to the pub as soon as I've checked things out. He may want me to set something up here.'

'I would have thought Erskine would have got his skates on and been here himself by now. Warns *us* off the Nadhouri case, says it's all political, and when this so-called terrorist strikes again Erskine's busy at the Folies-Bergère.'

Judith linked arms with Arnott and steered him along the corridor, well acquainted with the man's world-class irrascibility. 'Let's go and have breakfast,' she said.

The refectory had taken on a semblance of normality and a sizzling plate of Mossy's sausages and mushrooms soon put Arnott's temper back in line.

'I was searching the house for you last night, Pullen. You would think there'd been a four-minute warning the way the place cleared. Where did you scoot off to?'

'When I left you and Charlie Flood in the library, I went up to the Shaws' apartment in the west wing. I wanted to phone Pixie. I knew she would be utterly broken up about Madeleine and I needed to talk privately, soften the blow as far as I could. I couldn't break news like that on a pay phone, feeding in coins every five minutes. I knew the Shaws would understand. Nancy was in a terrible state, devastated that she had allowed herself to be duped by that hoax caller and thinking herself partly to blame, sending Maddy off like that in the middle of the night. I tried to

251

calm her down. It clearly wasn't her fault. Anyone would have been taken in. Teddy Shaw was at his wits' end and had decided to call in the doctor to give her some tranquillizers or something. Once I arrived, she latched on to me like a drowning person, begging me to reassure her in some way. Because I was there when she gave Madeleine the message from the hospital, I suppose. She wanted to go over and over it with me. It was all perfectly ghastly, not least because in her hysterics she was blaming herself for absolutely everything – even for sending Maddy out in the pouring rain to meet the taxi at the gate so as not to disturb anyone.'

'Poor cow. You can see her problem, Pullen. It's like a traffic accident, worse for the driver than the poor bloody corpse in the road.'

'I stayed there with them for ages and eventually she quietened down. Nancy Shaw's actually a very nice person, Arnott, when you get to know her. She made me promise to go along with her today to see Victor, to help her explain to him personally how it happened. I said I would. They've known the Pendleburys for years, she was telling me about Victor's father. Teddy's arranged for us to call this afternoon. Victor's on his own, which makes it worse for the poor man. His sister and that secretary of his, Tricia, have gone up to London to clear up Madeleine's things at the flat.'

'Don't waste any time these vultures.'

'It was almost midnight before I managed to sort things out with the Shaws and use their phone. By the time I got through, Pixie had heard the news on the radio. I was too late.'

Arnott leaned across and squeezed her hand. Judy made a supreme effort to put a good face on it and smiled weakly.

'I won't forget about driving you over to book in somewhere else. Can't say I blame you. Once the minibus leaves, the place will be practically empty. I'm hoping to drive back to London tonight myself. My new boss could hardly believe it when I rang through this morning and said I was caught up in yet another killing. What are you going to do?'

'I'm stuck here waiting for Charlie Flood. It's a last toss at this arty mob before the lot of 'em disperse. Once the statements have been signed they'll all bugger off back to London and the chances are we'll not catch up with them again. No one can be detained on any charges but that business of you nabbing the Canadian woman searching Mrs Pendlebury's suitcase got me worried. Charlie's going to put his official hat on and we may shake some truth out of one or the other of 'em. I've no standing here. I have to rely on Charlie and he's got more than he can deal with just now.'

Judith felt a twinge of sympathy for her ex-inspector, the poor old devil was used to calling the tune. Having to ask favours of Charlie Flood must really stick in his gullet. She rose, fiddled with her watch and murmured excuses about 'things to do'. 'Why don't we have a sandwich at this pub of yours after you've booked in? I'm not due to go to Finings with the Shaws till three. What's it called, the pub I mean?'

'The Crown. Will Smith's staying there. He said it's in the next village, so I reckon we'll soon track it down.'

'Isn't he going back in the minibus?'

'Poor sod's all broken up about Mrs Pendlebury. Wants to stay and see it sorted.'

Judy was about to walk away when she suddenly turned and said, 'One thing that came out in the course of Nancy Shaw's catharsis last night bothers me. I jumped to the wrong conclusion when she came to Maddy's room to pass the message from the hospital about Victor.'

'The man she spoke to who said a cab was on its way to pick up the Pendlebury woman?'

'Yes, but—'

Judy spun round as Valerie touched her arm. 'Excuse me, miss, but Mrs Shaw told me to fetch you quick, miss. There's an urgent phone call for you from France and she said you was to come to her office and—'

Judy snatched up her bag and started to rush away. Arnott lurched to his feet upsetting his tea, calling across the room with an explosion of pent-up frustration which sent Mossy's girl scuttling back to the kitchen like a rabbit down a hole.

Judith turned, looking distracted. 'What now, Arnott?'

'Don't sod off leaving me standing here like a pillock, Pullen. Finish what you was saying, girl!'

'Oh, that ... It was *my* silly mistake. I had assumed the "doctor" she spoke to was a man. But when we were going over it last night she corrected me. The hoax doctor was a woman.'

Nineteen

Arnott paced the circular drive fronting Chevenix Park anxiously watching Dr Tyler loading suitcases into the back of the minibus. He checked his watch yet again, cursing the 'no-show' of Charlie Flood. It was already nearly noon. He turned to go back inside to try phoning the station again; it must be Special Branch jamming the works. Charlie would never let him down.

With a scatter of gravel Will Haydock-Smith raced up on his bike, almost hurtling into the side of the bus. He looked more like a straggler in a cyclecross, his clothing mud-spattered, his unshaven face grey with fatigue. He threw down the bike and approached Ken Tyler and they withdrew to the porch, deep in conversation.

Arnott watched the two men keenly but their exchange was unremarkable, merely a staff résumé of the weekend course. After a few minutes they sorted through the luggage and Tyler extracted a box of slides and several text books which Will stuffed in a duffle bag. They shook hands and Will retrieved his bike, suddenly seeing Arnott. He strolled over and after a few words they walked off together, Will pushing the bike between them.

They had only gone fifty yards when a police car speeded up the drive, braked hard to avoid them and, much to Arnott's relief, Charlie Flood nipped out smartly, clapping the older man on the shoulder with a gesture of operatic bravura. Will cycled off, a lanky figure on the fold-up bicycle, which was never designed for rough country roads.

The two policemen veered off the drive and disappeared through a gate in a wall which led into a kitchen garden. The area was entirely enclosed, espalier fruit trees clamped to the brickwork like hostages. A gardener was working in the hothouses on the far side but within the walled garden all was peace, the sounds of imminent departure as Ken Tyler assembled his passengers, muted. Arnott and his companion paced the concrete path in the lee of the wall out of the wind like a pair of monks in a cloister.

Arnott was doing all the talking and, judging from Charlie Flood's impassive reactions, his argument was not altogether convincing. They walked up and down, Arnott's gestures becoming increasingly florid until, at last, flinging up a hand in mute surrender, Detective Chief Inspector Charles Flood agreed to participate in one last charade. Just for old time's sake.

They turned back and Arnott hurried things along, the two reaching the front entrance of Chevenix Park to find the passengers all settled, Tyler making last-minute arrangements with Chiaroscuro's major-domo, Foxton. Bruce had weathered the catastrophe with admirable fortitude and now shouldered the entire operation, Sophie Neuman having succumbed to deep depression, her moon face staring out at the bleak January landscape from her seat inside the minibus.

Flood squared his shoulders and interrupted Bruce's final instructions, loudly insisting – for everyone to hear – that two members of Chiaroscuro were not free to leave.

'But all the statements have been cleared. Inspector Palmer said we could go,' Bruce spluttered, his patience exhausted.

'Sorry, sir. But *my* investigation is *not* closed. Please ask Ms de Blanc and Ms Krantz to come to the interview room. Immediately.'

'But the bus is just leaving. These people are innocent bystanders. They have already been delayed for eighteen hours.'

The faces peering out of the windows of the vehicle were strained. No one had got much sleep the previous night and this was the last straw.

'Your driver need not wait,' Arnott put in.

'We may be some time.'

Ken Tyler pulled Bruce aside and after a whispered discussion they put it to the inspector that they would delay the departure for twenty minutes and then, if necessary, Foxton himself would take the two women to the railway station if the bus had to leave without them. Everyone was desperate to abandon the situation and, like passengers occupying the only lifeboat after the ship has gone down, were more than ready to sacrifice Lucie and Fenella in order to leave immediately. An argument broke out in the bus and in an effort to quell the mutiny, Tyler climbed aboard and tried to smooth things over. The atmosphere was electric, Lucienne tearful and vociferous in her denials, Fenella grimly obdurate. Only Sophie Neuman took no part in all this and sat on, zombie-like, welded to her seat.

The inspector stood in his long dark overcoat waiting for his instructions to be carried out. Suddenly the two girls were ejected. A sigh of relief went up all round. Arnott smiled, the sly grin which so infuriated Judith Pullen, and followed Charlie Flood and his two captives through the front door and into the empty interview room.

Charlie took off his coat and sat at the desk, Arnott at his shoulder, the two women, reluctantly perched on the empty chairs, nervously glancing at the minibus clearly visible through the window. Arnott ostentatiously switched on a recording machine, droning the official preamble before Charlie Flood began his interrogation.

It started with a summary of the security problems at the Chiaroscuro clubhouse in London, Flood outlining his colleague, ex-inspector Arnott's investigation of a number of thefts from members' lockers. Fenella lit a cigarette and leaned back in the hard chair, bored by his longwindedness. Flood's diatribe had the opposite effect on Lucie, who became increasingly agitated. Arnott lugubriously read out a list of stolen items and gave Charlie a signal to move in on the hapless Belgian, now pale with anxiety.

'Ms de Blanc, are you acquainted with the serious charges which are likely to be brought against Brenton George?'

Lucienne shook her head, tossing a mute appeal at Arnott.

'Yes or no, miss?'

'No,' she whispered.

'Brenton George has admitted stealing the items Mr Arnott just read out but has made a sworn statement which involves a woman here. He has an arrangement with this person – she handled the stolen goods. She was his "fence" if you take my meaning?'

Lucie sprang to her own defence.

'But things were taken from my own locker! Does Brenton accuse me? He's an

260

addict. People like that cannot be believed.' She half rose from the chair, her eyes wide with alarm.

'Claiming something had been taken from your own locker could have been a blind. Would you object to emptying your handbag on to the desk, Ms de Blanc?'

'Why?'

'Just to eliminate you from our enquiries, miss. Cocaine was traced to Suki Nadhouri. Other people are involved. This is an extremely serious matter.'

Arnott had to hand it to Charlie, his po-faced handling of this needle match was a classic.

She rallied, angry now.

'I could never afford to support a coke habit. See for yourself!'

She dropped her bag on the desk with a flourish. Charlie sifted the contents and then replaced them apart from a bank cheque card which he examined as if it were a precious museum artifact. 'Mrs Pendlebury was a careless lady, I regret to say. She kept her pin number in her wallet. I hope you are more sensible. The late Mrs Pendlebury apparently delayed reporting the theft of her service card to the bank and several illegal withdrawals from cashpoints were made.'

'Madeleine had more money than sense. I would not lose money like that and not question it.'

'Me neither. But she was slow to react. As I said, a careless lady. Unobservant, too, it seems. More important things on her mind perhaps?'

Charlie Flood nodded sagely and replaced Lucie's card, returning the handbag to her. Outside, the minibus started up and tension in the study was almost palpable.

'One more thing before I let you go, Ms de Blanc.' He pulled out a plastic sachet and emptied the garnet ring on to the desk. 'Can you identify this?'

Lucie snatched it up, obviously delighted. 'Yes, of course! It was stolen from my locker like I said. It belonged to my godmother.'

She put it on her finger as Charlie held up his hand.

He said, 'For the present I must retain this as evidence, Ms de Blanc. I'll give you a receipt, then you may leave.' He placed it in the centre of the blotter, where it gleamed, the garnets dull as flecks of dried blood.

Lucie stood, smiling broadly. 'Where did you find it, Inspector?'

But Charlie had turned away, conferring privately with Arnott. Arnott scribbled a message in his notebook, tore out the page and left the room, leaving the door ajar. He could be heard shouting for Rambo and, after a few minutes, returned looking rather pleased with himself.

The minibus revved up and the two

women rose, Fenella stubbing out her cigarette with a look of contempt at Lucie, who was speaking to Flood with animation, her anxieties apparently dispelled at a stroke.

'Forget the receipt, Inspector Flood. I have to catch the bus.'

She rushed out before Arnott could stop her but he caught Fenella's arm as she tried to follow.

'One moment please,' he said, closing the door.

Charlie was mumbling into the tape recorder, concluding the interview with Lucienne. Arnott indicated the empty seat and moved back to the door. With a shrug of wary acquiescence the girl slumped into the chair, watching through the window as Lucie climbed aboard just as the minibus was about to leave. It gathered speed and drove away. It had started to rain again and the claustrophobic little room perceptibly darkened. While Charlie examined his notes, the sound of the front door closing was followed by Bruce Foxton's sqeaky tread on the oak floorboards outside. His footsteps diminished along the corridor leaving a strange quietness.

The chief inspector looked up. 'Now that little bit of official business is over shall we get down to brass tacks, Ms Krantz? I do not propose to caution you at this stage. Your unofficial cooperation will be much more helpful, I feel sure. We understand each other?' He offered her a cigarette.

Fenella accepted, her black eyes watchful as roaches waiting for lights out. Charlie fingered the garnet ring, shooting mischievous glances at his hostage, blessing his luck that these two foreigners had not stood firm on their rights.

'You have more taste than Ms de Blanc. Brenton tells me you will have no truck with trash like this.'

Fenella inhaled, ignoring the jibe, and stared out at the rain.

'Mrs Pendlebury didn't go in for the genuine article either, did she?' Flood persisted.

Fenella's tart response was as expected. 'Madeleine preferred fashionable pieces. Flashy paste stuff to wear and then discard. She was interested in style not worth. The rich are like that, Chief Inspector. By some people it is now considered vulgar to flaunt real diamonds.'

'You don't agree?'

'I hate false modesty in all its forms.'

'I have information from Judith Pullen that you inferred the deceased was an addict.' He paused and then quietly continued, his lugubrious expression accentuated by the long creases marking the corners of his mouth. 'Ms Krantz, you lied about that. The pathologist found no evidence of Mrs Pendlebury's addiction and there is nothing to back up your accusation. If Sergeant Pullen discovered you searching the murder victim's suitcase and the excuse that you were looking for drugs is invalid, it leads me to wonder if your love of jewellery got the better of you.'

Her laughter was brittle. 'Stealing Madeleine's jewjaws, Flood? I've already told you, the lady *had* no valuables.'

'That being so and bearing in mind Mrs Pendlebury was never a user, what *were* you looking for? Before you answer that, I must remind you that if I chose to make an issue of this, the consequences would be grave. Sergeant Pullen is an experienced officer, her appearance in court would carry much weight.'

Fenella stubbed out her cigarette, her demeanor unruffled. Arnott sighed. He and Charlie had underestimated the opposition. This woman was no fool.

After a full minute, she spoke again, this time including Arnott in her cool assessment.

'OK. I agree the water's deeper than anyone expected. If this is strictly on the side–' and she nodded towards the tape recorder – 'I'll come clean. It's not much of a story. I am not a petty thief, whatever Brenton George has to say. Madeleine was in the process of divorcing her husband. This was triggered by a stupid mistake, a trifling matter which only Madeleine could take so seriously. Victor is a charming, intelligent man but he became bored and by mischance a gold bracelet belonging to a friend of his dropped into Madeleine's lap and she refused to give it back. If you're searching for a jewel thief, Flood, Madeleine Pendlebury was exactly that. Victor and I have been friends a long time and when she declined to return this bracelet he asked me to help. You see, Victor had discovered that she had hidden it at Finings over Christmas but he couldn't lay his hands on it. He searched her room and so on. No luck. Madeleine called at the house on Saturday afternoon expecting everyone to be away. She said she had come to pack her belongings but Victor guessed she had come to get the bracelet and, sure enough, she returned here with a suitcase full of loot. Victor was determined to do the honourable thing and return the wretched object to its rightful owner; it was of considerable sentimental value he told me, had been in the girl's possession for years. Victor telephoned me here early Saturday evening after Madeleine had left Finings and asked me to meet him for a drink in Bath. I got a taxi and we had a brief talk. That's when he told me about the bracelet and I agreed to take this last opportunity to recover it for him. Once Madeleine returned to London nobody would have access to it.'

'And you took on this criminal proposal for friendship's sake?' Arnott sceptically interjected.

'Actually, he offered me a thousand pounds if I agreed to try. I needed the money and Victor, quite correctly, claimed Madeleine had no right to keep this bracelet.'

'And a further sum on delivery,' Arnott hazarded.

She nodded, unabashed at the admission. 'A perfectly normal arrangement. Victor spends a fortune on his horses and his women. He could well afford it. The value of the thing itself was well in excess of four thousand and was irreplaceable for sentimental reasons.'

'And so?' Arnott moved in from behind to face her.

'And so nothing. It wasn't there. When Miss Nosey Parker Pullen caught me in Madeleine's room, I came out with the first excuse which popped up.'

'You said you were looking for cocaine.'

'Actually, she suggested it.'

Charlie Flood let Arnott have his head and relaxed, watching the play.

'Because she had recognized your voice, having overheard a conversation in the women's room at Chiaroscuro. Pullen knew you were implicated in Suki Nadhouri's dealing.'

That shook her. For the first time Fenella was flicked on the raw.

'Nonsense! Your little sergeant saw nothing at all. I emphatically deny that. You can't involve me in the Nadhouri murder. It was political.'

'Perhaps it was. Perhaps not. But we have something else here apart from coke dealing, which puts you on the spot, Ms Krantz. Madeleine Pendlebury is dead and a woman made the call which placed her into that fatal situation. There was a female accomplice.' Arnott leaned on the desk, the menace of his charge undermining her defences entirely.

She crossed her legs in a show of indifference but her knee trembled.

Arnott pressed home his advantage, hanging in there like a terrier.

'Two people enticed Mrs Pendlebury to her death, possibly unintentionally, but nevertheless threats or blackmail attempts were the reason for an elaborate kidnapping that ended fatally. When you telephoned Victor Pendlebury to tell him you couldn't find the bracelet in her room, Ms Krantz, perhaps he suggested you played your part in posing as a doctor and phoned to give the victim a fake message? There is no reason why you couldn't make the call on the housekeeper's phone in the kitchen or even from Mrs Shaw's office. It's open house here as far as locking up's concerned. No one would see you slip downstairs in the early hours and ring the Shaw's personal ex-directory number. Victor knew the Shaws socially, he could give you all the information you needed in that respect. In most murder investigations the killer is known to the victim and in the Pendlebury case I believe the murder was dressed up to look like Nadhouri's. Did you know that?'

Genuine incomprehension clouded her eyes and she stared at Arnott open-mouthed.

Charlie Flood stepped in smartish. Arnott had gone too far. Details of the Nadhouri murder were still Top Secret. And anyway, the Canadian had a cast-iron alibi in the Pendlebury case. She had been with Dr Tyler till nearly three in the morning after the quiz show. It was all in the statements if the silly old bugger had bothered to check it out before pushing him to take part in this farce.

Charlie wrapped it up, giving Arnott no more rope.

'Ms Krantz, I think we must conclude here. I have your address in London. I shall be in touch if I need to speak to you again. As we agreed, our chat has been informal, for background information only, of course.'

Don't ring us, we'll ring you, Arnott muttered to himself as Charlie ushered the woman out, calling loudly for Rambo to go in search of Mr Foxton. Arnott had blown it. The game was over. Fenella was dumped in the hall, her luggage at her feet, looking for all the world like a dazed air traveller who had just been through the mincer with two over-zealous customs men.

Charlie went back into the study, slamming the door after him and pointedly unplugged his tape recording equipment, pocketing the casette.

'Bad luck, Ralph,' he said stiffly.

'Win some, lose some, lad. Thanks anyway.'

'We'll have a jar when you get back to London. I've got to go back into Bath. Want a lift to the station?'

'I'm staying on a bit, Charlie. Give myself a breather,' Arnott replied, anxious for a bit of peace and quiet in which to pick up the pieces. 'Tell you what though. Could you drop me off at a garage? Place where I can hire a motor for a drop of sightseeing?'

Charlie's long face briefly rearranged itself into a sort of smile and he buttoned the awful overcoat and pushed Arnott ahead of him out of the house.

Bruce Foxton watched the two men depart. He had settled by the window in the library, a glass at his elbow and one of Shaw's excellent coronas scenting the room with cigar smoke. The house was deadly quiet, the only sound the muffled clacking of a typewriter in the interview room off the hall. He had withdrawn to the library after the departure of the minibus, his mind curiously at rest.

The entire enterprise was blown away by Madeleine's murder, of course. Everyone knew it. But it did free him from Tyler. Sophie was all to pieces but, for himself, the failure of the art club was almost a relief. He still owned the premises in Chelsea, the debts could be laid off somehow and his agreement with Tyler was finally smashed. Tyler had told him he had already decided to accept an offer of a job in Toronto and seemed in one hell of a hurry to shake the dirt of Chiaroscuro off his feet.

Bruce drew on his cigar, the faint aroma of leather bookbindings and brandy lending the Shaws' library the ambiance of a gentlemen's club. A club as destitute of members as Chiaroscuro would now be. He smiled, at peace with what was, by anyone's reckoning, a financial disaster.

He should never have employed Ken Tyler in the first place, knowing he was into small-time drug dealing. A false economy. But, at the time, Tyler had convinced him that it was no big deal to the few well-heeled club members already into what they considered a casual recreational vice no more harmful than some sort of mood enhancer. Bruce had agreed to turn a blind eye to any contacts Tyler made through Chiaroscuro on the strict understanding the business was discreet. In return, Tyler, a key member of staff and popular with audiences, would accept a share of the profits in lieu of salary for the duration of his three-year contract. Once the club found its feet, Bruce was confident he could dispense with Tyler with no bad feelings on either side and, in the meantime, the club accounts would be relieved of a considerable burden. Sophie suspected nothing. In fact, she congratulated Bruce on a financial coup. Dr Kenneth Tyler was a class act, well thought of in academic circles.

When Suki had been killed and the cocaine discovered in her car, Bruce had been terrified Tyler's little sideline had blown up in their faces. But everything was miraculously hushed up and they had agreed to let the dust settle. Play it cool. This second murder would allow no dirt to be pushed under the carpet and, ironically, Madeleine Pendlebury had, Ken assured him, never been on his books. But the chill wind of a second investigation would certainly blow the Nadhouri joy dust back in their faces. Tyler assured him there was no risk but he was wasting no time getting out, was he? Fortunately, he knew next to nothing about Tyler's customers, so dissembling would present few problems.

Bruce refilled his glass from the decanter, savouring this moment of calm in the eye of the storm. It couldn't last. The Shaws would surface again very soon and he must make his way back to London. He thrust aside any thoughts of what he might do when he got there. Roll over and play dead? The bank would be consulted as a matter of course and he must eventually make a settlement for poor old Sophie Neuman. But Bruce had been in tighter spots before. He would eventually think up something else. A garden design school perhaps? Sell the Chelsea place and set up in a country house setting – like Finings even? Manor houses were going for a song since the Lloyds' names had come such a cropper. He drew on his cigar, gazing round at the book-lined walls, the rain blowing fitfully against the glass, diffusing the winter sunlight, refracting the harsh glare of reality. Oh yes. A nice place in the country would suit him very well.

Twenty

Arnott felt a lot better with a set of wheels under him. The hire company had produced a red Fiesta, which seemed a bit of a skateboard compared with his own recently acquired boneshaker in London, but the weekend with Chiaroscuro had convinced him never again to rely on any but his own transport.

He called back at the murder squad HQ and managed to persuade Charlie Flood to let him have a look at the signed statements. Brenton was with his solicitor and likely to get off lightly he was glad to hear. Arnott then drove on to Chevenix and put his foot down till he reached the next village, hoping that Pullen and Will Smith had not given up waiting. He swerved into the forecourt of the Crown with a flourish, delighted to spot the green VW in the car park.

He burst into the smoke-filled saloon, perky as a turkey cock safely into New Year. The two of them were sitting at a corner table, each with a plate of sandwiches in front of them, neither displaying much of an appetite. After a hearty greeting, he went up to the bar to order a round. He knew what Pullen liked, wishy-washy white wine, virgin's piss as he called it, and, glancing over to their table, guessed at Will Smith's tipple. He shoved his way back through the lunchtime crowd, the drinks on a tray together with three bags of crisps, and sat down heavily, puffed out with all the rushing about.

'You got my note then, Pullen. I don't trust that spotty Rambo. Giving messages to a shifty blighter like that's as good as sending an SOS out to sea in a milk bottle.'

'Did you get a lift from Inspector Flood?'

'He took me into the city and I've hired myself this little red runner for a couple of days. Book me in here, did you, Pullen?' She shook her head.

'You're staying for the inquest then?' Will Smith's colouring, never at its rosiest in January, was ashen.

'I was hoping they'd got a spare room here. What's it like, lad?'

'Oh, all right. Shall I speak to Mollie about it for you? How many nights?'

'Two for starters. Thanks, mate.'

Will pushed past the people standing at the bar and disappeared into a back room. Arnott nodded after him and said to Judith, 'He's taken it hard and no mistake, poor bugger.'

Judith nibbled a piece of parsley from the garnish on the sandwiches and grimaced. 'What kept you?'

'I fixed up a floor show with Charlie Flood. Tape recorder, the lot. Thought, between us, we'd be able to shake down the Krantz woman and Lucie. Give them a touch of the frights and see what fell out when we set them up in the same room.'

'Any joy?'

'Not much. Lucie identified a ring I got hold of after a hunch about Brenton but there's no way of proving Krantz was fencing for the poor bloke. Her word against his and no one's going to take any notice of a boy with previous.'

'Well, it doesn't really matter now, does it? Chiaroscuro will probably fold anyway. Sorry I got you involved, Arnott. I never dreamed a part-time security job would turn out like this.'

Arnott took a swig of bitter and tried to perk her up before Misery Smith came back with his bag of woes.

'We did get her to admit that coke was not Mrs Pendlebury's little weakness, you'll be glad to hear. Though we already knew that after the PM report. Still, it gave us something on Krantz to lean on.'

'It was stupid of me to suggest it to Fenella in the first place. I seem to jump to all the wrong conclusions lately. It's not having you around to keep my feet on the ground,' she added with a wry smile.

'It wasn't entirely a waste of time but it don't look as if we can pin anything on Krantz drugwise merely on the strength of your eavesdropping in the ladies' lav. Pity you didn't take a proper dekko at the time. That's the trouble with your policework, Pullen. Hamstrung by all this fancy etiquette you picked up at school.'

Will Smith returned and sat down again, looking degrees more cheerful after a few minutes coddling from the motherly Mollie.

'I was telling Pullen here I got nothing much out of the Krantz woman. You knew her, didn't you, Will? A real hard nut, take my word for it.'

'I've known Fenella since I joined Chiaroscuro the year before last. She seems OK. Runs a flat-finding agency – I guess you have to be pretty determined to succeed in a cutthroat business like that. Sophie gets along with her all right, they help each other out with clients, I think.'

'Charlie and me got her in a corner about Pullen catching her up to her elbows in Mrs Pendlebury's suitcase – did you hear about all that, Will?'

'I told him,' Judy said. 'What did Fenella say, Arnott?'

'She agreed, cool as a bloody cucumber, that she wasn't snow clearing. Then she comes up with another fairy story. Says Pendlebury put her up to it himself.'

'Victor?' they burst out in unison.

Arnott nodded and helped himself to a sandwich. 'Krantz maintains Pendlebury asked her to reclaim a bracelet belonging to a ladyfriend. He said he was almost sure his wife had put it in with her own stuff when she packed on Saturday afternoon when you three all went to the house together. Krantz was told Mrs Pendlebury got hold of this item and had decided, out of spite, to hang on to it. Krantz says she was paid to recover it for him. I'll give the woman "A+" for thinking on her feet. Fancy concocting something like that off the cuff! Might even be true.'

Will's expression hardened. 'Oh, it's true all right. I can't say Victor's involved but the charm bracelet exists all right. Madeleine was terribly distressed about it.'

Judy added her own confirmation, rapping the beer stained table in emphasis. 'Madeleine came to see me at home. She called at my flat after a row with Pixie and told me she had discovered Victor was having an affair. She recognized the bracelet, you see. Madeleine had seen the girl wearing it. That put her in a state of total shock. She asked her father, Alain Lambert, to go over to Ireland and check it out. It seems to have been a long-standing relationship.'

'Well, blow me down, Pullen! Why didn't you tell me all this before?'

'It was confidential. I'd almost forgotten about it. Maddy intended to retrieve the package from Finings on Saturday and couldn't because Victor and Genista hadn't gone to Newmarket after all.'

'But the husband assumed she *had* packed it in her case and he paid Krantz to get it back...' Arnott looked as if light had slowly dawned. What a bloody parlour game this was. Sounded more like Pass the Parcel every minute. 'Where is this French bloke? You'd think he'd be here by now, his daughter stabbed to death.'

'Alain probably doesn't know about it yet. No one's sure of his exact whereabouts. He's abroad – it may be days before he's inform-ed.'

Arnott's face clouded. 'What evidence has this man got?'

Will filled in a few more blanks and gradu-ally Arnott formed some ideas about the mystery of the disappearing charm bracelet.

'Did Mrs Pendlebury tell you who this other woman was, Pullen?'

'She wouldn't say. She was desperately shocked by it all. But Alain asked the hotel manager for a description of the "Mrs Pen-dlebury" who had stayed there with Victor.'

'But why is this bracelet so important? Cheaper and less trouble to buy another one than pay Krantz to get it back.'

Judith shook her head. 'Victor's not a rich man, far from it. Finings is a run-down place and all his money and a whole lot of Madeleine's was sunk into the horse venture. Don't you see, Arnott? Madeleine had evidence to prove Victor had been unfaithful for years and—'

'Once Maddy divorces him, the money dries up,' Will put in. 'She could call in the loan on the new stable block.'

'Madeleine inherited a fortune from her grandmother last year,' Judith explained. 'Once she met Will, she realized she no longer wanted to share everything with the Pendleburys for the rest of her life. She didn't even like horses. Madeleine controlled all the spare cash.'

These last words sounded like an epitaph and Will slumped in his chair pale as a corpse himself.

Judith decided they were all sifting the dirt to no purpose. Everyone had suffered enough. She said, 'Well, anyway, it doesn't matter now, does it? Victor's affair remains private and, with no divorce, he inherits all Madeleine's money and that's that. Why rake it over now? I've got to get back, Arnott. I promised Nancy Shaw I would drive over to Finings with her to explain things to Victor.'

'And you still think Pendlebury is innocent?'

Arnott's questioning of the dotty lives these rich people led dropped like a stone between them.

'Innocent?'

'Of murder.'

Will looked stupidly from one to the other. 'You are not suggesting Victor *killed* her, are you?'

'Six to four when a wealthy woman croaks it's Hubby who "done the dirty deed". That true, Pullen?'

She reluctantly agreed, puzzling out the permutations in her own mind. 'When I spoke to Laurence this morning he assured me that they have no information that this Sioux organization is involved. Madeleine was not a political animal.'

'And if Maddy had discovered anything about Suki's death she would have told me,' Will said, sure of that at least.

'She didn't tell you everything though, did she, lad? She didn't say who the other woman was.'

'But that was obvious! Madeleine had no need to spell it out, did she, Judy? We all knew who it was. It was Victor's secretary. We all guessed about Tricia Carroll.'

Arnott relaxed. They were getting somewhere at last.

He said, 'Suppose you guessed wrong? What if Fenella Krantz was Pendlebury's playmate? She's known him for years, she admitted that, and sticking her neck out to steal back something belonging to his secretary takes some swallowing. Even for money it was too big a risk. The Krantz woman's a born liar. She wouldn't know the truth if she fell over it. I've got a gut feeling about this female. I reckon she was looking for the bracelet off her own bat. A hefty bundle of gold charms sounds more up her street than something belonging to a bloody typist. You never seen this item of jewellery either of you?'

They both shook their heads, regarding Arnott with astonishment, bowled over by this audacious leap in the dark.

He continued, leaning over the table like a conspirator. 'Suppose we recover the bracelet ourselves? The Frenchman's the only one with any sort of description of the other "Mrs Pendlebury" and he's missing. Without the bracelet as evidence the hotel manager's vague say-so is useless, be laughed out of court even if we knew who he was. Why not get it back on our own?' Arnott's eyes gleamed with this exciting proposal.

Will felt it was time to put in a word of common sense. 'We don't know where it is, that's why. Victor has turned Finings inside out without finding it. I'd bet on Fenella's thoroughness when she searched Maddy's things and—'

'Pixie told me Madeleine always kept a

diary, ever since school, she said. Maddy was very shy about anyone seeing *anything* she wrote because of her dyslexia, so it was locked away in the wall safe at her flat, never toted around on holiday or weekends because she was embarrassed about her spelling. She made no secret of it. Madeleine was rather lonely and immature. I could well imagine her confiding in a schoolgirlish thing like a private journal.'

'And the secretary, this Tricia, has gone to London with his sister to search the dead woman's flat for it!' Arnott crowed. 'By 'eck, that's it! Once the diary's destroyed they only need the bracelet to scotch any rumours *before* the inquest. There's no motive otherwise. They've got to get it back before the Frenchman turns up with his half-baked story about his daughter's divorce being in the pipeline. It's not much of a tale without any proof and as he's already known to be on bad terms with his son-in-law and probably cops the victim's estate if Pendlebury is accused, Lambert can hardly claim to be unbiased. If we could hand over the bracelet and the covering letter from the hotel manager, Inspector Palmer would have something to go on when Lambert surfaces with *his* story. The oldest motive in the book, Pullen. Money.'

'But everyone you come across in this scenario is seriously in trouble financially –

even Bruce Foxton and Sophie will be in Queer Street with Chiaroscuro after this second murder,' Will insisted.

Judy felt thoroughly confused, Arnott's appalling suggestion that Victor might be involved altered everything. She muttered, 'Fenella said something to me about all this. She said, "Evil flourishes on obsession". Victor isn't obsessive, just over-anxious to avoid the embarrassment of being exposed. Anyway, I know where it is.'

'What do you mean, lass?'

'The bracelet. Madeleine told me she'd left it in the French desk. It has a hidden drawer. She put it back there after showing Alain. It was the only safe place. She wanted to get it when we went to Finings on Saturday but Tricia was typing in the morning room so Maddy had to abandon the idea. The bracelet's still there.'

'You've seen this drawer?'

'Oh, yes. Sophie showed us all at the party before Christmas.'

Judith drew a sketch of the bonheur-de-jour on her serviette and showed it to Will, describing the mechanism of the hidden compartment.

'Ah, I've seen that sort of cabinetwork before. It's not uncommon.'

The barmaid called 'Time' and Arnott stood with the two empty tankards in his podgy hand. 'In that case, Pullen, there's no other way forward. It would give the murder squad a lever to screw more info out of the husband even if he didn't kill her himself. We've nothing else to throw at him so far. He could even have paid someone to nobble her for him. It's been known. Seeing as you know all about it, Pullen, you'll have to get the thing yourself.'

And with that he hurried up to the bar to get a last round before closing time. They sat listening to Arnott's cheerful banter with the barmaid, open-mouthed at this latest out-landish suggestion.

He returned and resumed his seat, swig-ging a substantial draught of bitter before elaborating on his crazy scheme.

'While you're hobnobbing with the gentry this afternoon, love, you make an excuse, leave the Shaws and Pendlebury crying on each other's shoulders and nip into the next room and get the packet.'

'Oh, yes?' Judy's hollow laughter sounded thin in the rapidly emptying saloon bar. 'I just say, "Excuse me, folks, while I rifle Madeleine's desk".'

'Come on, girl, be resourceful! What about when the four of you are on the doorstep saying cheerio? – bearing in mind the griev-ing hubby's on his own while the sister and his secretary are in London stripping the poor cow's flat. You pretend to have left something behind – your fags or something

– and go back to the room and snatch the goods. Easy as falling off a log! Only take a minute. A bloody chimpanzee could do it.'

Will warmed to the idea and put in the clincher. 'Madeleine was stabbed, Judy. She was then scalped to make it look like Suki's murder, just another Sioux killing, and you said yourself Erskine's ruled that one out. I think Arnott's on to something: Victor *is* involved somehow. Maddy was terrified of him.'

Judith scrambled to her feet, white with shock. 'But Victor didn't *know* Suki had been scalped. Nobody did. It is *still* a police secret. Come to think of it, if you knew about the scalping in the Sioux murder, you could have killed Suki yourself!'

'Kill Suki? Why on earth should I get involved in a political assassination? Good God, Judy, I don't even vote!'

Will took a deep breath and plunged in, making a clean breast of it.

'I overheard the details when the police were discussing Suki's head injuries. I had come back to Chiaroscuro to get my puncture kit from the locker. I'm afraid I couldn't keep my mouth shut,' he explained to Arnott. 'I told Madeleine the scalping was a secret from the media but later, when everything had blown over, she let the cat out of the bag.'

'When was that?' Arnott barked.

'On Saturday afternoon Judy and I went out to the stables with Genista. We left Maddy alone with Victor. She was in a terribly nervous state and Victor was arguing about the divorce. It all got pretty acrimonious she said. Victor was bitter, felt he had been left to carry the can, I suppose. She told me she rushed upstairs to get away from the wrangling and Tricia followed her and watched her packing. She wouldn't leave Madeleine alone for a minute, pretending to be sympathetic, saying how upset Maddy must have been about the Chiaroscuro murder and everything and that perhaps she ought to take a holiday, think things over quietly. Just to shut her up, Madeleine started telling her all about it. Madeleine didn't realize the police were still covering up the details of the ghastly business. I should never have mentioned it. It was my fault. Maddy was always featherbrained. In the course of Tricia's shakedown for gossip Madeleine mentioned the scalping and later felt a bit worried about it and told me. I said it probably wasn't important – Tricia was hardly going to run to the newspapers with the story and anyway, as Suki's murder was more or less written off as a terrorist killing, it wouldn't matter a jot.'

Arnott glowered, sifting the garbage in his mind, knowing all too well that the muck was spreading in all directions.

'For me,' he said, 'the snag in all this rigmarole is nothing to do with any divorce. What worries me is the scalping. Even if Will told Mrs Pendlebury about the Nadhouri injuries and she passed it on as women do, Will wasn't the only one who was in on it.'

'Who else then?'

'Bruce Foxton. He was in the know from the start. The black boy, Brenton George, was kept well clear when the body was examined – *he* thought Nadhouri had been bashed about the head and no one filled *him* in – but if you cast your mind back to the night of the first murder, Foxton was in the room with us when Erskine was reading the Riot Act to Will about keeping the info about the scalping under his 'at.'

Judy and Will were stunned into silence. Arnott trundled on with his hypothesis.

'If you put the Pendlebury lot next to Foxton and that hard-faced cow, Fenella Krantz, I'd lay odds on the pair most likely to set a trap for a rich woman with not a lot in the brains department.'

Judith felt he had gone too far as usual. 'Hold on, Arnott, Maddy wasn't that stupid. And Fenella was with Ken Tyler all evening after the quiz packed up.'

'She could have put through the hoax call. Or Tyler could have lied. If *you* spilt the beans about the scalping, Will Smith, how do we know Foxton didn't tell Tyler? They're 'hand in glove, ain't they?'

'Bruce wouldn't hurt a fly. But Tyler is a black belt... And he is a big spender on that collection of his.'

'And Fenella thinks he was the one supplying the cocaine to Suki,' Judy put in. 'He had plenty of reasons to frighten Madeleine into keeping quiet about any drugs in circulation at the club.'

'Just supposing we've been barking up the wrong tree. Say, the fake call was merely a device to get her out in the wilds in the middle of the night to frighten the lights out of Mrs Pendlebury like Pullen says? To soften her up for a bit of blackmail even? Krantz puts through the emergency call and Tyler's waiting in the Nissan, which he's nicked and when he's driven off with the poor woman, he pulls her out of the car and threatens her with a knife just to focus her attention while he explains the rules. Tit for tat. Tyler knows she's carrying on with Will here while Victor plays the white man who's not going to contest the divorce and whose girlfriend is being named in the petititon. Krantz has already had a tête-à-tête with Pendlebury in Bath that night when he had to explain why he had to get the bracelet back. Someone with evidence against *Mrs* P. could sell it on to Victor for "loadsamoney" and these days rich wives sometimes have to share the dosh when there's a break-up – pay alimony even! Anything against the wife would be worth a packet to the lawyers but as hubby's skint Tyler might decide it would be easier to change sides and squeeze Mrs Pendlebury, especially if she's the silly sort who pay first and cry later. Tyler could even pretend he's got the bracelet package everyone's so hot under the collar over and offer to trade if she keeps mum about his little business arrangement with Nadhouri. Mrs P. wouldn't know if he had or not, she wasn't certain *who* had it at that point.'

'But why kill her?'

'Could have been an accident. Tyler's desperate to keep out of the Nadhouri investigation, which Flood's still flogging. If he's been distributing drugs, he's really for the high jump. The victim gets all hysterical and tries to escape and the knife gets in the way. Once a violent situation gets out of hand like that, covering it up to look like a copycat killing would be the only way out. Officially brushed under the carpet like Nadhouri.'

'Whew! That's quite a big "if", Arnott. And there's nothing to link Fenella and Ken Tyler, is there, apart from being an alibi for each other Saturday night?'

'Just thinking aloud, mate. You have to look at things from all angles in this game. I'm in no position to go over to the Finings place and make up my own mind about the set-up.

I have to rely on what you and Pullen tell me. And it just don't ring true, especially this rubbish that no one names names. Fornication's hardly headline news any more, is it? Why was Pendlebury being such a gent?'

'Victor's old-fashioned,' Judy explained. 'He would feel bound to defend the girl's reputation if he could. Anyway, if his long-standing relationship was with Fenella – not his secretary after all – I doubt whether Fenella would want to be tied to him permanently, especially if he was broke. Depends if he got any sort of settlement, I suppose. But Victor's the last person to force a high-profile litigation, of course. Both Ken Tyler and Fenella preferred things as they were, I should say. No loud denunciations from Madeleine about cocaine or adultery.'

'Is this Fenella married? Is that the problem? No bun in the oven or anything like that?'

'Not that I know of.'

Arnott glanced from one to the other, weighing up the pros and cons.

'You're right. I'm up the creek. The only solid thing we've got to go on is this bloody bracelet everyone's so keen to lay their hands on. But it would give the local bobbies something to put in the motive slot and there's no other lead.'

Judith suddenly capitulated. 'OK. OK. If you think it's so important, I feel I owe it to

Maddy at least to try. I'll see what I can do. I'm making no promises, mind, but I'll try to think up something when I'm at Finings this afternoon.'

After she left, Arnott and Will sat on in the deserted bar finishing their beer. Both absorbed in their preoccupations, small talk was desultory. In an effort to lighten the mood, Arnott ribbed the younger man about his name.

'Willy Smith I can take – a good old British handle – but Haydock! Your dad a book-maker or sommat?'

Will smiled, glad of a temporary respite. 'Quite the reverse. Mum was the punter. She got good odds on an outsider running at Haydock Park the day I was born. It won. Like all gamblers she's very superstitious. She thought "Haydock" would bring me luck.'

'Lucky she didn't call you after the horse then. William Red Rum Smith'd take a bit of beating.'

'Yeah. I never thought of that ... Bruce Foxton put in the hyphen when I got the job with Chiaroscuro. He thought plain William Smith too suburban for one of his lecturers. Haydock-Smith had more of a ring to it, he said.'

'What was the nag called?'

'Oedipus,' he replied with a guffaw.

Arnott blinked and changed the subject,

suspecting the joke was on him. The landlord's wife was beginning to take a close interest in her two new boarders and Arnott went outside to fetch his bag from the car. She showed him up to his room at the back of the pub, a nice double bed and a sturdy pair of armchairs, much more up his street than the dinky wallpaper he had had to stare at at Chevenix. After unpacking, he knocked on Will's door and invited him in to share a bottle he had bought in Bath. It was going to be a long wait: Judy wouldn't get back to them till well after five.

Arnott felt bad about putting her up to it. It was a bloody risky move which could easily backfire. Too late now. Will Smith slunk in and dropped into one of the chairs. He, too, was on edge and inevitably they reverted to talk of the murder.

'Tell me about Pendlebury.'

Will's expression hardened and he thought for several minutes before answering.

'Victor is exactly like Goya's portrait of the Duke of Wellington. Do you know it? It's in the National.'

Arnott sipped his whisky from a tooth mug and let the lad ramble on.

'Ah well, I'll have to explain. Most portraits of military men emphasize the power and the regalia. Reynolds would have made a production number of it. Goya was much more subtle. He didn't even use the famous

293

hawk-like profile. The duke of Wellington, probably our finest commander, is shown head-on – up to his neck in medals, of course, but the fancy dress is secondary. Goya shows the face of a man of strong sensibilities, dark eyes all too aware of public admiration but harbouring secrets. Whether the secret was his inner turmoil at the bloodshed he, as a soldier, had unavoidably promoted or some private guilt is up to us to decide. But the picture leaves a lasting impression of a man with something to hide, a weakness he himself dare not acknowledge.'

It was hardly a photofit. Only an art historian would give a crackpot description like that. But despite having never set eyes on Victor Pendlebury Arnott felt he had learned something at last.

'You're convinced he's involved in his wife's murder, too, ain't you, Will?'

'Oh, yes. I am.'

'What's this secretary bird like? Pretty?'

'Tricia Carroll? I've only seen her once. Bossy little party but quite attractive. Much more organized than Maddy ever was and certainly no idiot. It's difficult to imagine her helping Victor to threaten Madeleine in any way but it's obvious she thinks the sun shines out of him. Has worked for Victor for years apparently.'

'Let me think aloud for a bit, chum, and

see how it strikes you.'

Arnott lit a cigarette and started speaking, his bluff Yorkshire burr taking the sting out of an unpalatable synopsis.

'We know that Pendlebury is desperate to protect his lady-love and the only concrete evidence is tied up with a charm bracelet the woman left at a hotel. The real meat in the sandwich is the fact that Mrs P's the one with the money.'

'She told me she'd guaranteed substantial sums since he launched the horse-trading operation.'

Arnott leaned back in the chair, his head wreathed in smoke as he stared up at the ceiling, deep in thought.

'Right. Pendlebury can see the writing on the wall. But I thought this bloke's old man was a fraudster who secretly salted away his winnings?'

'Bloch? Madeleine didn't know very much about all that but if there was any nest egg Victor must have spent it by now.'

After a pause Arnott rumbled on but a knock on the door interrupted further speculation. Mollie handed him a letter, grimly eyeing the half-empty bottle of scotch.

'The boy from Chevenix Park cycled over with this for you, Mr Arnott. Said it was urgent,' she said, closing the door behind her with a bang.

He recognized Judy's scrawl and his heart sank. Bad news for sure. After scanning the brief note he glanced up, looking relieved.

'Pullen didn't make it to the Pendlebury tea party, son. Her sister rang. There's been an accident. A fire in the pottery workshop, the kiln backfired or sommat. She's gone straight down there. Romney Marsh – a bloody long drive from here, by gum. The mother's in a bad way, Pullen says. Looks like we'll have to snaffle the bracelet and the hotel manager's letter on our own, Willy Smith.'

Twenty-One

The whisky helped, of course.

An hour later Arnott had almost squared it with his conscience. Being retired softened the edges of any moral dilemma. After all, he was supposed to be a private detective on this case, wasn't he? Freelancers could bend the rules a bit – that was why the public called them in instead of the police half the time. He tried out this argument on Will Smith, who wasn't much of a drinker and now, cruelly sober, was impatient with Arnott's prevarications.

He took away Arnott's bottle and emptied it in the hand basin.

'I thought you were a professional, Arnott. If we're going to break in, for Christ's sake, let's get on with it. What you need is something to eat and some fresh air. Let's walk into town and stoke up.'

Arnott reluctantly agreed and put on his sheepskin coat and thick boots. He looked like a Michelin man and Mollie, watching the two set out across the car park, had to smile.

It was a good idea. By the time they reached the bright lights Arnott felt more his old self, buoyed up by Will's hard-headed determination to nail Madeleine Pendlebury's husband as a hypocrite if nothing else. Arnott had to hand it to the lad. He had misjudged him, shoved Will Smith in the same box as the rest of the arty mob at Chiaroscuro. But the floppy first impression was a cover. Under the boyish charm, Will Smith was a man as pigheaded as Arnott himself.

They tramped back under the stars with a detailed plan dissected against any flaws. Arnott was even beginning to look forward to it. He had got out of the way of taking chances. Being out in the cold without the legality of the police force behind him had forced him into taking risks he would never have needed to consider as a serving officer.

Will Smith suffered from no such heart-searching. The terrible attack on Madeleine was his first and probably his last brush with violence and he was haunted by it. It was essential for his own peace of mind that he did his utmost to bring some sort of justice to bear, to clear her name at least. It had become his obsession. Perhaps Judy had been right when she had said something about evil flourishing under obsession. He had never felt such deep malice before and was certainly the last to resort to lawbreaking but the cruelty of Maddy's death had stirred a latent fury which only retribution could soothe.

They went back to Arnott's room to go over the plan yet again.

'If you like, Arnott, I'll do it on my own. You need not get involved at all. I know the layout of the house and I know how to trigger the secret drawer.'

'And I know how to break in like a real housebreaker, lad. For all we know the place is festooned with tripwires.'

'I doubt it. Victor spent nothing on the house and there's no guard dog, not even in the stables. That's where all the mod cons are. If Victor has installed a burglar alarm it's at the stables. Considering the investment involved he should have put an electric fence round the horses.'

'What about the stable manager? Hard

man, I bet. He'd be alert to any noises round the house.'

'The stables are a good quarter of a mile away and he's got a staff cottage near the horses. The housekeeper has a place of her own, too. They don't live in and the stable lads are from the village. The Pendleburys prefer having the house to themselves according to Madeleine. Very keen on their privacy apparently. It's a pushover, Arnott. I'm surprised Finings hasn't been turned over before. Though, come to think of it, there didn't seem anything worth pinching apart from some Scottish watercolours Madeleine promised to show me.'

'And you say everything's round the back?'

'They don't use the rest of the house in the winter. It's all a bit dilapidated, you know what these country houses are like, thread-bare hangings and crappy old furniture just to show you're not "nouveaux". Sort of shabby chic. It reminded me of a place in Dorset I went to last summer with a dealer to look at a supposedly undiscovered Vermeer. The house was a shambles but the chap had spent a fortune on his collection of vintage cars, all in perfect nick.'

'Finings is nothing like Chevenix Park then?'

Will chuckled. 'Chalk and cheese.'

'And you reckon this ramshackle conservatory built along the back is the weak spot?'

'Here, let me show you.'

Will sketched a rough ground plan of the house and jabbed his pencil at the diagram of the adjoining rooms behind the disused conservatory.

'The middle room's a winter sitting room and leading off from it is Madeleine's morning room where her desk is. On the other side of the sitting room is Victor's study. I thought we could slip into the morning room via the conservatory with no hassle. We went in that way on Saturday and from what I remember it was an ordinary glazed door with no mortice lock or anything fancy. Can you cope with that, Arnott? What about if it's bolted at the bottom?'

'If it's a glazed garden door I can easily cut out a pane and put my hand through to reach a bolt. I bought a glass cutter and some rubber suction pads this afternoon while you was in the bike shop. Lucky for us there's no live-in staff.'

'There is one snag I forgot to mention. Victor sometimes sleeps in his study. I couldn't make out if it was since his estrangement with Madeleine or whether it really is doctor's orders. Victor's supposed to have a heart problem, though Genista poo-poos any suggestion he's not a fit man. If Victor's sleeping downstairs we shall have to be bloody quiet getting in. If we leave it till the small hours he should be snoring by then.'

'Pullen said the doctor had put him on tranquillizers since his bereavement, probably sleeping pills as well. It's usual these days – the quacks think they can dose you up with pills to blot out anything,' Arnott said with bitterness, Peg's death still vividly painful to him. 'He should be out for the count by the time we get there.'

'The secretary's gone back to London with Genista. Tricia will have to stay in town to organize the lampshade workrooms. Maddy said she more or less keeps the business running and there's a chance Genista will stay on overnight at least. There must be plenty to sort out at the flat.'

Arnott looked grave. 'We shall just have to keep our fingers crossed, lad. You still on?'

'Sure! It will only take five minutes once we get there. Have you got a torch? I don't want to fall over the furniture.'

They spent the evening watching television in the snug, Arnott, much to Mollie's confusion, sticking to low-alcohol lager. Having discovered her two lodgers swigging whisky upstairs, the landlord's wife was put out to find them so abstemious once the bar was open.

While the car park was still full, Arnott slipped out and moved his Fiesta half a mile down the lane to be well out of Mollie's earshot after midnight. Will was all for cycling over to Finings on his own but Arnott, while confident of Will's resolution, was far from sure of his abilities as a housebreaker. They turned in and tried to get some sleep before setting out but neither was successful, Arnott quietly panicking at the prospect of being caught red-handed and hauled off to the local lock-up. He could well imagine Charlie Flood's face if he had to call on him to bail them out.

In desperation, he tried to read a dog-eared copy of *Scott's Last Expedition*, which he found in the drawer of the bedside table. All that snow and ice and old-fashioned loyalty grabbed Arnott's attention all right, though it was the last thing to put him to sleep. He grew quite angry reliving the organizational cock-up it had turned out to be and felt at one with the poor sod who had walked out into the blizzard and put an end to it.

Will knocked him up just after two, suitably togged out in a dark-blue tracksuit and trainers. The old man had no sporty gear and, worse, no soft shoes but as his role was merely to break in there would be no call upon Arnott to creep about.

The night was still and cloudy with a damp drizzle in the air which chilled to the bone. By the time they had walked to the parked car another problem had etched itself on Arnott's worry list. How were they to get

302

back inside the Crown without a key? Getting away on the quiet had been difficult enough. He shook his head and kept mum – there was no point in worrying Will about it now.

They drove off as the church clock struck the half hour, leaving the car in a lay-by well away from their destination. Arnott's corns were beginning to throb: he wasn't used to all this hiking about. The sudden emergence of Finings through the drizzle thrust aside his proliferating doubts and Will led the way, keeping clear of the white fence rails of the stables. Dense shrubbery grew close to the house, which stood massive in the darkness, unlit and apparently uninhabited. The door of the conservatory stood ajar and the thin beam of Arnott's torch flickered over the two garden doors leading into the house.

Will silently pointed out the morning room entrance and they edged forward. It was all as quiet as the grave, only a barn owl hooting in the bare treetops on duty.

Will tried the handle, which was secured as they expected. He stood aside waiting for Arnott to get to work on the lock but, cautious as ever, the older man felt his way along the slimy conservatory staging and tested the other door. After a lifetime of officially investigating break-ins Arnott was never surprised at the general public's carelessness about security; it was as if people had become fatalistic about robbery and the ones with the most to lose were often the worst, especially those whose trust in the wholesomeness of country life blinded them to unpalatable statistics.

Arnott briefly shone his torch at the sitting-room door and gingerly turned the handle. It gave without a sound and, grinning like a toby jug, the cunning old blighter gave Will the thumbs-up. He slid past and disappeared before Arnott could pass him the torch. Arnott breathed heavily, straining to hear Will's progress inside but the lad was a natural, his presence in the creaking old house as soundless as a ghost.

Arnott propped open the door an inch and stepped aside, anxious not to impede Will's exit. He shuffled along the staging and stumbled against a cold metal obstruction between the two garden doors. Curious, he shone the torch, discovering the rusting office desk inappropriately shoved outside.

Incurably nosy, Arnott tried each drawer, peering along the narrow ray of light as it played over what looked like stacks of mildewed account books. He opened one of the ledgers and found it to be some sort of gardening record, lists of horticultural references and dates with detailed notes on plant species. Arnott was not green-fingered and the day-to-day memoranda of the late Mr Bloch's snowdrop breeding was lost on him.

He cocked an ear, listening for Will, but the night continued silent as before apart from the persistent hooting of the owl. Driven to fill in the anxious minutes with any sort of activity while he waited, Arnott tried the bottom drawer, which slid open without a sound. He felt about inside, alert for any sort of activity inside the house, only half attending to his own gropings. The lad was taking his time about it and no mistake.

His fingers touched a box and he shone the torch inside the drawer. It was a brown cardboard collar box, the sort he had not seen for years. Arnott used to have them himself when stiff collars were sent to the laundry. He chuckled, reckoning even the Governor of the Bank of England wore soft collars to work these days. He opened the box expecting to find more gardening rubbish but inside was something wrapped in tissue paper. The package had none of the musty smell of the rest of the items in the desk and, tipping out the contents, he focussed the pencil beam of light.

He gasped, knocked sideways by his shocking discovery.

Lights suddenly blazed in the house and he almost dropped the torch, swivelling round towards the racket which had broken out. A scuffle and a woman's piercing demands were loud and clear. He bundled his find into his pocket and crept up to the lighted windows of the winter sitting room.

The scene inside turned his bowels to water. Will stood with his back to the garden door facing a furious female in a diaphanous nightdress levelling a shotgun at him. Behind her, the door to Victor's study gaped and beyond this the man himself was struggling from a tumbled bed. Bloody hell! – Will had stumbled into the love nest. Pullen had been right all along. Fenella Krantz was in the clear, Victor's fancy pigeon was Tricia Carroll! She had come back from London and Pendlebury was caught in bed with his typist, poor bugger.

Arnott froze, waiting to see how Will would tackle it. The situation was far from lost. Pendlebury would be in no rush to call the police and expose himself to humiliation and ribald comment, his wife barely cold on a mortuary slab. And bang goes your snow-white reputation if you blow the whistle, Saint Victor, Arnott reflected.

The woman aiming the shotgun looked far from stable and Arnott judged his own sudden emergence might startle her into accidentally pulling the trigger. He decided to stay put and let Will have a crack at it first, let the atmosphere cool a bit before introducing himself.

Her voice was shrill with fright and Arnott grimly acknowledged that his preconception of Pendlebury's little bit of fluff had been way off the mark: this one was a bleeding virago!

Victor scrambled into the room looking every bit his age, his hair tousled and bearing the glazed expression of a man awakening to a nightmare. He stood in the doorway clutching his silk dressing gown to his chest, blinking at the lights. The woman railed on, ignoring Victor's attempt to conciliate. Will hadn't got a word in yet but, having recognized the interloper, far from lowering the shotgun, she grew visibly more menacing, her vituperation woundingly accurate. Arnott bided his time, pressing himself close to the wall outside, trying to catch every word. His ear stung with the unstoppable invective.

'—and what more are you after, you stupid gigolo? Haven't you lined your pockets enough with Madeleine's handouts?'

Will took a step forward and tried to speak but she jabbed the gun at him, forcing him back, her eye unwavering. This woman meant business.

'I came for the bracelet,' he said quietly.

Arnott gave a silent cheer. The lad was handling the situation like a pro, keeping his cool, calm despite all the insults.

'How dare you! Madeleine knew how much it meant to me – every single charm on that chain has a special memory for me. Hand it over.'

Victor attempted to intercede and touched her bare shoulder, muttering inaudibly. Arnott struggled to hear but only the woman's voice was clear as she shrugged off Pendlebury's efforts. Arnott threw aside caution and peered in through the glazed door at the escalating confrontation. Nobody noticed, all three inside the room intent on the bitter exchange.

'Will Smith is nothing but a common thief, Victor. Here, you! Put the bracelet down there.' She indicated a small wine table and steadied her aim.

Will stiffened and even from his awkward viewpoint Arnott sensed the lad's rising anger as he looked at the package in his hand and then deliberately zipped it inside a pocket of his track suit.

'You can't shut me up like you did Madeleine. No wonder the poor girl was so disgusted, Victor. You're nothing but a sham.' Will turned and took a step towards the conservatory.

For a split second Arnott felt the lad might actually pull it off, just walk away and let Pendlebury stew in his own juice.

'Let him go, darling,' he pleaded.

'Victor, can't you understand? We can't let him get away with it. Madeleine wouldn't give in, you see. I tried to make her see sense, my dear. What good would come of telling the lawyers about us? How dare she pass judgement? She was no angel herself. It was such a little deception to ask of her. Just a little patience would have been enough.' Her voice had grown soft and persuasive as she spoke, it might have been a different woman entirely. Arnott stiffened, sensing her mood veering strangely off balance.

Her light tone ran on, confidential – as if Will were of no consequence whatsoever.

'I did not intend to, Victor – at least, I don't think I did – but Madeleine was so stubborn, my love, so stupidly determined to expose us. Such spite! I couldn't bear that. Afterwards, I sat for a long time in the car, wondering what to do. Perhaps it had been in my mind all along, ever since I heard about the murder at the art club in London ... It took only a moment, like skinning a rabbit almost ... Then I came home.'

Arnott was totally confused. Perhaps he had assumed too much? Or misheard? He pressed in closer just as Will stepped forward, screaming incoherently at her, breaking the spell.

The woman's fury erupted, igniting a final incandescence in her brain as she aimed the shotgun.

'Don't move another inch, Will Smith! Stop him, Victor! You can't let him ruin us now – not after all I've done for you, for God's sake. He broke in here in the dark – no one will blame us for shooting a burglar.

How was I to know who he was?'

Then she fired.

Arnott threw himself into the room as the deafening explosion reverberated, cannonballing into Will, who had caught most of the shot in his shoulder, sending them both crashing into the wall. Victor let out a cry of anguish as he ran forward and suddenly all three men were entangled.

Will sank to the floor, bleeding heavily and, as Arnott bent over him, Pendlebury spun round and attempted to wrest the shotgun from her. She jumped back, holding him at bay, her eyes filling with tears.

'Genny, my darling, what have you done?'

Arnott struggled to his feet, his eyes darting from one to the other, comprehension slowly dawning. He looked down at Will slumped against a chair, spattered with blood, alert to Arnott's unspoken question.

'Yes,' Will whispered, his voice barely audible. 'This is Genista. Genista must be the other woman Madeleine was going to cite. It never entered my mind – no wonder poor Maddy couldn't bear to talk about it...' he said, the words fading. He clenched his fist in pain.

'Pendlebury and his sister—?' Arnott muttered in disbelief, staring at Victor, who returned his gaze with a dazed acknowledgement, his mind still struggling with Genista's rambling confession.

Arnott withdrew the package he had found in the cardboard collar box, laid it on the wine table and unwrapped the tissue. His rough fingers smoothed the lock of hair, which glinted under the light like a skein of gold thread rooted to a jagged piece of scalp now stiff with dried blood.

'Oh, my God,' Victor gasped. 'Madeleine ... Then it's true, Genny...?' His voice petered out and he reached out to hold her. The gun fell to the floor. Victor tried to speak but seemed racked with physical pain, clinging to her, speechless. He slowly collapsed at her feet, uttering an ugly choking cry. She crouched down beside him, sobbing uncontrollably.

After a swift glance at Will, Arnott made a move to retrieve the gun but before he could reach it the garden door burst open and a man in breeches ran into the room, brandishing a heavy torch.

'Mother of God! I heard the shot. What—?'

Genista cried out in relief. 'Paddy! Quickly, help me. It's Victor. He's had a heart attack.'

Arnott kicked the gun into a corner and crowded in to have a look. Pushing the man aside, he knelt down to feel Victor's pulse.

Arnott tried everything.

'He's gone,' he said at last, struggling to his feet.

Genista shoved him aside and frantically tried to resuscitate her brother with the kiss of life.

Arnott and the stable manager stood uselessly in the background, regarding the woman in her flimsy nightdress desperately fighting to breathe life into the dead man. The explicit movements were all too much for Paddy Frith, who roughly pulled her off.

'You bloody witch,' he shouted. 'Leave Victor alone, can't you? Haven't you ridden him long enough? Give the poor man some peace at last.'

He grabbed her, pinning her arms, and turned to Arnott, his weatherbeaten cheeks wet with tears.

'I don't know who you are but get an ambulance. There's a phone in there,' he said, pointing to the study.

Will crawled forward and took possession of Madeleine's bloodstained lock of hair, holding it to his cheek, his face ashen.

Twenty-Two

When the police arrived the five of them were still ranged about the tumbled sitting room at Finings; one dead, one riddled with lead shot and the only woman curled in Victor's armchair silently staring at the catastrophe her obsession had brought about.

Arnott had fetched her dressing gown from the study after making the emergency call and now gently draped it over her nakedness. She sat unmoving as if her life's blood had seeped away. The men all averted their eyes from the body on the floor and Arnott tried to assess the extent of Will's injuries. He now seemed oddly numb to the pain, a matter of alarm, but, determined to keep the atmosphere as calm as possible, Arnott confined himself to patting the lad's arm in an awkward gesture of comfort.

In the brief time at his disposal before the police machinery came into play, Arnott impressed upon Will the necessity to draw a veil over their presence at Finings. 'I'll explain everything,' he assured him, 'leave it to me,

313

son.' In fact, Will's consciousness was fading fast and the chances of Inspector Palmer obtaining Will Smith's version were ebbing.

When the police burst in, Arnott drew the inspector into the study and attempted to describe the events leading up to Victor Pendlebury's fatal coronary. But Palmer impatiently urged Arnott to get on with his account of finding the scalp. His subsequent revelations that Mrs Pendlebury had been murdered by her own sister-in-law, who had then shot Will Smith, temporarily cancelled any residual curiosity he may have had about Arnott's presence at Finings and he accepted, for now at least, that Arnott had merely walked into the house behind Will who had come to demand a missing bracelet.

'Why's this bracelet so important?'

'It's in a package with documentation proving the funny goings-on between Pendlebury and his sister. Will Smith's got it zipped up inside his top. You'll need it as evidence, Palmer.'

The inspector had more than enough to worry about and curtly shut him up, striding back into the sitting room to supervise Will's departure in the ambulance and to orchestrate the police procedure. A WPC was despatched upstairs to fetch some clothing for Genista and to get her dressed for the drive to headquarters. The woman had no fight left in her, allowing herself to be led like an automaton. A few minutes later, she reappeared, fully dressed and utterly calm, the extraordinary aquamarine eyes dull as pebbles. Arnott and Palmer followed the two women outside, thankful for Genista's passive acceptance of being in police custody. It was almost as if she had died with Victor.

They watched the departure and then re-entered the house to examine the dreadful memento of Madeleine in its tissue wrappings which Will Smith had reluctantly relinquished before passing out.

'You and the stable manager stay here with my team, Arnott, while I follow Miss Pendlebury to the station. I'll get Charlie Flood over to sort out some of this mess. He deserves to be in at the kill, though, strictly speaking, it has little bearing on his own investigation into the Nadhouri case.'

'The scalping was a clumsy shot at linking the two murders, don't forget. A casual investigation might have passed it off as killing two birds with one stone – with one political motive, any road. The sister-in-law may even have planned it that way – something as barmy as scalping the victim is practically unheard of, a pity to waste it. When Pendlebury's secretary gossiped they knew very well there had been a news embargo on the Nadhouri mutilations.'

'And how did it get leaked?'

'Ah, that's a long story.' Arnott gave a brief

run-down of the part Tricia Carroll had played in all this and congratulated Palmer on co-ordinating the two investigations, playing up the subsidiary role of Charlie Flood, whose support he still needed. Arnott found all this buttering-up stuck in his craw but, since his retirement, the old vulture had been forced to share the pickings.

Palmer shrugged, unwilling to hand the Met any morsel.

'Incest, you say, Arnott? By God ... Lucky the other witness, Smith, was only peppered with shot; he can back up your statement. The Irish jockey, Paddy Frith, burst in *after* the shooting you say?'

After a further curt exchange, he hurried off, leaving Arnott to return to the sitting room. The stable manager had not moved, afflicted by a paralysis of shock. The police surgeon was supervising the removal of the body at last.

Arnott sank into the armchair, feeling the bitter chill of the house close in around him with the sounds of departing police cars. A sergeant had been left to hold the fort, awkwardly aware of Arnott's quasi-official capacity: a former CID inspector from London, even an old codger like this one, was not something to be trifled with. Arnott prevailed on him to go and make a big pot of tea.

Paddy Frith slumped on the sagging sofa,

316

his head in his hands. Arnott offered a cigarette and the man's hand, brown and sinewy, trembled as he held it for a match. He raised his eyes and the two men recognized their mutual acceptance of the terrible events. Arnott guessed Frith assumed him to be with the police contingent and he did not enlighten him. He had come across witnesses like this Irishman before, fiercely loyal and normally uncommunicative but, once the tap was turned on, a surge of pent-up emotion was released.

'Genny couldn't help herself in the end, sir,' Paddy muttered. 'It had been going on too long, before they came back here from Argentina after their mam died. It's not as devilish as everyone seems to think, brother and sister drawn together like that. Poor people would never have been so hard on them...'

'Were you the only one who guessed?'

'Reckon so. Old man Bloch never realized what he had done to them – all that nasty talk, prison an' all. Holy Jesus, their mother made it worse forcing them to pretend they was no kin to the crooked old jailbird. It threw them together sharing that secret. Young lives twisted by all the deceit, sir, like a pair of veal calves reared in the dark. Nowadays, who cares two farthings about swindlers like Bloch? But you have to have worked with the family like I did to see it

Genny's way. A stable lad I was when I first came here. Old Roger Pendlebury, Victor's grandpa, sent me over with a hunter he bought in Tyrone. A very strict Protestant family the Pendleburys was, sir. Not a morsel of human kindness for sinners.'

'Did Miss Pendlebury always keep a shot-gun under her bed?'

'That's Victor's. He used to take pot shots at the rabbits out of the study windows. Kept it by him all loaded up ready. Mr Bloch used to bang away at them rabbits eating up his prize snowdrops and Victor just kept it up out of loyalty to the old devil. The only violent thing poor Victor ever done.'

The young sergeant came back with a tray and Arnott passed Paddy a steaming mug of strong tea topped up with a splash from Victor's decanter. Arnott pulled his chair up close, putting himself between the sergeant and the stable manager, warning off the young man with a fierce dismissive gesture.

'Why do you think Miss Pendlebury killed her sister-in-law? Was it jealousy? Or for her money, do you think? To keep the stables?'

Paddy's eyes glimmered in his weather-beaten face.

'No, no, sir. Nothing like that. Victor could have got by. He talked about having to draw in our horns if his wife left. Tragic it didn't work out that marriage of Victor's. He tried to get free of Genny when he brought his

318

new young wife to Finings but she wouldn't let him be. Mrs Victor was a pretty lady but no match for a Pendlebury woman. He should have chosen someone who could stand up for herself – it would have helped the poor man to lead a decent life. No one could rein in that filly Genista, not even her mam. Victor and I understood each other, sir. His wife only turned away when she found out about him and his sister. You can't blame the poor soul, she was too innocent to see it for herself and Genista can be very cruel. Mrs Victor would have been generous to him if his woman had been anyone else. He said there was likely to be a divorce but he had enough of a stake to pull through.'

'Mrs Victor could not forgive him then?'

'He told me he *tried* to pull her round for Genny's sake. I was the only one he could talk to about it. It was making him ill, caught between his wife and that she-devil. He loved them both, sir. What Genny could not face was being splashed all over the papers. That was what had made her hair go grey in her teens, you know, the scandal-mongering. And now Mrs Victor threatening more shame, a repeat of the hounding she and her brother had suffered when their pa went to prison. Genny had always got her own way with Mrs Victor before, she thought the poor creature would give in. If you had seen that girl break in a young stallion you'd know what Mrs Victor was up against. Sheer will-power. If the silly lady had agreed to keep quiet about his sister and call out some other woman as Victor tried to coax her, Genny could have let it be. It wasn't the money. Oh no, sir. Genny *wanted* Mrs Victor to leave them to themselves here. Genny was just too proud to have their family name smeared all over the county. She shied at that. How could they give up everything and run off abroad again? It didn't work that first time, did it, sir? They belonged here, poor sad babbies.'

Tears welled up once more and he blew his nose on a filthy rag of a handkerchief. Arnott said nothing. After a few moments Paddy's soft brogue continued, this time in a whisper.

'I had my doubts about Genista all along, sir. I heard someone in the stables the night Mrs Victor was attacked. I looked out and in the moonlight Genista was clear as day, riding off on that fold-up bike.'

'On her own? Are you sure?'

'Do you think I wouldn't know that girl anywhere? She had on her old riding mac and a rough tweed cap she wears for early morning exercise. Where would she be taking herself off to after midnight? And she with her own car? Next morning the bike was back behind the loose boxes, caked in mud it was, sir, but it made me worry, you know...'

'And when Victor confided in you about his divorce there was no suggestion he would take any desperate measures to stop it?'

'Victor? Jesus and Mary! That poor man never raised his hand to a dog. No, no, sir. That was Victor's trouble. He let Genny have her head in all weathers but Victor would never have let her hurt his wife. Did you not know the man?'

Arnott shook his head and was about to speak when heavy footsteps in the uncarpeted passage stopped him short. The sergeant sprang into life and whipped open the door. It was Charlie Flood and another uniformed man. He strode into the room in his long overcoat looking like the wrath of God.

'Bugger me, Ralph, is that broken nose of yours into *everything*?'

Arnott nudged him outside, closing the door on the two policeman and Paddy Frith.

'Keep your hair on, Charlie. If it wasn't for me putting in a good word for you with Palmer you'd still be snoring your 'ead off.'

Mollified, if unconvinced, the chief inspector followed Arnott along to the kitchen. It proved to be set in a Victorian time warp complete with a black-leaded range and copper pans. But it was marginally warmer than the rest of the house and after riddling the dying embers Arnott set about finding himself some breakfast. A raw red dawn was just beginning to break.

Knowing when he was beat, Charlie Flood waited impatiently for Arnott to assemble a pile of bacon sandwiches and a fresh pot of tea. After taking a bite from his deliciously steaming wad, Arnott nudged his reluctant ally and fixed him with a twinkling eye.

'Palmer give you the gist of it, mate?'

'Too right. Bloody incest he says. That true, Ralph?'

' 'Fraid so, Charlie. The sister killed that poor blonde right enough. Put the scalp in her father's old desk in the lean-to glasshouse out the back. Lucky I found it. Can't see Palmer's boys turning out every bloody garden shed looking for the evidence. I'll give you a red-hot tip, Charlie, so don't say I never pay my debts. Only thing is I'm relying on you to smooth things over when it comes to Will Smith and me being here in the middle of the night.'

'Come out with it, Ralph. What you keeping back from Palmer?'

'You go round to the stables, Charlie, and get hold of a folding bike. Stash the bloody contraption in a plastic bag and hand it over to the forensic boys. When they compare the mud from the Nissan boot I bet you a fiver it'll match up with the muck on the bike.'

'Straight up, Ralph? You wouldn't set me up, would you?'

'I owe you one, mate. Fact is Will walked in

through the back door and I followed, just to prevent a felony you might say. No break-in, I guarantee. No big problem there, is there, Charlie?'

'OK, OK. But where did you get the tip-off about the bike?'

'The Irish bloke saw Genista Pendlebury sneak off on it on Saturday night. My guess is she'd picked up a few useful tips from the ex-Borstal boys they employ at the stables but you could always shake them down about that. She biked into town, nicked the Nissan, stuffed the bike in the boot and then phoned the Shaws, setting up the fairy-tale hospital run. Bundled up in some wet-weather gear and posing as a taxi driver, she picks up the sister-in-law and drives off quick before the silly bird wakes up to it, stops off in a quiet bit of country and threatens the poor cow with a knife, thinking she could force her along as she had always done before.'

'Force her along what?'

'Make Mrs Pendlebury agree to name some other tart in the divorce caper. Anything to keep Genista clean in the sticky world of horse-trading. Every bloody tout wetting himself laughing once the "Brother and Sister Love-In" story got about. Sniggers round all the parade rings from here to Doncaster Races. Can't you see it, Charlie?'

'But to knife the poor bitch?' Charlie

Flood retained an old-fashioned horror of deviations and doubted the depths to which even incest would drag a respectable-looking woman like Genista Pendlebury.

'Well, jealousy was festering over the years. Mrs P. was a pretty little lady, rich and stupid. The sister probably hated her guts and, if the killing had passed off as another political rub-out, there was always her money, which, whatever anybody says, I still think is up front in any horse-trading lark. Can't dabble in the gee-gees with no loose change. You should know, lad.'

Charlie Flood was worried. He liked things nice and simple. All this female psycho stuff – what did Ralph Arnott know about women?

His long face betrayed a flicker of indecision and Arnott rose, brushing the crumbs from his sheepskin coat.

'By 'eck, if you don't make a move soon we'll be frozen here like some bloody Antarctic expedition. I'm going outside now and I may be some time,' he added with his old foxy grin, relishing the joke lost on Charlie.

Galvanized into action, Flood strode out of the kitchen and bawled along the passage for his sergeant.

'Go and stand over a fold-up bike stowed at the back of the stables. Don't let anyone touch it, you hear me? I'll be talking to the Irishman.'

The bacon sandwiches had done their worst. Arnott's eyelids felt lead-lined. He unlocked the back door and stumped off alone through the gates and along the lane to get his Fiesta, still parked where he had left it, it seemed, forty sleepless nights ago.

Twenty-Three

Laurence Erskine was unable to deliver the mate of Judith's single Christmas earring until Valentine's Day. It was their first opportunity to meet since Madeleine's murder. He flew back to London for a few days' leave and magically acquired two tickets for an *Oklahoma* revival. Two seats in the stalls on February 14th no less. Such amazing good fortune normally only falls to the ones who always lose at cards. Lucky in love. It was all too true.

Afterwards, they swanned back to her flat on a raft of lilting melodies. Judy had prepared one of her Italian dishes and it only took a few minutes to whip up a salad and heat the tortelloni, the air fragrant with fresh basil and warm ciabatta. Laurence opened a bottle of wine and lit the fire. Judith grinned at him as she lit the candles on the table and he quickly bent over his glass, swirling the Chianti, his expression inscrutable.

To Judith he looked good enough to eat. His winter tan had faded in the weeks he'd spent since Christmas tied to the coat-tails of the leader of a British trade delegation, a politician easily tempted by Washington hostesses and, despite every warning, determined to teeter on the edge of the diplomatic danger zone. Erskine wore a casual tweed alpaca jacket which made his spare frame seem almost cuddly. She soon pared down all this superfluous padding and, in the space of just a few hours, their mutual trepidation was thrown to the wind, the relationship frisking along like a sail boat suddenly caught in a summer breeze. Judith fingered the silver earrings, abstract squiggles playing hide and seek in her long hair.

They didn't bother with the washing-up. Who would? Later, in the afterglow of a perfect evening, Laurence broached the touchy subject of Madeleine Pendlebury's death.

'Something's cropped up,' he said.

'Not now,' she murmured, nuzzling his ear. 'Let's forget all about it. It's over with, darling – just too horrible to think about...'

He persisted, his voice a lazy drawl, like a man being boring about his hard day at the office. 'It's not something likely to hit the headlines but you might as well hear it from me. I got a whisper on the grapevine. That lecturer bloke's been found dead.'

She stiffened, rigid with shock. 'Will Smith?'

'Eh? Who?'

Judy shook his shoulder, irritated by his sleepy response. 'The lecturer, you said. At Chiaroscuro? Will Smith's killed himself, you say?'

'Suicide? Who's Smith? Oh, I see what you mean. No. The senior man. Tyler. Dr Kenneth Tyler, the china expert.'

'What happened?'

'A mugging in Toronto. No witnesses.'

'No!'

'Oh yes.'

'Took them a couple of days to identify the body. His wallet and everything personal had been snatched.'

Judith snapped on the bedside light. Her eyes narrowed. 'What do you mean, no witnesses?'

Laurence yawned. 'Hey, keep your hair on. It was just a mugging. Thought you'd be interested, that's all.'

'Oh, sure. Since when have you trawled the back pages of the Toronto press just to fill me in about street crime.' She paused, choosing her words, familiar with Erskine's little evasions. 'You think it was Nadhouri's doing, don't you? Someone out to get Suki's supplier.'

He shrugged. 'Couldn't prove a thing against Tyler. Brenton George refuted any inference he'd seen any dealing going on and Fenella swore she knew nothing about any cocaine at the club. There wasn't a scrap of evidence. Flood's spitting in the wind over that drug business and Bruce Foxton's in the clear. Facts are just not forthcoming and the political involvement is irrefutable. Anyway, it's on the cards the Sioux lot will be rounded up in a couple of days – we've tracked down one of them at least, someone remembered seeing a motorbike zooming off along Goff Street the night Suki was snuffed out. A Harley of all things. It's been traced. The drug connection is a very minor aspect of the case – a private grudge of Nadhouri's is possible, I grant you, Morton's still on the payroll, but it's hardly the sort of thing likely to land him on the mat for a mugging thousands of miles away.'

'And your lot now turn a blind eye to any possible Nadhouri involvement in Tyler's death. The man may have been innocent, for God's sake! No wonder Flood's getting nowhere with Brenton George and Fenella.'

'Judy, have a sense of perspective, love. It was a mugging. Happens all the time. It's up to the Canadians to look into it.'

He pulled her close, wishing now he'd never brought it up. And the evening had been skimming along before all this. She tensed in his arms, her mind in turmoil. He reached across and doused the light, murmuring meaningless phrases of reassurance, finally muttering gentle enquiries about her mother's accident in an effort to avert a slanging match. His luck held.

Grudgingly, she filled in the details. 'As I told you on the phone, the kiln just blew up. Took the roof off the studio and practically gave Pixie a heart attack when she heard the explosion. Claire's gone off to Zambia with them for three months' holiday while the studio's being rebuilt. The publicity probably did her good. There's talk of an exhibition of her work being included in a craft show at the V & A at Christmas.'

'She was insured, I take it?'

'Oddly enough, yes. Under all that vague arty exterior, Claire's quite astute, you know.'

'Lucky your sister was there when it happened.'

'God, yes! Claire's hands are still affected but the burns will be quite healed in a few months. One funny thing – she lost her eyebrows in the blast and it doesn't look as if they'll ever grow back. Her hair's OK but this bare forehead of hers makes her look strangely nun-like. Mysterious.'

'They say the only thing that makes the Mona Lisa look mysterious is the fact she's been painted without any eyebrows. It's not the Leonardo smile at all. It's having no eye-brows that does it. Perhaps it'll catch on. Suddenly, it'll be all the rage.'

They giggled, hugging each other and stifling the laughter like children after lights out.

'An air of mystery cuts no ice with my sister. She can't stand secrets. It's the one thing about Claire that really gets her goat.'

'She still on about tracing her dad?'

'Given up on that, thank heavens. Gave her enough of a fright when she found out about mine.'

'Did Claire call out for her lost love while she was semi-conscious?'

'Not on your nelly. Tight-lipped even in delerium, my mother. Don't ever let on that we found out, will you, Larry? She'd be furious. It slipped out at Madeleine's funeral.'

'But Claire couldn't go to the funeral, surely? Wasn't she in hospital?'

Judith nodded, suddenly wistful. 'It was Madeleine's father – Alain Lambert – who let the cat out of the bag. Poor man was in a terrible state, hardly knew the time of day, and the funeral was a tremendous ordeal for everyone. We were all desperately upset, of course, and the atmosphere was electric. The Shaws were wonderful. Nancy Shaw's a real Trojan. Felt partly to blame, I suspect, having given Maddy that cruel message about Victor being ill. She organized the funeral at

Chevenix, Alain being totally incapable of taking charge of *anything*, poor devil. Afterwards, a few of us went back to the Shaw's place. I didn't want to go, couldn't face it to tell the truth, but it seemed the least I could do and Pixie had to stick by the poor man.'

'I thought your sister was ill herself?'

'Luckily, she was over the worst when the kiln blew its top and, strangely enough, having to tackle the fire and get Claire out and off to hospital and everything seemed to pull her together. She even coped with Maddy's death better than I did. Entirely her old self again, thank goodness. That virus or whatever it was seemed to turn her mind for a couple of weeks ... It was only Pixie and Nancy Shaw who dragged everyone through that terrible funeral. Arnott came, bless him.'

Laurence snorted, never a fan of Judy's old boss. 'How did Lambert manage to pull your family skeleton out of the cupboard then? Too much booze at the wake?'

'He *was* pretty groggy, as a matter of fact. Did you know he had an assignation with Claire in Dover the night Madeleine died?'

He laughed, clasping her to him in a whoop of derision. 'Don't say *Alain's* your long lost papa!'

Judith shoved him in the ribs. 'I should be so lucky! No, it turns out that at Claire's urgent insistence, Alain met her on his way back to France that night. He'd returned to London to fetch his car and was driving down to Dover to catch the night ferry. The police checked it all out, just to make sure he couldn't have been involved in Maddy's killing, I suppose, but, of course, Pixie wouldn't let it rest. Finally, got the whole story out of him at the funeral – why on earth Claire made him meet her that weekend. He told Pixie everything.'

Laurence lit a cigarette, suddenly alert.

'You knew about this stupid campaign to bully Claire into putting names on the family tree?' Judy muttered. 'Turns out, all this feverish nagging over Christmas finally got Claire on the run and she insisted Alain meet her on the quiet that night. To ask his advice, he said. They'd known each other, through Madeleine, for years. Claire kept her eye on her at boarding school when we lived at that staff cottage and Alain was always grateful. Fancied her himself, so he said, the old bumchaser. Anyway, they met up near the ferry terminal and over supper Alain tries to reason with Claire, takes Pixie's side, says she should have come clean years ago. Eventually, she admits, she can't.'

'Christ Almighty, Ju, does anyone care about all this old family history after all this time?'

'Pixie does! It was just as I thought all along. Claire is far from certain *who* Pixie's father is. She was pretty wild in her heyday and apparently got carried away with some guitarist at a rock festival and by the time she woke up to the fact that she was up the spout, he had moved off on the hippy trail and she never made any effort to run him to earth.'

'Very romantic,' Laurence dryly retorted. 'But having dragged all this out of Alain, why didn't Pixie let it go at that?'

'She'd waited too long to let him off the hook even at the funeral. She can be implacable that girl! She doubted she'd get the chance again.'

'Alain knew Claire's second fiddle then?'

'Oh yes. That was the cause of the dilemma. Claire told Alain she could hardly tell me about *my* father and admit to Pixie – who was, in fact, the one badgering to know – that she couldn't put a name to hers. Alain begged her to be honest, he said – we were hardly children, after all. Strangely enough, he was the one who introduced Claire to this other romeo, a man called Frank Sachs, a cameraman who worked on several of Alain's films. But he never suspected they'd got so involved. I suppose that was why Claire had to nab him that night – he was the only person she *could* confide in. Sachs was killed in a car crash in LA years ago, apparently. She hadn't told him about me. He never knew he had a daughter. I wonder why?'

Laurence held her close, brushing away the tears.

'That's obvious, darling. She's like me. Wants you all to herself.'